Lady's Children

BOOKS BY RHIANNON HELD

THE SILVER SERIES
Silver
Tarnished
Reflected
Wolfsbane
Death-Touched

STAND ALONE
Hound and Key
Mirror Bound

Lady's Children

A collection of short fiction from the world of *SILVER*

Rhiannon Held

To Brandy, Eileen, Cyrena, Alicia, Kim, Michele, Amber, Yonara, Johonna, Erik, Kate S., Ross, Jessie, Bob, Lorelea, and Chris.

And all the NWAA archaeology folks back in the day.

Contents

Mistaken Captives

We begin with our archaeologist. This novella is set simultaneously with the first half of DEATH-TOUCHED, and features the first appearance of Faith and the return of Laurence. Laurence was introduced way back in SILVER, along with Rory, the former alpha who still looms large in his life.

1

Faith's GPS smugly announced that she'd reached her destination beside the state park's impressive, carved sign, about a mile and a half of indifferently paved road before she actually found the venue. Fortunately, good old-fashioned road signs directed her the rest of the way to the hall. Half a gate was shut over her lane at one point, announcing the park was closed, but she followed her boss's directions and drove around. The day was working up to be a hot one—in Seattle terms—but the sweep of shadows from the evergreen boughs overhanging the road made all the difference when she opened the car windows.

The hall was pretty obvious when she reached it. Blending into the landscape with the same weathered wood siding and dark green metal roof as the other park office buildings she'd passed along the way, it looked big enough to host a substantial crowd for whatever public classes, presentations, or other events the park wanted to put on. The parking lot was packed.

When she'd gotten the details about this job, Faith had thought it was a weird place to hold a wedding, especially a summer one, but maybe the couple hadn't had many choices with this many relatives. She'd bet it was less expensive than some ballroom downtown.

And had better ambiance, in her opinion. The forest was quiet and beautiful, especially since she wasn't looking at it with all her gear on her back, wondering how many more shovel probes she could finish that day. She couldn't see any empty parking spaces, so Faith turned the car down the service road leading to the back of the building and pulled off onto the shoulder.

A couple of guys were just heading inside from consultation with a third, who headed in her direction instead. Faith would have expected from their location that this would be the smokers' huddle, but the air was clean and the guy coming up to her had empty hands.

She stepped out of her car, but stayed standing behind the open door. "Hey, I'm with the catering company." Not that her bland black slacks and white shirt didn't shout "server" already. A lock of black hair slipped out of her professional ponytail, and Faith shoved it quickly behind her ear. One of the perils of changing her mind between layered short and ponytail long: the growing out time was a pain in the ass.

"Can I park back here, do you know?" She didn't see any of the company's vehicles, but they usually encouraged the employees not to take spaces guests might want.

"We don't need any servers. We already told your company that." The snap to the man's tone made Faith's eyebrows go up. She looked him over again. He was a little small for what she expected of bouncers, but he looked well muscled despite his slim frame. Taller than her, but that really wasn't hard. He was the kind of guy with such a washed-out blond coloring that he probably wouldn't show a five-o'clock shadow for three days. What was his problem?

He seemed to read from her silence that he'd overstepped. "It's a private party." His voice warmed with a little embarrassment. "Maybe they didn't remember to tell you? We already hashed out the miscommunication when they first showed to set up."

Faith leaned back over to grab her purse from the passenger seat, and checked her phone. No new voicemails or texts. Then again, she was one of the most sporadic servers, picking up hours between field projects. She wouldn't be shocked if her boss had run down the list of people she had to notify and forgotten about Faith. But she didn't even know who this guy was. Why should she take his word for it?

"Let me call my boss." Faith held up a finger while she listened to the line ring, and the guy subsided against the wall beside the door. No answer. Now what? She bit her lip. How much due diligence did she do before blowing off the stupid wedding she hadn't really wanted to work anyway?

A happy kid laugh dopplered toward her from somewhere inside. A six-year-old boy sprinted through the doorway and launched himself off the threshold like a superhero who could clear the concrete step down from the door in a single bound. He smashed into Faith's knees and then fell back on his butt. His face creased for half a second with the quintessentially kid expression of trying to figure out not how hurt he was, but whether it was worth bursting into tears about it. Apparently he liked his audience, so he did.

Faith slipped her phone into her pocket and lifted the boy gently with a grip under his arms. "Sorry, kid. You've got to look before you leap. Where're your parents?"

A new man arrived in the open door and gave the kid an exasperated look. "Just inside," he told Faith. He was tall and striking, almost intimidatingly so in a celebrity sort of way, though she didn't recognize him. Maybe an actor, with those two white locks of hair at his temples.

A hand lightly on his back, Faith ushered the boy up onto the step, and the bouncer guy made a strangled noise of protest. Now she could see inside a little, through the open door, oh no! Faith really didn't understand the problem—so it was a private party. What made this wedding so super secret? If they were pinching pennies by refusing servers, she doubted they had the money to employ bouncers, even short, clean-cut ones.

Now her curiosity was aroused, and she angled herself to get the best view inside she could. The decorations did look more inexpensive than many weddings she'd seen in the months since she'd picked up the second job with the caterers, but Faith liked them better for it. Small discs of cut glass had been hung in all the windows to catch the sun. The only tables were the banquet tables around the edges, so apparently everyone was going to stand to eat—and for the ceremony as well. Faith didn't see any chairs for that. The banquet tables had white cloths, which picked up the rainbows nicely. Small strings of crystal beads were strung along the edge of the tables, alternating circles and half circles.

The guy in the doorway smoothed the boy's hair, then turned to guide him firmly into the hall. "Edmond, you've got to stay inside, all right? Go find your father." The kid resisted for a moment, wanting to stare at Faith, but finally he gave in and bounded off.

He slipped into a crowd that was fairly informal to match the decorations. Most of the women were in blouses and skirts rather than dresses. It made one woman stand out at the edge of the crowd, though Faith supposed up close her hair was probably platinum blonde, not actually white. Her dress was very elegant, with a long skirt of fabric light enough to waft around her ankles, dark blue with points of white and gold embroidery like stars. She had her hand stuffed into a pocket on one hip that completely spoiled the line of the dress, but Faith supposed some women just didn't know what to do with their hands.

The crowd was also very diverse, much more than she would have expected when most weddings had such large contingents from the same families. Everyone also seemed somehow really energetic or graceful or something. Maybe one or other of the couple was a sports star, with teammates past and present attending. Soccer, maybe? Some of the men looked bulky enough for football.

The guy in the doorway shifted to block it, and Faith settled her weight back before her curiosity could get rude. "I'm—I'm one of the servers. This guy said there was a mix-up and you don't need anyone?" She tipped her head to the bouncer guy. Maybe it was also a little rude not to take his word for it, but all of this just seemed slightly weird somehow. "I mean, they didn't leave me a voicemail or anything, but I don't work as many events as everyone else, so I guess it's not that surprising. So it's a pretty exclusive event?"

The guy in the doorway relaxed a little, like he finally understood what she was worried about. Maybe he'd worked in the service sector before himself. "Yeah, Laurence is right. We told them that when they arrived to drop off the food. I'm sorry it didn't make it to you." He got out his wallet and pulled out and offered a couple bills. "For lost tips."

Faith brightened. "Thanks, I appreciate it." At least the drive out here wasn't a total loss. On her way past where Laurence was propping up the wall, she offered him an apologetic smile.

She hoped he could go in soon and enjoy himself.

Instead, he pushed off the wall to trail after her at a polite distance. "You do many weddings?" His voice was awkward, and Faith suddenly wondered if he was hanging around to hit on her. That was...well, really flattering, actually. He was pretty good looking, and she'd been using her variable schedule at work as an excuse not to bother dating for too long. He'd been an ass at first, but right now he seemed faintly apologetic. He'd probably just been following his boss's directions. She flicked her eyes down. No wedding ring.

She checked her phone's clock while she decided whether to plead urgent chores at home to let the guy down easy. But she found she liked the idea of chatting for a bit, so she slid the phone away again rather than use the excuse. "Nah, I just pick up hours when I'm not out in the field for my main job." She braced herself. This guy looked like the bullwhip-joke type. Which was preferable to the serious-questions-about-dinosaurs type, at least. "I'm an archaeologist, actually."

Laurence shoved his hands into his pockets. "That sounds cool." Faith waited for his next comment long enough that he started to look uncomfortable. "I'm, uh, kind of between jobs at the moment myself."

Faith dipped her head in a quick apology. "No, sorry. I just couldn't believe you didn't make an Indiana Jones joke. Or ask if I'd ever been to Egypt." She laughed. "You kinda just won yourself major points with that, by the way." And she'd better hope he didn't have a girlfriend because she'd let herself in for awkwardness now if she'd misread his initial comment.

"Oh. Uh, good." Laurence looked at his feet. He seemed pleased in his awkwardness at least.

Faith decided to change the subject. "You here for the bride or the groom?"

"I've known him longer." Laurence pulled a face and rolled his shoulders like maybe he didn't care for the groom, then tried to turn the gesture into a shrug. "Sorry if he was a bit intense. He's like that." He looked back at the hall.

He meant the man with the white locks of hair, Faith realized. That was the groom? He'd been wearing a sport coat, not a tux. "Was the bride the woman in blue, then?" She'd been the most formal of those inside, without similar dresses anywhere to mark bridesmaids. But the bride should have been in the back somewhere, before the ceremony, shouldn't she? But Laurence nodded. Huh. "It's interesting they're not going too traditional. Not even a pastel color."

Laurence wandered a few steps closer, in a casual pacing way. "Pastel? What are you talking about?"

As she tried to puzzle out his confusion, Faith suddenly realized her mistake. This was obviously a reception. Her boss had miscommunicated that as well. "I thought this was the ceremony, so I was surprised she wasn't wearing white." That didn't seem to help. Faith didn't expect him to know all the ins and outs of the garter and something blue, but she'd have thought white wedding dresses were pretty pervasive, if he'd been part of Western culture long enough to have accentless English.

More awkward silence fell for a beat. "So, archaeology, huh?" Laurence said finally.

Faith leaned a hip against the car. "Not like you're thinking. I'm a shovelbum. When the government or a developer has some big construction project, it's the job of the company I work for to check the land first, to make sure they're not going

to destroy any archaeological resources when they start digging. Or hurt any historical buildings either." She gestured off
into the trees. "So mostly it means a lot of tromping around and
digging test holes without finding anything in them."

Laurence's gaze followed her gesture. "Is there a lot of stuff
to find around here?"

"Pre-contact, there's a ton—Native American before contact with Europeans, that means. Prime real estate is prime real
estate, so most places we want to build now, like on the water-
front, were places where people used to like to live. And there's
more historic resources than people might think. The remains
of early cities under the foundations of modern buildings, and
things like homesteads and logging railroad grades. It's not as
old as on the East Coast, but there's certainly stuff to find."

Someone moved on the trails among the trees to their side.
Laurence turned as two men stepped out onto the gravel of the
access road behind him, one black-haired like a Native himself,
Inuit maybe, and the other with darker skin. The Native guy
raised a hand in vague greeting and Laurence gave an "ugh, you
again" grimace and pointedly looked away again, back to Faith.
A couple other guests, clearly.

"What's the coolest thing you've ever found?" Laurence
asked her.

Faith laughed, and rubbed at her lip as she stalled. She
hated that question. There were a lot of cool things that she'd
found—and a lot of things that didn't seem cool on the surface,
but were scientifically important. And a lot of garbage with no
scientific value. She never quite knew how to convey that middle category to laypeople.

Since her car was taking up a good portion of the gravel,
the two new men had to thread past the two of them on their

way to the main parking lot and presumably the front entrance. She leaned into her car to give the first one a bit more room as he passed.

But rather than following, the second guy stopped behind Laurence. Faster than Faith could process, he had one hand around Laurence's mouth. In the other he had a knife he slashed diagonally up Laurence's abdomen so blood spattered as far as her and a shiny red mass bulged out of the cut and Laurence struggled but the man was much taller and had a good grip on him.

Faith could hardly—think, but she couldn't just stand there stunned; she had to scream, to run for help. She drew a breath, but there was the other man, the one she'd forgotten, and he was behind her. He got something over her mouth, and when she tried to breathe, the world spun and then fuzzed out.

2

Faith's cheek was smashed against something unyielding and chill. She was lying on something hard. That much came to her in a half-awake haze, and then adrenaline burst through her body. Her heart pounded as her eyes snapped open. Those men. They'd killed Laurence and kidnapped her.

She was lying on industrial tile and staring at an industrial table leg bolted to the floor. Beyond it, there were floor-level cabinets under a counter at the edge of the room. Everything was lit with the slightly harsh wash of cheap fluorescent light banks, though with a hole of dimness in the center of the room like a single bank had burned out. Faith sat up, swiping at her mouth and nose, though of course there was nothing there now, and the weird lingering chemical-y scent in every breath was just her imagination.

Everything was silent, but she peered into every corner anyway. Nothing moved, no sign of the kidnappers, though there was a person-sized lump on the floor on the other side of the table. Faith's pounding heart made her peer into every corner a second time, before she moved. God, if that was Laurence's body she'd probably puke or something, but she absolutely had to know.

He still had a cloth over his mouth and nose, slid slightly off center, so maybe the chemical smell wasn't her imagination after all. Faith yanked it off and tossed it as far as she could. He was breathing. She could see that even before she took his pulse. It felt strong enough, but she didn't have much basis for comparison, especially since her hands were shaking so hard she wasn't sure she had her fingers placed exactly right on his neck. He was flat on his back, though his arms were flopped, one on his chest, one up near his head, like someone had dragged him in by the ankles and not worried about how his arms knocked around.

His shirt was completely soaked with blood from chest to hem, the fabric bunched up around the jagged tear crossing it. The top of his jeans was black and damp, though it looked like the denim hadn't wicked as far. Reminded of the splatter, she looked down at her own shirt, but the brown dots there seemed so polite in comparison.

Faith groped for her first-aid training, but her thoughts felt like they were shaking at the same frequency as her hands. Put pressure on the wound to stop the bleeding, but the blood she could see was browning, drying. So the bleeding had already stopped. You weren't supposed to ever remove the compress, just keep up the pressure until help arrived, but when were they going to get help? She knew she should leave it alone, but she couldn't help herself. She needed to know how bad it was. She took one side of the shirt between thumb and forefinger and lifted it away, wincing at the blood sticking it down.

Nothing. Bloody skin, yes, but it looked smooth. Faith moved around to kneel at Laurence's side, and carefully rolled the shirt fabric as high as possible over his chest. She couldn't see even a scratch. But that couldn't be right. It had to be under there somewhere. She reached out to wipe at the blood, but stopped herself. She was in enough danger from disease as it was. She pushed to her feet. Maybe there was something around here to wipe with, before she went so far as sacrificing her shirt. She didn't think kidnappers usually left paper towels lying around in their basement prisons, but basement prisons didn't usually have sturdy tables and cabinets.

When she surveyed the room again in the patchy light, she suddenly realized what it reminded her of: Chem 101. It was like an abandoned classroom, or maybe a low-level industrial lab. Something with a lot of workspace and supplies, but no facilities for really heavy chemicals.

There were three doors. One behind them, which Faith set aside for the moment. Laurence's head was pointed in that direction, so whoever had dragged him in had probably left the same way and locked it behind themselves. That left one door at the back of the room, and one at the side. She went around the other side of the huge central table to avoid stepping on Laurence, and arrived at the back door first. As she got closer, she saw it even had an official exit sign above, but smashed so it no longer illuminated. She tried the handle, and it turned like it wasn't locked, but the door wouldn't move a millimeter. Blocked. Faith kicked it experimentally, and it thudded dully. No give. Her brain caught up a second later, and she stopped breathing for a second. What if the kidnappers heard the noise and came running?

She forced herself to take a breath. Come running to see what? That their kidnappees were banging around, trying to get out? That couldn't be unexpected. If they didn't trust all the doors to hold, they would have tied them up.

If the kidnappers had meant to let them go, they would have hidden their faces. Faith braced herself on the door handle again as the thought bubbled up. The light-headedness was probably left over from the chloroform or whatever had been used to knock her out, she told herself. Where did she know that from? Somewhere real, or a mystery novel? Or worse, her far-too-extensive *CSI* viewing habits? She knew better than to accept those as the full truth.

Anyway, it didn't matter. She could still scout their prison. And help Laurence.

The second door had no handle, but when she hooked her fingers into the hole where the entire assembly had been removed, it opened onto a tiny, windowless bathroom. The room had a toilet, a mirror, and a sink with an eye-wash attachment bolted onto the side. And a stack of one-ply institutional-looking toilet paper rolls in the corner. Faith grabbed one, ripped off the outer wrapper, and wrapped herself a nice wad around her hand before dampening it at the sink.

When she returned to Laurence, the blood resisted her, too sticky to wipe without so much pressure that the toilet paper wore away. But she managed to remove enough to be sure.

He had no injury. Whatsoever.

Faith sat back on her heels and shucked the bloody mass of paper off her hand. A voice at the back of her head lectured about washing her hands immediately, but she ignored it. Had this been *staged*? Was Laurence working with the kidnappers? They'd slashed some fake blood pouch and then—dumped him in here with her? Why? He could be off showering and then giggling with his compatriots over a hot meal while she assumed he was dead.

Faith pinched the inside of Laurence's forearm, digging her

fingernails in. He had better not be faking unconsciousness. He moaned and weakly pulled that arm away, ending with it only flopped a little closer to his body.

"What the *fuck*." Saying it out loud helped Faith focus a little. She had some questions for Laurence, so maybe it was time to help him wake up. She stood and returned to the bathroom to wash her hands thoroughly. She drank straight from the faucet, and then cupped her hands underneath for lack of anything better to carry water in.

Most of it leaked out before she made it to Laurence, but enough remained to spatter his face when she opened her hands. On the second trip, she had more success, and opened her hands fast enough the water fell all at once and made a satisfying splat noise.

Laurence sputtered, coughed, and dragged his forearm over his face to clear the worst of the water before he opened his eyes. "Lady."

Faith presumed he meant her. She stepped back a little, to be out of range if he sat up and reached for her. "What? I needed you awake. You have some explaining to do. What was all that with the fake blood? Are you with those guys?"

Instead of sitting up, Laurence fanned fingertips over the side of his face like his head was killing him. "Fake—?" His other hand went to this stomach, and slid over the damp, smooth skin. "No, they definitely got me—small cuts can still bleed—" His excuse stumbled over itself, like he was trying to remember a script through a hangover.

Locks clunked on the other side of the door Faith had picked as their entry point, and she ignored Laurence to retreat to the end of the table farthest from that door. She had nowhere to go if the kidnappers did come after her—the bathroom door swung outward, so she could hardly barricade herself in there—but she felt at least a little better with the table between her and them. She gritted her teeth, and told herself that if they'd wanted her dead, she would be dead. Or raped. Or maybe they'd wanted her to wake up first—fuck. Faith clenched her fists. Just let them try.

The dark-skinned man entered alone, a huge dog at his heels. It was whitish gray and lean like it was a wolf cross. The dog growled, a low, warning sound rather than something that sounded like a prelude to an attack. In contrast, the man held his hands open, pretending he was nonthreatening. "You're awake. Good." He nodded to Laurence, who struggled into a sitting position, panting as if in great pain. "Sorry you got dragged along, but you were in the way. Don't worry, though. When the Roanokes ransom Susan, we'll throw you in for free." He laughed. "Think of it like a vacation."

Faith tried to measure the man's distance from the open door behind him from the corner of her eye, but the dog looked at her and paced over to stand more directly in her path. It was like he'd sensed she was thinking of making a run for it. She focused her attention on the man again. He didn't sound like a kidnapper. He sounded like a frat boy assuring a school administrator that the beer he'd just dumped on his head would wash out, barely able to hold in his snickers long enough to get the words out.

It took her longer than it should have to process that, because it made no sense. "Susan? What the fuck are you talking about? I'm not Susan." Did she even look like Susan? She hadn't seen her own doppelganger in the crowd, but she hadn't had long to look. There had been other women with Asian features, but Faith's had been diluted since her Thai grandmother. She'd have thought she could never be mistaken for white or Thai.

Laurence got a good grip on the table and hauled himself up. He growled, sounding remarkably canine himself. Once there, he swayed, deathly pale, and failed to launch himself at the kidnapper in a whirlwind of violence, as had clearly been his intention.

The kidnapper chuckled. "I'd heal up for a bit before you try anything, if I were you. We had to keep adding chloroform for longer than we'd intended. You probably lost some brain cells." He paused, and Faith's words finally seemed to catch up with him. He frowned at her, seeming to see her properly for the first time. "Oh, please. The only human at the Were wedding? You think we're stupid?"

"Shut. Up." Laurence got paler, if that was possible. "She's not Susan. She's some—waitress."

The kidnapper rounded on the dog. "You said it was her, Amak!"

Faith drew in a deep breath. Insane. At least one of their kidnappers was stark fucking nuts, blaming his pet when things went wrong. Maybe that was good? Maybe it meant he'd make more mistakes? Her heart was beating so fast she could hardly breathe, though. She had a terrible feeling that insanity in her captors would make her situation even worse.

And then the dog sort of—stretched and twisted and then there was a naked man straightening to his feet, and Faith backed up until she hit the counter behind her. In the movies, reality blipped like that and you didn't even blink, but she was looking at this with her eyes, and deep in her mind she *knew* that and so her brain ground to a stop. It couldn't—the dog hadn't—

"You saw her too," the naked man said. He had black hair, like the second kidnapper. He was the second kidnapper. "Talking to her son." He tipped his nose up, inhaled deeply. "It's not like you can mistake the scent."

"But what if she's the *wrong* human?" The dark-skinned man whined.

Amak crossed his arms. He seemed to be answering his friend, but he looked at Faith as he spoke. "If she is, we'll have to find somewhere to dump the body. She just saw me shift, after all." He shook his head with simulated frustration. "What a pain in the tail."

Clarity snatched Faith up and held her above the situation for a breath, two. If she wasn't Susan, these men would kill her. Right now he was just threatening her to make her drop what he thought was an act, but something told her they really would carry out that threat if they became convinced of the truth. Laurence was in no shape to do anything, and she couldn't take the kidnappers on unarmed, two to one. Ergo, she needed to be Susan.

Two to one when one of the men had been a dog. Or a wolf.

Faith ruthlessly pushed that aside. She could think about special effects or hallucinations after anesthesia later. Right now, she needed to be Susan, and stay alive. "All right, fine. We can stop the act, Laurence. It's clear they're not going to let me go." She curved her lips up in an expression that was nothing like a smile at Amak. "Can't blame a girl for trying, can you?"

Laurence twisted to face her, a complicated maneuver involving both his head and how he balanced his weight against the table. "You're not—"

"I am Susan," Faith spoke over him. She wanted to scream at him to play along, but she didn't dare even glare at him.

"Thought so." Amak crossed his arms and looked smug.

"Well, both of you can get comfortable. The Roanokes may take some convincing." He gestured and the as-yet-unnamed kidnapper went back to the doorway, leaned around into the hall behind, and straightened with a couple stuffed fast-food bags held in one hand.

Amak strolled up to Laurence at the same time. He laid his hand against Laurence's throat, thumb against the hollow, fingers lightly cradling the side. "If we are forced to hurt the little fragile human, it'll be your job to explain it to the beta. But there's no need for that if you don't cause any trouble."

Given the way he'd fought his way to his feet, eager for violence, Faith would have expected Laurence to have snarled now, snapped at the man. Instead, Laurence folded, cringing like an abused dog. Amak smiled, malicious in his enjoyment, and then walked back out of the door as his friend tossed in the food and closed it with a *thunk* behind him.

Faith walked over to the bags, but didn't pick them up. She stared down at them until her eyes got tired of focusing and she let them slip to blur. "Did you see that too?"

Laurence tried to make it to the floor in a controlled manner, and ended up just slumping down to hands and knees, too fast. "I—see what—?"

Again, it sounded like he was desperately trying to cling to a script that had long since stopped fitting the situation. Faith strode over. "Don't lie to me!" she screamed down at him. "It was real, wasn't it?"

Belatedly, she thought about the kidnappers hearing her, and then it hit her. They could have cameras in here. They could be watching everything. She spread her palm at Laurence. "Don't answer that."

Laurence's expression looked briefly like he'd received a stay of execution. He lowered himself to the floor to rest on his back, one arm beneath his head. Faith did a circuit of the room, climbing onto counters and table to peer into every corner of the ceiling and walls. Then she opened all the empty cupboards set into the counters, checking for listening devices. She couldn't find a single thing that looked remotely electronic.

"They won't have thought of cameras." Laurence's voice came from a different direction than Faith had expected, and she pulled her head out of a cupboard to find he'd crawled to the fast-food bags and spilled one out over the floor to form a small sea of paper-wrapped burgers.

The sight wrenched Faith's attention off herself, finally. Laurence may not have had a huge, bleeding gut wound, but he looked terrible. She hurried over and unwrapped a burger for him, and helped him to scoot so he could lean his back against the nearest table leg to eat it.

She pulled the other bags over and peered into them. One was nothing but fries, and the third was full to the top with more burgers. "How many people do they think they kidnapped?" she said with weak humor, and frowned at the scribbles on top of the paper. The burgers apparently came in several different varieties.

Laurence fumbled for another burger, and she unwrapped one that looked like chicken, though it was hard to tell when it wasn't fluffed for an ad camera. It disappeared in a few bites, as did a third, and a fourth. Faith wondered vaguely where he was putting all of them. He was not a big guy. His stomach seemed to agree, because it rumbled and gurgled suddenly in protest.

Laurence squeezed his eyes shut and tilted his head back. "Lady, I forgot about gut wounds."

Faith looked down at the sesame seeds dotting the bun half exposed on the next one she'd been unwrapping. She almost wished she still was confused, that all that was wrong was one moment that could have been an optical illusion. Things fit to-gether too much. A guy who had all the blood from a wound, but no wound. A guy who ate like a much bigger guy. Like, for instance, he'd healed a lot and needed energy. "When he cut you, I could swear I saw intestines. Then again, if I'm trusting my eyes, I saw a dog turn into a man."

Laurence looked pained, pressed his lips together, and didn't answer. Even with digestive difficulties, his color seemed to be returning slowly. Faith set the burger she had in her hands on his lap, and started sorting through the rest to find one she might like for herself. Most of them seemed to have cheese, and she hated fast-food processed cheese. "So here's the thing. Either I'm dreaming—or hallucinating so comprehensively that I might as well be—or this is really happening. If it's really happening, if I don't play along, I might get killed. If I'm dreaming, I'm passed out somewhere and I can't do a damn thing about it. So better I play along like it's real."

"You're very practical." Laurence spread the paper on his burger wide, corner by corner, like a flower.

"It's that or go catatonic." Every time Faith tried to trace the other possibilities too far, her chest felt too tight to breathe. When she focused on practical action, the clarity felt artificial, like too much caffeine after a week of all-nighters, but better that than the alternative. "Unless this is some kind of stunt, or-ganized by crazed horror-movie fans."

Laurence's look at her was so incredulous that she laughed. Only a little bit hysterically. "Okay, not that, then."

"The—" Laurence scrubbed at his jaw. "The people this is aimed at. They won't leave you here. You can ignore all this weirdness, and then you'll be back to normal life soon enough."

Faith gave up on her no-cheese search and munched on a fry. She was too keyed up to be hungry, and everything was stone cold anyway. "And you? They'll be happy to leave you?"

Laurence dropped his head, though not before she saw him set the muscles in his jaw. "No. I mean, it seems rather like Lady's justice that I got hurt, after what I did…But they won't leave me. They're not like that."

"Good." Faith knelt up and pressed her lips together. Here went nothing. "Look at me." She put as much intensity as she could into her voice, and waited until he followed the order, surprised. Even then, he avoided her eyes, keeping his gaze near her ear or over her shoulder. "I can't just forget it, though. They think I'm Susan, and Susan obviously knows all of this stuff, or they wouldn't have been talking like that in front of her. So I have to know everything Susan would know."

Laurence dropped his head, face settling into stubborn lines. Faith wasn't surprised. Clearly everyone involved in this was trained to lie instantly and comprehensively, and to keep it up as long as possible. "Everything!"

Laurence hunched his shoulders, letting silence be his answer. Faith settled back on her heels, and tried to turn her caffeine-hangover thought processes to another approach. She could just act like she knew what was going on? Smile—well, frown—enigmatically? They'd talked about a beta—and "Were" for that matter. And with that healing and impulse to violence, it had to be werewolves she was dealing with. She wasn't wearing any silver, unfortunately.

But what about all the other crap? Roanoke and all that? Maybe she could brazen it out, but Faith didn't want to rely on that. She didn't want to *die*, just because her boss had forgotten to phone her and tell her not to show up to the fucking were-wolf wedding.

Laurence's gaze jerked to her like her emotional outburst had been out loud. Something about his expression eased more sympathetic.

Faith decided not to waste the opportunity. "So what does this have to do with Virginians?" She settled down cross-legged and leaned forward over her lap.

Laurence looked blank for a moment, then understanding dawned visibly. "Oh. Roanoke. It's a title. Nothing to do with the city. The couple getting married. Silver and Andrew Dare. They're the Roanokes."

Faith waited, but he seemed to actually think that was a real answer. "And the Roanokes, everyone at the wedding, even you, are…werewolves." She felt stupid just saying it out loud.

"Yes." The word sounded dragged out of Laurence. With that admission made, the rest of his words tumbled out. "The title comes from the colony. Those were the first Were to come to North America. Now we're all part of the united Roanoke pack, but organized into sub-packs. Sub-alphas take the name of their city. I used to be Richmond."

The bitterness in his words when he said "used to" held an entire other story, but Faith didn't have time to do more than note it for later before he continued. "Susan—you—are mar-ried to the Roanoke beta, John. You two have a son, Edmond."

Faith looked down at her hands. She didn't normally wear rings, so she didn't have anything to switch to the correct finger. She'd have to keep her left hand out of sight and hope their kid-nappers weren't very observant. "Is Edmond a werewolf too?"

"Werewolf blood always breeds true." Laurence's attention went internal for a second. After that pause, he started eating again, with no digestive protests this time. "You know, I don't think I could tell you everything even if I wanted to. The Roanokes and, therefore, their betas are based out here in Seattle. I live...back East." Again, bitterness. "I've only met Susan a few times."

"Probably more times than those assholes." Faith waved a hand toward the door. She thought she'd convinced Laurence to talk. Was she going to have to pause and reconvince him every five minutes? But then she noticed he hadn't picked up another burger, and his eyelids were sliding lower. "I guess it can wait a while, though."

"I need to..." Laurence stalled by crumpling up several burger wrappers into a huge ball and tossing it as far as he could. Unaerodynamic, it flopped about three feet. "I mean..." He actually flushed.

Faith flipped through her vague cultural knowledge of movies. Why hadn't she read more horror? Detective novels weren't pulling much weight at the moment. Laurence had been injured, and he was still acting like he needed more time to recover. So it was either something like "eat of human flesh," or... "You need to turn into a wolf?" Was it a full moon tonight? Was it even evening? The wedding had been in the afternoon.

"Shift." Laurence stood and then shrugged out of the bloody remains of his shirt. A thought seemed to strike him, and he nudged the bag still full of burgers toward her. "You should eat a couple before they go bad. I wouldn't put it past Alaskans to forget we need to eat more than once a day." He leaned his weight on the table as he pulled off shoes and socks. He seemed to sense rather than see her opening her mouth for a follow-up question because he answered without looking up. "That pack isn't part of Roanoke. They're wild and independent, which mostly just means they run around in wolf most of the time."

He pulled off his jeans and boxers next, apparently with no modesty at all. Faith jerked her head to the side and thought hard about the Alaskans instead. She seemed to remember that wolves only ate every few days or something, so if the Alaskans were wolves most of the time, that must be why they forgot about three meals.

And then she heard the ear-flapping, fur-shaking noise that dogs made when they shook off water droplets or shed hairs into a cloud. Faith looked back quickly, but her politeness about the nudity had already missed her the chance to see another...shift?

The wolf flopped onto its side, flaked out like any domestic dog. It was a mix of gray with washes of lighter color, especially on its belly. Faith couldn't tell precisely with it lying down, but it looked smaller than the other one she'd seen. It looked asleep already.

Faith scooted closer and reached out to touch—who was she kidding anyway?—him. Laurence. His guard hairs tickled her fingertips, not soft but very smooth.

He certainly felt real.

3

Faith circled the room at least twice over while Laurence slept. She kicked the wall—the drywall dented like there was concrete beneath—and tried to loosen the bolts on the central table, should it be any use as a ram. All that got her was smarting fingers. Finally she gave up and curled on the floor, head pillowed on her arm, and stared at the cabinets. The concrete below the tile sapped her body heat, so she climbed on the table. She lay there until she felt like she'd go crazy from staring at the same wall while her thoughts circled around with the sluggishness of sticky-eyed exhaustion that still wouldn't let her sleep. Werewolves. Werewolves.

In the end, she must have dozed, because the passage of time stopped being quite so excruciating as to seem like physical pain. She opened her eyes when she heard Laurence snuffling around in the pile of abandoned burgers. She waited without getting up for him to turn back into a human, but he seemed content to slurp and gnaw away the wrappers, like a real dog. At least, that's what all the noises sounded like.

Faith sighed and sat up. She ached, and rubbing her eyes didn't do anything to dispel the vague fog in her vision and brain. "Let me," she said, and jumped down to unwrap a row of cold burgers for him. He snarfed them one by one, while giving the impression that if she hadn't been there, he would have tried to eat them all in one mouthful.

Not wanting food poisoning herself, Faith dug into the fries instead. They were fairly unappetizing, but better than nothing. At least they were starchy enough she could close her eyes and think of real breakfast foods, like hash browns.

Laurence grabbed his underwear and jeans in his mouth and padded off to the bathroom. He must have turned back into a human in there because she heard the toilet flush and the sink turn on. The water continued for long enough that she figured he must be washing as much of the remaining blood off as he could. She wondered why he'd bothered hiding out to—change? Shift? She'd seen it already. But maybe this was like the kind of drunken one-night stand that made you overly modest in the morning out of general regret.

Faith wished everything were that simple. He could just suck it as far as his insistence on secrecy, though. All her thinking overnight had only made her more sure she needed to continue with her plan to be Susan.

Laurence padded out in just his jeans and went to pull on his socks and shoes, one hand braced against the counter. He looked completely healthy—better than healthy, deliciously muscled—but Faith pushed that thought away. "What time is it?" she said.

Laurence looked up after pulling on his second shoe. "Why are you asking me?"

Trying to find the words to explain something she'd blurted out without really thinking, Faith flushed. She gestured vaguely at the ceiling. "You know. The moon. And stuff."

Laurence scrubbed his face, and his skin rasped on bristles that, as Faith had expected, were too light to see from her distance. "Lady, how did John put up with this?" The husband, Faith remembered after a beat. "First—" Laurence held up a finger. "The moon's also up during the day. Second, I have no idea if it's up or not. It's still *there*, whether our time zone is looking at it or not. It's nearly full, if you happen to care."

"John probably helped the process by not being rude." Faith skewered Laurence with a glare, and he dropped his head immediately, apologetic. "I'm sorry, but I don't know anything, so it's hard to even structure questions." She set down the bag of fries and detoured around the other side of the table to use the bathroom herself.

Washing her face and swishing out her mouth made her feel a bit more alert, at least. When she returned, she sat on the table and swung her feet as Laurence walked around doing all the same things she had—kicking the wall, shoving at the locked door, testing if the table could be moved—and chiseled out of him a few basic facts that seemed relevant to their situation.

Werewolves were a separate species, so their captors couldn't turn her with an accidental bite. One horror movie worry laid to rest. Faith still felt like her cop shows were standing her in better stead—or leading her completely astray—with this kidnapping situation. Laurence could heal a hell of a lot of stuff, given food and rest, as she'd seen, but he'd still die from the heavy stuff, like being shot in the head. He especially didn't want to admit to that, but Faith got it out of him by loud-ly wondering how he could possibly hurt their captors when they could heal practically everything. Silver burned them, and didn't heal, but she was fresh out of that, so it wasn't much help.

And werewolves could apparently hear really well. Lau-rence didn't say that, but he suddenly interrupted her with a growl as he stared at the bolted door. Faith stared at it too, until the locks scraped and Laurence gestured her urgently behind him. Faith wasn't going to cower behind anyone, but Laurence was the one who could magically heal, and besides, keeping out of reach of the kidnappers was just a good general strategy. She thumped off the table and took up her earlier place with the length of it between her and the door.

A new man entered, with two dogs—wolves, Faith remind-ed herself—behind him. She recognized one from before, so she assumed the second was the second of the two kidnappers. The new man moved like a serious martial artist, smoothness combined with the subtle threat of violence. His dark gold hair was cropped short, still a little raw like it was a recent change from a longer style.

The two wolves focused on Laurence at a gesture from the new man, and backed him slowly into a corner. Laurence looked from one to the other, arms held loose like he was con-sidering the attack possibilities, but fortunately seemed to real-ize the odds were against him.

The new man strolled around the table, passing in and out of the dim bar from the dead bank of lights. Faith backed up until her back was against the counter, but then she tried to make her body language casual, like she was just leaning against it. She wasn't any good for a kidnapping exchange if they killed her. She repeated that to herself several times.

"You don't look like much," the man said. "Small even for a human." His Russian accent was so thick and unexpected that Faith almost burst into hysterical giggles. God, he was just like a TV crime family heir, swanning around with an immaculate suit and product-filled hair in a room full of thugs with prison tats and shaved heads.

"Who are you?" Faith asked, when the worst of the inappropriate impulse to humor had passed. Her voice shook a little anyway.

"Someone doing his job." He reached out and took her chin. He did it slowly enough that Faith let him. If he wanted to grab her in some immobilizing hold, she doubted she'd see it coming. He was gentle enough as he tipped her head from one side to the other, and Faith almost expected him to check her teeth like she was a racehorse he was considering buying. "I can't promise your time here will be short, I'm sorry. The Roanokes may take some time to be reasonable. But I see no reason to hurt you. At the moment."

With as little warning as Faith had feared, he was suddenly holding her against him in a parody of a romantic embrace, tipping his head to whisper into her ear. She froze as her heart raced absolutely out of control. "We get what we want. Always."

"Get your Lady-fucking hands off her," Laurence spat, and just before Faith couldn't stand it anymore and shoved herself away from the Russian, whatever the consequences, he was suddenly gone and over by Laurence.

The Russian got a good grip on Laurence's throat and slammed his head into the wall with a crack that made Faith feel like gagging. "Watch your mouth. Show some respect."

Laurence blinked several times as if stunned, and Faith dragged her attention away to the open door. But the two stooges wolves had moved over to cover it when the Russian took over for them in menacing Laurence. No opportunity for her to make a run for it. What the hell did Laurence think he was doing, provoking the Russian?

"What?" Speech and a cocky smile came back to Laurence simultaneously. "The Lady fucks, doesn't She? Otherwise Death would have been pretty disappointed, back before he was exiled." The Russian's lip lifted in a rolling snarl, but Laurence just kept right on going. "I mean, obviously he found a chase on the side, or we'd never have had many-legged Fenrir—"

"You need the Lady's grace, it seems," the Russian growled, his accent getting thicker. He reached up under his jacket at his side, into some sort of sheath Faith couldn't quite see. It looked like it was shaped wrong, and when he withdrew the blade, she could see why. It curved in a sharp half-moon from one side of the hand to another, held with a bar across the palm like a cross between a punching dagger and brass knuckles. "If I must, I carve it into your skin." He caressed Laurence's chest with the flat of the blade while the other man held very still.

The Russian sheathed his blade and slammed Laurence into the wall again, but this time he slid down with a smear of blood to lie in a heap. "North Americans," he said, contempt in the line of every muscle. "I hope you won't make that necessary for you, human." He lowered a hand to indicate Laurence.

Faith pressed the side of her fist to her mouth to hold in any reaction. She didn't plan to. Not least because she had the feeling that the Russian had no idea that the treatment he'd just given Laurence might well have killed a human. God, she was shaking all over.

"No." The word wavered so much that the sheer embarrassment of it finally kicked Faith into gear. Fuck this Russian werewolf. *Fuck* him. She refused to let him make her that scared.

Maybe he could kill her, but she couldn't let him think he had her cowed. "But I need some more food. The stuff from yesterday will have gone bad by now. It'll make me sick if I eat it."

"Mm." The Russian collected himself and returned to something of his earlier grace of movement as he paced a few steps to look down at the few remaining burgers in the mess of crumpled wrappers and bags they'd left on the floor at one side of the room. "Amak," he said, and that wolf trotted out into the hall and returned nosing a couple boxes of doughnuts stacked atop each other. One spilled off at the end, but it looked like the lid didn't gape enough to let any doughnuts touch the floor. Faith made no move to rescue it.

"Until later," the Russian murmured, and swept out of the room with the wolves following.

Faith stayed right where she was until the locks had been thrown home. Then she ran to Laurence. He was already rousing, but she ignored his grumbled protests and took his head in her hands to examine the back carefully anyway. Blood matted the hair, but not very much, and he didn't react as if the spot were tender when she touched it carefully.

"What was *that*?" she demanded. He grumbled again and pushed her away, so she let him go this time.

"Everyone says Russians are very religious. I was curious if I could get to him." Laurence massaged the side of his head like he had a headache all over. When he reached the bloody patch, he brought his fingers forward to see, then winced.

"Why? How could 'getting to him' possibly do us any good?" Faith didn't realize she was shouting until she heard herself doing it. She wrestled her voice under control. "Unless it gives a window of escape, pissing him off just means he's going to hurt us more while we're stuck here."

Laurence dropped his head and looked so defeated that

Faith started to regret her anger. Maybe he'd been doing it out of nerves, same as she'd wanted to giggle. They were neither of them in a good situation here. She sat back on her heels, and then switched to sitting cross-legged as silence stretched between them. "Wasn't it the horse that had extra legs, in Norse mythology? Not Fenrir?"

Laurence glowered at her. "Humans always think they own stories."

Faith held up her hands. Geez, no offense.

After a beat, Laurence subsided again and sighed. "My grandparents came from Germany. They'd tell the kids all the stories that no one approved of here, either." He smiled slightly at the memory. "That one's about how Death sired a cub on a mortal wolf. He had eight legs, and he grew so large that all the human warlords competed to entice him to fight for them."

"You guys seriously have your own mythology?" Faith coughed when Laurence started to glower again. "Religion, I mean." Seeing as religion usually ended up meaning *your* stories, and mythology was everyone else's.

"The Lady created the Were as her children. The humans were made by their own gods." Laurence shrugged and tried to get up. Faith held him down with a light pressure on his shoulder.

"You stay there. I'll get breakfast." The type of food certainly suggested it was morning, unless the Russian was putting a lot more effort into fucking with their heads than Faith really believed he was. Faith gave Laurence one whole box and kept the other to herself long enough to choose two of her favorite varieties.

"I should be taking care of you," Laurence grumbled low under his breath as he opened his box, and Faith pretended not to hear. If the plain old human knew not to antagonize her captors to no purpose, maybe it was the other way around.

He cleared his throat and spoke in a normal tone. "I'm including you in my prayers to the Lady. If you want to include me in yours." He said it diffidently enough that Faith couldn't read if he meant it, or if he was poking dry fun at the idea of taking religion that seriously.

"I'm pretty agnostic." If she even thought about it. She'd never gone to any kind of religious services as a child, and never encountered anything that changed her mind as an adult. "Thanks, though."

Then Laurence broke the moment by getting a huge puff of powdered sugar down his chest when he made the mistake of exhaling just before taking a bite of his latest doughnut. Faith's giggle felt like it was probably from nerves again, but she allowed it.

She needed the release of laughter at the moment.

4

Dust sifted down onto Faith's head as she moved the acoustical tile aside. A mutant dust bunny apparently born of the mating between a spiderweb and powder drifted down in a more leisurely fashion to kiss her hair. It stuck there when she swiped at it.

The space above her was relatively clear, what she could see with poor light and her low angle. She was standing on the table, but while that was plenty high to lift the tile aside, it didn't let her see very far. She wondered what the floor above was made of. Could they punch through? She was dubious, especially since they lacked tools of any kind. The empty space just begged to be crawled through, over into the next room, but the metal struts holding the tiles creaked when she even started to lift her feet as she held onto them. No way they'd hold her weight, never mind Laurence's.

"Will you relax for a few minutes?" Laurence was one to talk, because he was pacing slow circles of the room, around and around the central table. Faith was somewhat sympathetic, because she could feel the way they were feeding off each other, but at least she was working on something *useful*.

"These guys are not exactly hardened criminals. They have to have forgotten something that will allow us to escape." Faith took another couple swipes at the dust bunny trying to eat her head, and imagined she must look like a dog pawing ineffectually at the piece of tape some owner had stuck on its ear. The moment she thought of it, she dropped her hand. She didn't want to think about canids at the moment.

"Or we could just wait for the Roanokes to negotiate our release." Laurence finally seemed to realize he needed to put his money where his mouth was and relax. He stopped with an effort, boosted himself up onto the table, and patted it beside him.

Faith gave him a baleful look, then slid her tile back into place and sat. She swung her legs, whether to annoy him or because she really did need that physical relief valve for her fear, she didn't know herself. "Negotiate with what? Money? Pretty much anything else, I assume we really don't want the bad guys having it. Unless it's the Roanokes who are the bad guys in this little werewolf summer stock production of *The Sopranos*." Saying it, she realized she had no idea, except for her instinctive feelings about people who minded their own business at their weddings versus people who gutted their enemies and then smashed their heads into walls.

"No!" Laurence whipped his head around to glare at her. "The Roanokes can be too piously helpful, but they have noticeably decreased the fighting in North America since they took over." He clenched his jaw over the last words, like he hated making even that lukewarm admission of approval. "Maybe they want the Roanokes' hostage back. She's Russian."

Faith almost demanded to know what his deal with the Roanokes was, but again, so many other things seemed like they should be higher on her priority list. "They have a Russian hostage?" A prisoner exchange did make a certain amount of sense. But again, who were the rebels, and who was the evil empire in this situation? "So the Roanokes decrease fighting. Is this hostage the reason you're not fighting with the Russians?"

Faith pressed her lips together hard as she considered the permutations of that. It fit, if she finally gave in to thinking about the sides in this conflict as different crime families. Neither was on the side of the angels, but the one that preferred less bloodshed had holds on all the others to make sure things stayed quiet.

"In that case, they're going to be weighing whether some random woman they don't know and a guy who doesn't seem to be making himself their best friend are worth a whole war." Faith pressed her fingertips to the corners of her eyes. Dammit. Hearing it out loud, even though she'd been the one who'd said it, had just hit her hard.

Laurence stared at her, lips slightly parted from where he'd started to interrupt her and then stopped. "I—" he said at length. "Hadn't thought of it that way."

"Well, try it for a while. See if you don't start poking at the ceiling too." Faith got back up to her feet. "Besides, when that Russian guy smashes you around, you don't die by mistake. So don't talk to me about sitting around and waiting for rescue, okay?"

Laurence had no answer for that. He pushed off the table like he was planning to pace again, but he growled low instead. "Company. Here." He gestured her over to the edge of the table and then boosted her down like she weighed nothing at all.

Faith imagined female ballet dancers must feel that way, soaring but grounded by firm support.

"Lunch, maybe," Faith murmured, but the door opened before Laurence could answer.

The kidnappers were both humans, and empty handed. Or at least their hands were empty of food or anything threatening—the phone in Amak's hand was so mundane Faith didn't register it for a beat. They shut the door behind themselves before coming only a few steps into the room. Faith supposed that even with the door unlocked, the time to open it would give them a chance to stop any escape attempts.

"Hi," she said, and stepped cautiously forward. She doubted they'd believe her if she smiled at them like they were her best friends, but she could at least be pleasant and cooperative. Maybe she could get them to talk a little. If they felt more relaxed around their captives, they might make more mistakes later.

"Hi." The dark-skinned guy checked her out a little bit like it was pure habit. She didn't feel slimy, anyway, the way she had when the Russian got so close.

"You know our names, but I don't know yours," Faith said, and eased her neutral expression a little closer to a smile. She held her hands loose and open by her sides.

The guy she'd already heard called Amak looked dubious, but let it give way to amusement. "Suppose there's no harm. I'm Amak and that's Chuck—"

"Charles." The dark-skinned guy shoved Amak's shoulder, and they tussled with mock punches for a couple seconds.

"Chuck," Amak insisted, and retained the last word this time. He lifted his phone. "You made our friend forget to take a picture, so we're going to send him one."

Laurence crossed his arms with a glower. As if it would steal her soul or something. Honestly. "Why?"

Faith ignored him and held out her hand. "Where's the newspaper?"

The kidnappers looked at each other and then at her. "What?"

These guys clearly had *no* idea what they were doing. "You need my picture to prove that I'm okay, right? Well, how do—" Dammit, she had too much new stuff crammed into her head to remember everyone properly. "The Roanokes know that you didn't take it yesterday and I'm dead right now? You have to have something in the picture with me that didn't exist yesterday, like today's newspaper."

Chuck still looked dubious, but Amak's face cleared. He seemed pleased with the simplicity of the solution. Faith didn't bother to point out that the credit wasn't hers. "I guess we'll have to go grab one."

"Or you can pull up a news site on your phone and take the picture with Chuck's. The webpage will still have today's headlines." Faith held her hand out for the phone like it was the most natural thing in the world that she'd pull it up for them, but her heart was pounding at the thought of them figuring it out. Amak gave her a narrow-eyed look and held the hand with his phone against his chest.

Well, she hadn't really figured that would work. Speaking of newspapers, though…Faith waited until Amak was paging through menus to try to plant her suggestion as casually as possible. "Like *The Seattle Times*," she said. Amak nodded distractedly, and Faith held her breath.

"There." Amak showed her the screen. Faith squinted at the main headline. Something about Boeing and a big order being in question. Nothing like "23-year-old Seattle Archaeologist

Still Missing."

Faith didn't know if she was disappointed or relieved. She hadn't even thought about it until just now. She'd been so busy being Susan, she hadn't thought about who would miss Faith.

She wasn't sure anyone would, at least not for another couple days, anyway. Or people would miss her, but she didn't think anyone would freak out. Work would get annoyed if they called with a field project and she didn't answer, and her friend would be pissed if she missed coffee on Sunday without canceling, but none of that would be weird enough for anyone to go to the police. The perils of being single and having a job where projects came and went, she supposed.

All that was beside the point, though. She wasn't going to wring her hands about whether her people would notice and send help while she sat on her ass, waiting. She'd do whatever she could for herself.

"Looks good," Faith said, nodding to the screen. Her server shirt had long sleeves, so she popped the buttons on the cuffs and rolled them up to her elbows. There were a couple bruises here and there on her arms and legs—she presumed from where they'd lifted her when she was out—but otherwise she clearly hadn't been beaten. She stepped beside where Amak was holding the phone up, and Chuck took the picture. She didn't smile.

When they pulled apart, the men put their heads down over their phones, presumably closing the browser and sending or saving the photo. Laurence shifted his weight in the most casual of movements, and Chuck looked up and growled. Laurence subsided again.

"So that Russian guy is pretty intense. How'd you guys get hooked up with him?" Faith kept her eyes on rolling down her sleeves. Get them to talk; get them to relax. And relax herself, so they didn't look at her like they'd done earlier when she tried to pull something over on them.

"Mikhail?" Amak shrugged. "Man shoots a mean game of pool. And I'd bet he could drink even Hugh under the table."

"Hugh?" Faith looked at the door, though of course it was still shut. If there were anyone else outside keeping watch, she wasn't going to see him from here.

Amak gestured dismissively and slipped his phone away. "He's just a friend. He was around for the wedding, but now he's off with his daughter or something." He shrugged, uncaring.

"So who's the Russian I'm getting traded for? Mikhail's girl-friend or something? Sister?"

"It doesn't matter—" Amak didn't finish his answer because he whirled to face Chuck as Laurence jumped the other man. He waded in to help, raining punches onto Laurence and then kicks once he was down. The two kidnappers looked like they got in each other's way a little, but that didn't matter because Laurence hardly got in more than a couple blows of his own before he was taking too much abuse to stay up. It was all so *fast*, worse than watching a shaky-cam fight scene on TV for giving her a sense of motion and violence and nothing more.

"Jesus fucking Christ on a pogo stick," Faith hissed under her breath as she backed up behind her old friend, the table, in case they started rolling around in her direction. She and Lau-rence were going to Talk about this, make no mistake.

The kidnappers stepped back and frowned down at Lau-rence, curled up on the floor. Chuck rolled his neck until it cracked, and Amak eyed blood on his knuckles and then scrubbed them off on his jeans. "Lady, you like pain, don't you?" Amak said. Chuck laughed, and they let themselves out.

Faith had meant to let her anger at Laurence carry her

along, make her stride over and start screaming at him about what a moron he was, if his fragile male ego couldn't let him keep still while she talked her way into a better situation for five minutes—but the anger swirled so easily into shaking reaction. She crouched, fingers and forehead on the edge of the table, and fought off tears.

"Why can't you just *stand still*?" Apparently the screaming was still there, bubbling below the surface. Faith managed to straighten and went to stand over Laurence. "For *five minutes.* Fighting our way out *isn't working.* Okay? If you keep attacking them, you're going to get yourself killed, or me hurt, or maybe they'll just decide we're both too fucking much trouble and they'll dump us and try for some other hostage—" And there were the tears. Faith pressed her fingertips over her eyes until they receded a little.

She took a deep breath, then another, expecting Laurence to jump in, but he only sat up slowly and let her collect herself. "Look." Her voice wavered, so she repeated it more steadily before continuing. "I can't heal like you guys. So let's keep this on a nonviolent footing for a while, okay? If they don't attack us, you don't attack them. I was trying to talk to them so maybe we could maybe find out something useful, or make them more relaxed later. I wasn't just chattering for no reason."

"Yessir," Laurence mumbled, maybe on a breath of humor. She couldn't find it on his face, though, so Faith reluctantly let things lie. She stalked away, but there wasn't anywhere to *go.* She wasn't going to hide in the bathroom. Much longer and she might start sleeping in one of the cupboards under the counter to get a little privacy, though.

Her attention snagged on the nearly empty box of doughnuts in her glance across the room to decide where to go, and she slowed and lifted it. She'd saved one, but now Laurence should probably have it. She took it over to him, opened the lid, and offered it out.

Laurence didn't stand, but he firmly shoved the box back at her, denting the cardboard. "You'll want that later."

Which made her feel a little bad for yelling at him. Faith wasn't sure whether to insist, or bow to her own biological imperatives. They probably wouldn't get another meal anytime soon after the last performance, and Laurence didn't look nearly as bad as he had after the gut wound when he'd inhaled so much food at once.

Thinking about the details of his healing triggered another thought, and Faith bit her lip. "The violence isn't a werewolf thing, is it?" If it was and she'd just yelled at him for something instinctive...well, shit.

Laurence scooted back until he was leaning against the cupboards, winced, and moved a few inches to the side to avoid getting jabbed in the back by a handle. He let his head tip back to rest against the edge of the counter and exhaled in dark amusement. "No more than it's a human thing. Or a wolf thing." He pressed his lips together, and a muscle in his jaw jumped. "You can't let people take advantage of you. You can't let them think you're weak."

"Or you can let people underestimate you." Faith's shoulders eased with relief as she closed up the doughnut box and put it away on the counter. If it wasn't a werewolf thing, he could be talked out of it. She hoped. He could always not listen, like a human, but at least he wasn't fighting some ravening monster in his mind. She'd sort of already guessed he wasn't, though. A short, slight guy who flirted awkwardly wasn't exactly a Hollywood Wolfman.

"Yeah, yeah, blah blah blah." Laurence glowered at the ceiling. "You're probably doing a better Susan than you realize. She's good friends with Silver, and that's what our dear alpha is always spouting. Her and Andrew both." His tone went singsong, like he was parodying a quote. "Talk to people. Understand them. Find what motivates them. Abstaining from violence is not weakness. Taking refuge in it is weakness." He returned to his normal tone, weary. "I've familiar with their talking points. And I'm sure they'll repeat them to me ad nauseum now they've busted me down from sub-alpha."

Faith's opinion of these people went up a couple notches, if they'd also noticed Laurence had this problem, and taken him out of a position of authority as they tried to deal with it. "A sub-alpha heads...a pack? Under the alphas?"

"Yeah. In Richmond, Virginia." Laurence clenched his hands, then flexed one open with almost as much effort. "But not anymore. The alphas in their infinite wisdom took my pack away."

Faith could hear when she needed to drop a subject. She stepped away to sit down in the corner between two cupboards, head tipped back against them. If his...alphas couldn't get through to Laurence about his behavior, she doubted she could. She'd have to watch him carefully around their captors and do what she could to manage the situation herself.

5

After a long interval—definitely longer than a doughnut could hold her, so Faith suspected they'd missed lunch, dinner, and started heading into the wee hours of the morning—food arrived, delivered by Mikhail alone this time. Faith tried not to look too desperate, or grateful, but her stomach was keeping her from being able to sleep.

It seemed like Mikhail wanted privacy, because Faith only glimpsed wolves out in the corridor before Mikhail shut the door firmly. She'd seen this episode, in which the crime boss pulled up a chair and offered expensive alcohol and smiles, though neither he nor his victim had any doubt who was in control.

Mikhail hadn't apparently thought to import any chairs, and Faith didn't see any bottles in the plastic bags of take-out containers, but he did smile as he set the bags on the table. "You are hungry," he said, a firm statement. It made Faith want to contradict him on general principle, but she made do with ignoring his words instead.

Mikhail popped the first two containers open invitingly. Mexican tonight. Or whatever time of day it was. One looked like fajitas and another enchiladas. Faith wondered absently whether he'd just ordered one of each thing on the menu. Maybe she was doing Russia a disservice, though, assuming its cities didn't have international restaurants like every cosmopolitan city. Somehow she didn't see werewolves as being attracted to big cities, cosmopolitan or not, though.

Faith picked the fajitas and started to push the enchiladas down the table to give Laurence room to eat. Then she thought better of it, and tugged it back right next to her. He could eat where she could smack him if he looked like he was thinking of lunging at the Russian. Laurence didn't even seem to notice. He settled next to her and dug in with his fingers.

Mikhail was hanging around like he planned to say something, but Faith could only stand to let the silence stretch so long before hunger ripped away her patience. She popped a few pieces of steak into her mouth with her own fingers to hold her while she wrapped up the rest.

"I have questions for you," Mikhail said, leaned his hip against the table, and warmed his smile a few degrees.

Laurence left off stuffing his face and growled. Faith presumed it was in response to the smarmy manner, not the idea of questions in general. She held out a forestalling hand, and he subsided.

Mikhail laughed, and Faith felt like the oozing smarm had left a slimy residue on her. "You are practical. Thank you. This will be easier." He pulled out another container, this one with tacos tucked neatly into a row inside, and oriented it so that either one of them could take a few. "How long have you known Roanoke Silver? Has she always spoken with Death?"

Faith froze with her last fajita halfway to her mouth, though the tortilla didn't get the memo about holding still and let slip a piece of pepper and a dribble of sauce to soak her fingers. The first question, she could brush aside with some kind of "long enough" answer, but about the rest? Speaking with Death? What did that even mean? Being suicidal? She'd tried to get information from Laurence, but it appeared it hadn't been the right information.

"Why should I tell you?" Faith set her fajita down and tried to put a bit of challenge into her voice. If she let herself look as terrified as she felt, he'd be sure to know something was wrong.

Mikhail touched a fingertip to the underside of her chin. "To keep man who feeds you happy."

"She's always muttered to herself ever since she was hurt." Laurence put a hand on her wrist, as if to say "I got this," and Faith wished she dared leave him to it. At least he was trying to help.

"And I suppose you would dismiss any miracles just as easily." Mikhail's lip curled and he stepped away from Faith. "And the human would not understand what she was seeing." He snorted. "Tell me this instead. How much freedom do they give Tatiana? Do they trust her?"

Laurence opened his mouth, but Mikhail made a dismissive gesture. "I am not interested in outer appearances. I want to know from close to the Roanokes."

Faith took a bite to give herself time to stall. Okay. She could be logical about this. Tatiana was a Russian name, and if her freedom was in doubt, she had to be the hostage Laurence had mentioned. Which only made sense. Of course he'd be curious how she'd been treated.

Which Faith didn't know anything about either. Maybe she could bullshit her way to something that would satisfy him, though. "They treat her just fine. Not so much freedom that I get to have heart-to-heart chats with her. If you want to know how she feels about how she's been treated, ask her."

"Mm." Mikhail dropped his hand to flatten his palm on the tabletop as he thought. "How does she get along with the alphas? Friendly?"

Faith rewrapped her tortilla, now thoroughly soaked through, as another excuse to stall. A hostage? Why would she be friendly with her captors? All these werewolves seemed far too badass to be worried about Stockholm syndrome. "What do *you* think? Of course not." Then she got it, all at once. He was worried that Tatiana had gone native. Or become a double agent. Or whatever cliché you wanted to use that meant she and this guy were no longer on the same side.

"Are you lying?" Mikhail pushed forward into her personal space. Faith abandoned her food once more to back up, but he kept coming inexorably until her back was against the door. Laurence kept pace with them, then edged up beside Faith so he was facing Mikhail too. Faith put her hand to his wrist. Mikhail had done this before. He was just trying to frighten her. He probably wouldn't do anything worse yet.

"She's been here for how long? Of course they don't have daily fights or torture sessions or whatever." Faith glared at Mikhail. She wasn't afraid. She wasn't shaking at all. She was just pissed that he was asking her stupid questions, questions she totally knew the answers to.

"Does she play chase with anyone?" When Faith didn't answer fast enough, Mikhail bared his teeth. "There is someone.

I knew it." He pressed against her and set his hand against her throat. When Faith squirmed to the side, his grip tightened, but it relaxed when she froze. She had a hard time keeping her breathing even when her heart was beating out of control. God, what was she supposed to say? She didn't understand.

"Why do you care who she fucks?" Laurence said in a low rumble.

Light-headedness swept through Faith for a beat when she realized that he'd just translated for her. Though how you got from a kid's game of tag to fucking she had no idea—but that didn't matter. Now she needed to come up with an answer that would sound plausible but wouldn't piss him off. "Oh, now I'm supposed to have a peephole into her bedroom? Not my husband, that's for sure."

"Or you, clearly." Mikhail brushed his free hand against her hip, dropped it again. "No, I am sure there is a woman…she probably looks sharp, not pretty. Speaks before she thinks."

Laurence made a muffled noise, maybe a laugh that even he found inappropriate, but couldn't help himself. Mikhail laughed outright, and Faith started to believe that they might make it out of this without a blow-up. "He knows which woman." Mikhail tipped his head to Laurence.

"Rumors," Laurence said, with an awkward shrug.

"That explains most of why she has not come home. Tatiana's voice always wavers with emotion." Mikhail turned back to Faith, fencing her in by resting his weight on hands on either side of her upper arms. "Now. Has she told the alphas anything about her real pack?"

"I don't *know*." Faith judged that the time for playing along had passed. Now was the time to appear to lose her patience and try to get out of this situation. She shoved at one of Mikhail's arms.

"You do." Mikhail moved the arm, but to her throat, so fast that she didn't process the movement until he was pressing down. Air came hard and Faith tried to cough or wheeze or she wasn't quite sure what, but Mikhail's muscles were like stone under her blows when she tried to grab at his arm and shove it off or even lighten the pressure. Jesus, help, help! She needed to—to kick, she remembered to kick, but he didn't seem to mind that either, and she didn't have much strength left for kicking harder.

And then Mikhail reeled back. Because Laurence had punched him, Faith put together after a moment of gasping. He was hauling back for another to the same place on Mikhail's jaw that was already showing a nasty purple bruise, but Mikhail dodged. He threw Laurence into the table with a crack that sounded like something in the table had snapped. Laurence keened with pain.

Faith put her hand up to her throat, an automatic impulse even though the slightest pressure stabbed pain through it. Air. Air was nice. She'd try to pull in as much of that as possible before things went south again.

When Mikhail turned away from Laurence, she scuttled to the opposite corner of the room. He let her, and jerked open the door she'd been standing against instead, muttering something in a language Faith assumed was Russian as he left and slammed it behind himself. Maybe something uncomplimentary about her. Or Laurence. Or Tatiana.

Which may or may not have been a good thing, but Faith's caring was utterly exhausted at the moment. She'd gotten out of this encounter alive; that's what she cared about.

Thanks in no small part to Laurence. Faith went to him and helped him straighten from where he'd crouched against the table, curled in around the side that had smashed into it. "Sorry," he muttered under his breath when she touched him. "Know you told me not to."

"I told you not to start anything!" Faith wanted to shake him, to hug him, as if that would help his massive bruises. Instead, she tried to be the best, most stable support she could be. "I'm *glad* you reacted when he was the one who attacked first. I wasn't—I'm not so naive I think anyone can manage no violence ever. But you can't be *stupid* about when you choose to use it. You know?" Faith pressed her lips together on further flailed explanations. The guy was hurting and she was lecturing him. Good going.

"Need to display good judgment," Laurence murmured, like it was a quote. Maybe from his alphas. His tone made it sound thoughtful rather than mocking.

Faith laughed raggedly. "Maybe later, after a good meal." She supported Laurence over to sit on the floor with his back to the cupboards, then handed the tacos down to him.

6

Faith finished eating fairly quickly, leaving her once more with her choice of terribly uncomfortable dozing positions to try to pass the night. Assuming she hadn't guessed wrong, meaning it was too early in the evening to sleep. Her thoughts felt more sticky than ever, but that could merely be due to stale adrenaline festering with the return of painful boredom.

In contrast, Laurence ate slowly. Which was really weird. Now she was watching for it, she caught the way he subtly hunched around his arm, as he did everything one-handed. She scooted closer and leaned out to try to see around his body to get a better angle on that arm. "You need to eat more before you can heal properly?"

Laurence looked up from his takeout container and frowned at her for a bit, like he was trying to decide what to say. Since it was probably some kind of information about Were, Faith made herself be patient and let him come out with it at his own speed. "It is healed. I didn't set it fast enough, so now it's crooked." He set the takeout container aside and held his arm out.

Faith gritted her teeth against the sight. It wasn't gruesome by any means, just subtly…off, in a way that turned her stomach the longer she stared at it and her mind became certain it wasn't just an optical illusion. His arm bent like a straight pencil refracted by the waterline in a clear glass.

He tucked it against his chest again quickly, like he was responding to her reaction. "I'll rebreak it soon. I just don't feel up to it at the moment."

"No shit." Faith hugged herself. "Maybe you should leave it until we get out of here and you can see a doctor."

"Getting out of here will be easier if I have two working arms to do it." Laurence watched her silently, and it took Faith several breaths to realize that he was saying that he was on board with her strategy of escape, rather than passively waiting for a rescue. She smiled despite herself, though only briefly before she remembered they were talking about rebreaking arms.

"If you'd be willing to help—?" Laurence gave her a hopeful smile, then winced. Faith assumed her "oh, God, what?" reaction had showed on her face. She'd had the first-aid course with every other field tech, of course, but that meant, at most, splinting a break to limp to help. Really, it had concentrated more on recognizing a break so you could call for help, not move the person, and wait for the ambulance to arrive.

"It's not actually that big a deal. If it was my leg, I'd do it myself in a moment. But the grip and leverage is just so hard on an arm. Werewolf healing—we get used to it. Popping stuff back into place, digging out bullets when they heal in." Laurence dredged up the smile again. "I can tell you what to do. I'll rebreak it, I just need you to pull, so it falls into place properly."

Faith took a deep breath and told her stomach sternly that it was welcome to keep the recent food as a congealed lump so long as it kept it. It couldn't be worse than seeing his intestines before. Besides, when she'd tried to do things like get eyelashes out of other people's eyes before, it had always been the other person's reaction that was the worst. When they winced, you freaked out. Laurence wouldn't even have to be ultra-manly, because it seemed like he legitimately didn't freak out as much at such stuff. "All right."

Laurence described everything she needed to do in detail— which didn't take long—and then again, while she didn't really listen but instead psyched herself up. By the time he wound down the second time, she was about ready. She gathered up the remains of the food for him to eat afterward, set it on the nearest counter, and nodded at him.

"It's easy," he asserted, for probably the fifth time, and then body-slammed the side of his arm into the edge of the table like the world's most juiced-up football player. The same crack sounded as before, which made Faith's stomach flip, but she grabbed his wrist when he shoved it at her across the surface of the table.

She braced her foot against the nearest leg, and he did the same on the opposite side, and then both pulled. Faith closed her eyes and whispered "c'mon, c'mon" under her breath. She would have cursed, but that would have made it sound like something was wrong, and really she just needed something to focus her adrenaline.

The pressure stayed constant for a long moment, longer than she could quite stand, and she really did pull as hard as was humanly possible for her. Then the pressure changed, let up slightly with a wet, crunching grind, and Laurence released an explosive breath. He gasped something that Faith only caught the end of. "…walk in Her light and Her grace."

Faith hurried around to ease him to a sitting position, though when she tried to get up to get his food, he held onto her wrist. "Thanks," he said, earnest.

Faith sat down with him. "Thought you said it would be easy." She looked down at his hand around her wrist. It was strong and steady, not shaking with reaction or anything. "You calculate based on a Were being able to pull harder and do it quicker?"

"No." Laurence tilted his head to look at the ceiling. "Hadn't ever tried to do it long enough afterwards the battle high had worn off. It's different when you're all keyed up from fighting."

He was silent for a few seconds, and then she hugged him. She wasn't quite sure why, but she wanted to do *something* for the poor guy, to acknowledge what he'd just been through. On her behalf, no less.

Far from pulling away or grumbling, Laurence hung on to her, like a shaking dog tucking close to your legs. She ended up staying there, leaning across his chest with her cheek on his opposite shoulder; when his arms came up around her too, she wasn't sure who was giving and receiving comfort anymore.

"Did you fight a lot as an alpha?" Faith wasn't sure why she asked, when the question could be taken so wrong. Something about their fragile moment together, stillness between violence, made her dare to ask.

"Sub-alpha. Yeah." Laurence paused like that might be all Faith got, but the moment pulled him along too. "Fought more when I was beta, though, under the former Roanoke." Her ear was too far from his chest for his voice to resonate properly, but when she moved with each of his breaths, she still felt immersed in his words.

"Not a nice guy?" It felt wrong to interrupt, but Laurence's rhythm seemed like he didn't know how to tell the story on his own. Faith didn't want to make this an interrogation, but she might as well prompt him with open-ended stuff until he stopped answering.

"No." Laurence laughed, low. "His father built the pack. He could hardly hold it, until Dare came along. He ruled all the sub-alphas from the Eastern Seaboard to the Mississippi." Faith didn't turn to look, but one of Laurence's arms lifted presumably to sketch that in the air. "When Dare won the challenge, he added the independent Western packs for the rest of the continent."

His arm resettled on her back. "Rory used to have a terrible time keeping betas. He'd get pissed at them or they'd get pissed at him, and suddenly there was someone new. That settled down when he pulled Dare in as enforcer. That actually worked well, for a given value of 'well.' Dare chose his battles, so he wasn't picking fights, but he wasn't rolling over for Rory's shit either. And he was off traveling so much, he and Rory couldn't snap at each other's tails."

"When in there were you beta?" Faith smoothed the side of her thumb against the bare skin of his back where her hand rested. For a beat, she worried that might be too sexual, but she'd been thinking of smoothing bristled fur on a dog, and he seemed to react that way as well.

"About halfway through Dare's time as enforcer. I'd been taking advantage of my pilot's license, doing some roaming." Laurence let a breath trickle out. "I was flattered when Rory offered me the position. It wasn't bad. I resented the fact that Dare outranked me in practice, even if he wasn't technically supposed to, but…" Laurence started to shrug, then seemed to realize it would disturb her. "And then Dare found Silver and they went running off together to take down the guy who'd attacked her, and told Rory where to shove his demand Dare come back and protect him instead. Rory's voice came untethered with the rage…"

Faith tried silently to parse that for a couple seconds before formulating a question, and Laurence anticipated her. "Um. I guess the human expression would be…lost his shit?"

Faith had to laugh. Okay, fair enough.

"He used to…" Even though they hadn't been looking at each other for the whole conversation, Faith got the feeling Laurence was telling this part really hard to the wall, not to her. "Lay into me some, when he couldn't take it anymore. Better me than anyone lower ranked. But losing control made him look weak, and looking weak made him lose control."

He fell silent and Faith reran his phrasing through her mind. What would "lay into him some" mean to a werewolf who was blasé about the idea of resetting bones? No wonder this guy had lingering issues.

She'd assumed with that admission, he'd be done, but he surprised her by starting up again after almost a minute. "I thought when I became sub-alpha, I'd do it *right*. But no one would *listen* to me, since I'm so small."

"Maybe a break from it is a good thing," Faith suggested tentatively. What did you say to a physical abuse victim who'd started abusing others? Other than, "I'll support you through therapy. So get some. Please."

Maybe her assumptions about what would be rude to make explicit in this situation were wrong, though. "Are there werewolf therapists?" Having tiptoed up to the topic from the side, nervousness made her chatter when he didn't respond. "I mean, you don't really think of that kind of thing, unless it was some kind of premium cable show, with too much full frontal and sex on the couch and no actual psychology. 'Therapist to the supernatural.' " She gave it a title card ring, and Laurence exhaled in slight amusement.

"Therapists for Were or Were therapists?" His hand moved against her back, not really directed enough to be a petting motion. "Neither, particularly. What would one of us even say to a human therapist? All the important stuff would have to be kept secret."

"I don't know. It doesn't actually sound all that crazy different at the core. Say he was your boss, that you got fired from a managerial position. Swap the details but not the substance." If not for the kidnapping, for the guy turning into a wolf right in front of her, maybe he would have done that to her when he was flirting. Unemployed, just visiting for his friend's wedding... It probably would have worked, too.

Laurence growled low, but not directed. "Normally, you'd just talk to your alpha. Sometimes I hate Dare for being so fucking perfect. *He* always does the right thing. Says the right thing. People listen to *him*."

"He can't be perfect. He hasn't rescued us so far," Faith noted, and Laurence's chest shivered against hers in what she belatedly realized was a laugh. If a lame joke like that could help him a little, good. She'd take it.

7

Laurence looked up expectantly when Faith came out of the bathroom, having decided to declare it morning and wash up. As she sorted out her thoughts, she combed her fingers through her hair, wished she hadn't, given how long it had been since her last shower, and fastened it back again. She had no idea how he could tell that she had another idea, but he waited as expectantly as any dog who'd heard the word "walk."

"What?" she said, and climbed up to sit cross-legged in the middle of the table.

Laurence leaned with his palms flat on the end. "You smell like you have some kind of plan." He ducked his head in sudden apology. "I mean, it's not like you have to come up with one. Especially after the way Mikhail treated you. Are you sure you're—"

Faith cut him off with a gesture before he could finish. Dwelling on all the things she had to fear in this situation would make her freeze up, so better not to even mention them.

"But you are better at plans than me," Laurence finished up, sheepishly.

Faith couldn't take the pressure, now her proto-idea had been set up as the best they had, so she drew up her knees to stall. Her work pants were getting unutterably filthy with all this rolling around on the floor. "It's only because I watch too much TV. If werewolves watched as much, they'd recognize my ideas."

Laurence frowned at her in mild annoyance. "We watch plenty of TV."

"Like what, *Shark Week*?" Faith giggled a little punchily. Lack of sleep was definitely getting to her. "I mean, like crime stuff."

"I liked *The Maltese Falcon*," Laurence said with great dignity.

Faith started to laugh, but then another thought occurred. Speaking of situations that happened often in movies—"You're not secretly several hundred years old, are you? Please tell me you're not."

"I'm thirty-seven," Laurence said, and then winced like she still looked uncomfortable. Well, he looked maybe twenty-five, so she was justified. But at least that wasn't as bad as she'd suddenly feared. "I like old movies, okay?"

"Okay." Faith flashed a smile at Laurence to try to make up for her discomfort, and his face lit up in response. "What I'm really cribbing from is the procedurals. A new crime every week. *CSI: Original Flavor* and *CSI: Extra Crispy* and all that."

She stood and pushed the ceiling panel aside again. "What we do is, we leave this slightly open like we knocked a hole somewhere up there or something and couldn't quite fit it back in place as we left. Then we hide in the cupboards until they come in and check on us. They go running upstairs to stop us, leave the door open, and we stroll out."

Laurence hooked his thumbs into his pockets and raised his eyebrows. "Cupboards?"

"I know I'll fit. I got through a dog door once, when we were locked out of my friend's house. And there's a good chance you will too, trust me. That's what makes the plan work, people don't really realize how much space is back there for someone who's smaller." Faith sat, hopped off the table, and opened one of the cupboards. She bent to demonstrate, but Laurence stopped her with a hand on her shoulder.

"I believe you." He took a deep breath, stopped, and then dropped his hand instead of speaking. "I—" He grimaced. "It's a good idea, but they'll smell us instantly."

Faith straightened, and picked at a small chip in the top edge of the counter. "Well, fuck." She tried to sort her Hollywood assumptions into enough order to ask him a question about the range of his sense of smell that wouldn't annoy him, and then the path to a solution occurred to her. "What would cover us up, just make everything stink? I mean, we don't have much to work with, but if we let some of the food go off or something."

"Maybe. They might ask what we were trying to hide, though, if we left perfectly good food lying around." Laurence frowned, and to her relief, Faith actually saw the wheels start turning. "Short of bleach or something, the best thing would actually be to put our scents all over the room, so they can't tell which patch is current." He stepped over to her, suddenly diffident. He pushed past that all at once, set his hands on the counter on either side of her hips, and held himself within an inch of brushing against her in multiple locations. "Stronger traces if we get sweaty."

A corner of Faith's mind noted that he hadn't ever bothered to put his ruined shirt back on and also he was absolutely the ideal height for her to lean forward and kiss him right now. The rest of her mind said stern things about times and places. She didn't push him away yet, though. "So we do push-ups?"

"Attraction has its own scent." Laurence tilted his head, but didn't kiss her either.

Faith grabbed onto the counter edge so her hands insulated Laurence's from her hips. She didn't—didn't know how to say this. Even if he'd been human and couldn't smell she was turned on, he'd have been able to see the way her back arched her slightly toward him without her meaning to. She kept thinking of what it had been like when he'd wafted her so effortlessly down from the table. "Not here." She coughed. That had been supposed to be a simple "sorry, no."

Laurence removed his hands, rocked his weight back. "Yeah," he agreed. Faith couldn't tell what he thought about her answer. He didn't look either annoyed or disappointed, at least on the surface.

"How about I cut myself, like it happened when we were climbing out?" Faith spoke too quickly, trying to get them out of the awkward moment as soon as possible. "Is blood noticeable enough? I guess I kind of assume it would be to a predator."

Laurence glanced at the open tile. "That would work. I think I should be the one to do it, though."

Faith shook her head. "You'll just heal up right away, won't you? I'm the one who'll actually spread enough around that they'd notice."

Laurence drew in a breath, perhaps to object, and then let it trickle out again. "And they'd probably realize that too. Better if it's human blood they smell, you're right." He went over to the table, and it took Faith a beat to realize he was waiting to boost her up. "Shall we?"

Faith licked her lips. She hadn't really quite gotten as far as thinking about putting the idea into action. If they set it up too soon, she supposed the blood might dry. But it wasn't like they could wait until they heard footsteps in the hall—well, until Laurence heard them—to set it up and dive into the cupboards. "Even if they don't bring us breakfast, you'd think they'd want to check on us each morning. Let's do it."

Faith wished she and Laurence could have holed up in the same cupboard, though that was absurd. She was already curled with her knees tight against the bar between the doors and her ass against the back wall. She kept having visions of one of the kidnappers yanking open the door and her being too wedged to do anything about it.

She didn't want to sweat with fear and make her scent any stronger in here either. Faith focused on deep breaths, and tried to ignore the throb in her hand as well. Getting a deep enough scratch to bleed properly had *hurt*, and the second time when they'd renewed the blood because the kidnappers hadn't come yet had made it even worse. She brought it up to her mouth to suck away any new seeping so that didn't make a noticeable smell either.

The door banged open, and a set of footsteps thumped in. The clarity of the sound made Faith hold her breath. If she could hear them, they could hear her. "Breakfast," Chuck said. "Where are you?" His voice squeaked with stress. "Fuck, where are they?" Footsteps, like he was running to the bathroom. That door crashed open.

Faith had to take a breath, but she tried to do it as slowly as possible. Don't hear her. Please, don't hear her. Or smell her.

"Amak!" The volume of the bellow made Faith wince. "They got out through the ceiling. We'd better cut them off upstairs. Now!"

The footsteps pounded out. Faith waited, listening, as hard as she possibly could, but there was no sound of the door closing.

She thought she should probably count to sixty, but she quickly revised that down to thirty because she didn't think she could stand any longer. Laurence yanked open the door she was facing at twelve, and she felt like her insides had been pressure hosed with adrenaline.

"Even if they come back, we need to get running." He was almost visibly vibrating with impatience. He seemed to recognize that pulling on her while she was wiggling out of the cupboard would only snag her and slow her down, but the moment she was out and standing up, he grabbed her arm.

Then they ran. Into the hallway, and they had to choose right or left. Laurence picked left, perhaps because he was already a little skewed in that direction, and Faith tried to register what she was seeing around her while still running flat out after him. The lights were stretched too far apart to see well, like they were on an after-hours or emergency setting. Was there a stairwell? An exit sign? No windows, just more doors with official-looking plastic number plates. One door even had a prosaic men's restroom sign.

Laurence reached a corner first, and then he was slamming back into her and they both went down in a tangle, him on top. She took most of the impact on her ass, fortunately, but even though Laurence wasn't a big guy, she'd have bruises from his landing for sure, especially on her belly, where one of his elbows had come down. He was wheezing too hard to roll off, so she shoved him and then finally took in Chuck, just lowering his arm from where he must have basically clotheslined Laurence.

"How stupid do you think we are?" Amak called, arriving from where he must have been covering the other direction in the hall, while Chuck just smirked. "The blood was a good touch, though. I actually had to think for a second."

"You must be exhausted, then," Faith muttered into Laurence's shoulder after helping him sit up. She might as well not have bothered, because Chuck knocked him right back down again with a precisely aimed kick to the jaw, then yanked him up with a hand under his armpit while he was too stunned to resist. Faith hurried to her feet and held up her hands in surrender lest Amak think anything similar was necessary for her.

He took a tight grip on her arm, but nothing more. Still riding high on his smugness, she suspected. Clearly, a plan based on physical logistics and blood wasn't the way to go with werewolves. Which left…well, a new plan she'd be coming up with any minute now. "Nice pursuit, but no kill, I'm afraid," he said.

"No cigar," Chuck corrected, and they both laughed. Faith thought hate hard enough at them she hoped they'd expire on the spot.

Amak shoved Faith back along the hall, Chuck following. She tried to use the time to gather more information about where they were being held, but she didn't see anything she hadn't seen on the way out. Numbered doors, low lights. A bulletin board that had been cleared of all content to leave its surface covered with odd patterns of holes.

At the door, Chuck undid the bolts and yanked it open only wide enough to shove Laurence through. Then Amak did the same with her, almost sending them both tumbling again with Faith on top this time. Fortunately, Laurence caught her, stuttered a step back, and then braced his feet to catch them both. A beat later, their captors shoved the morning's two doughnut boxes in behind them and the bolts slid home.

"It was a good idea," Laurence said in the succeeding silence, tone lifting as if he were hoping she could be jollied into optimism and her next escape idea would bubble right up.

Faith wasn't in the mood. Childish as it was, still shaken from her fall, she needed time to sulk. She growled, though the word didn't really fit the sound anymore now she'd heard Laurence and the others do it, and jerked away from him. "No, it really wasn't." The next one would be, however.

8

The trouble with this plan, Faith reflected as the beginnings of nausea made her cheeks flush, was the timing. If the kidnappers didn't show up this afternoon, she would have given herself food poisoning for nothing.

She curled her knees against her chest and rolled a different area of her forehead to rest against the cupboard door. It had originally been cool, but being only a veneer over particleboard, it didn't hold that temperature for very long. Nausea often made Faith feel like she had a raging fever as her body freaked out at the other sick sensations. She gritted her teeth and tried to think of something else. She didn't want to throw up and have it all be over with before the kidnappers arrived.

Still, despite its risk, she still felt this was a good plan. It had come to her when Laurence knocked the container with the remainder of last night's enchiladas out of her reach, saying it smelled wrong. No lunch had been forthcoming, and that had been the most recent of their leftovers. That got Faith thinking: what if she ate it anyway, and acted like instead of having food poisoning, she needed to go to the hospital? The "fake illness to get attention" trick was an old one, but it played into a werewolf blind spot, which was what she'd realized they needed after the last failure. They didn't understand human physiology, and Laurence's reaction only cemented her certainty. When she pitched the idea, he looked like she'd just suggested infecting herself with Ebola or something, completely ignorant as to what food poisoning actually entailed.

Of course, assuring him that she'd throw up after an hour or two of misery and then it would all be over sounded fine in abstract, but was much more visceral in the midst of the misery. Laurence's footsteps paced up behind her, and she waited for him to pass by, but he hovered. Faith finally gave up and twisted around to look at him.

"Are you sure you're okay?" He caught his lip in his teeth, and started to take his hands out of his pockets before shoving them back in again for lack of anything better to do with them.

"Peachy." Faith dry-coughed, pure muscular frustration at a stomach that hadn't quite gathered itself to fully spasm yet. She remembered this stage. This was the stage where she went and hugged the toilet and thought throwing up thoughts in hopes it would finally *happen*, and then it would *end*. But instead she needed to be holding it down now.

"They've been here at least twice a day so far. So they should be here anytime." Laurence spoke earnestly, like the information was news to either of them. They'd hashed that out before Faith had eaten the enchilada. Otherwise, what would have been the point?

"Why don't you get me a drink?" Faith flapped a hand to the bathroom where they kept the fast-food cups they'd saved from soda to refill with water. "I'll chug it when they get here, to hopefully set me off." She'd certainly had a couple memorable experiences where drinking too much water to counteract a stomach upset from alcohol had backfired spectacularly.

Laurence returned quicker than she would have wished, and she had to deal with his hovering again. "Go away," she said, coughed, and flapped her hand again. If he was so desperate to soothe her fevered brow, he could do it after she'd thrown up and was no longer a ticking time bomb of gross.

Laurence stood straight suddenly, making Faith think of a pointer dog. He must be able to hear them at the door. She grabbed the edge of the counter and carefully pulled herself standing. Her head swam and she dry-coughed several times. God, hurry up.

"He'll be glad we took initiative and helped him out," Chuck was saying as he entered. His face was creased with an exasperated frown. "Trust me." He strode over to Faith and shoved a phone at her. Her phone, she realized. "We need your password."

"He's much more likely to resent us interfering." Amak crossed his arms and glowered right back. They weren't so distracted that they didn't both look at Laurence when he just shifted his weight, though.

"It'll make a big difference if it works." Chuck shook the phone at her when she didn't touch it. "C'mon." When Faith gritted her teeth against a roil in her stomach and tried to take it from him, he kept stubborn hold. "No, you don't get to use it. We do. Just put in the password."

Faith supposed she should have carefully considered what damage they could do with her phone, but nothing occurred to her immediately and she really wanted to curl up in the bathroom so she just put in the code.

"I'm sure your husband won't be nearly so rational as the

alphas when we text him directly about the threat to your safety." Chuck said it loudly, pointedly aimed at his friend as well as his captives. "He'll demand they give our friend what he wants immediately."

Faith swallowed hard against a retch. God, she was close. What was Chuck saying? Susan's husband. What was his name? She couldn't remember.

"He's not here," Chuck said after a moment of scrolling through various menus. "It's not under 'husband' or 'beta' or something stupid, is it?"

Amak snorted. "Try 'puppy.' " He eyed Faith. "Or some other human pet name. What do humans use? 'Sweet honey,' isn't it?"

"Got that number memorized," Faith said lamely, and coughed. Amak finally seemed to see her properly, and he stared at her in confusion. Faith assumed that by now she had the metaphorical greenish cast that came with nausea.

Chuck ignored Faith and kept scrolling. "There's her dad— and mom. We can use one of those instead."

"Her human parents," Laurence snapped. "Sure to call the police if they get an unexpected ransom demand. Don't be prey-stupid."

Faith stopped listening. There. This was it, the feeling that preceded more than coughing. She'd have had just enough time to run for the bathroom, but instead she crouched and aimed vengefully in the approximate direction of Chuck's shoes.

He jumped back at the first splatter and stared at her in abject horror as she brought the rest of the enchiladas up and then dry heaved a couple times for good measure. She spat out a mouthful of acid, wishing she could do something about the burn that had wormed a little way up into her sinuses, then gathered herself.

"Oh, God, is there blood?" Faith had meant to sound terrified, but she ended up sounding more wrung out. It would have to do. "If there's blood—if I have E. coli, I have to go to the hospital—"

"Echo-lie?" Chuck shoved her phone in his pocket and stared at her with wide eyes, so she knew she'd judged her choice of jargon properly.

"You die from dehydration. Because nothing stays down—" She felt exhausted enough a few tears popped up from the sheer relief that finished off food poisoning, and she blinked her eyes to make them fall. "Please, you have to take me to the hospital."

"That would be an excellent opportunity for her to escape." Amak inched closer to where she was half collapsed on the floor, then rocked back, lip curling in disgust.

"Come on, smell her." Chuck, with splattered shoes, seemed to be taking this more seriously. "She's not going anywhere."

Amak sighed, surveyed them both for a moment, then pointed at Laurence. "But he's definitely fine. Get to the back of the room, or we're not taking her anywhere."

Laurence put up his hands, and docilely backed until he was up against the wall. Chuck moved to block the quickest path around the table to the door. When both had arranged themselves, Amak nodded and jerked Faith up. She hunched over her stomach, concentrating on appearing as miserable as possible. If they got as far as the hospital, she assumed they might think far enough to worry about her ratting them out to the authorities, but she didn't plan to wait that long. Someone would have to get the car, leaving her with only one guard. That would be her moment.

Outside in the hallway, door shut with finality on Laurence, they turned right this time. There wasn't room for three abreast, so Amak held Faith's arm and Chuck dogged—ugh—their steps. Around a corner, an exit sign revealed itself. The door below it led to a concrete stairwell that echoed creepily, until they arrived at the first floor and flat industrial carpet damped their footsteps. They passed tall window panels looking into an office, maybe reception, with abandoned chairs and a desk here and there, skeletons of its disuse, and then out through double doors. Cool air at odds with the bright sunlight slapped her in the face. An older parking lot spread out before them, with faded lines and cracks here and there, mature trees swallowing up the street lights along the edge.

"Get the car," Amak directed. Belatedly, he glanced around, overt about his check for observers or passersby in a way Faith didn't allow herself to be. He was relieved; she was disappointed. The neighborhood seemed decaying and quiet, unlikely to have much traffic at all, never mind the kind that would notice anything beyond the stretch of road in front of their vehicle. Chuck jogged to a battered SUV tucked off along the side of the building, probably to avoid drawing attention from the road.

Faith moaned and collapsed once more to try to loosen Amak's grip. No dice, so she remained bent over and prodded her abused throat muscles into a cough, working herself up to a retch. Real nausea tiptoed up around the edges of her guts, summoned by the faking. God, she felt gross, but freedom was right *here* in front of her, and she must have seemed believable. She worked up enough spit to send it toward Amak's shoes this time, and he let go of her to neatly dodge it.

Faith ran. She knew she could never outrun them normally, never mind while sick, but a road was right there. If she could get to it, flag someone down, or even be in sight of the cars when they tackled her, someone might notice—

Her muscles were shaking but that almost helped narrow her vision down and focus her. A few steps, a sawing breath, and no one had caught her yet, maybe she'd make it. She dared hope.

Teeth closed around her ankle. The pavement rushed up to meet her face as she was dragged backward and Faith tried to scream in the vain hope someone could hear it but all the breath had gone out of her in a huge *whumph*. Her teeth clacked together as her chin caught on a root bump and she belatedly started to flail. It didn't help.

The wolf must have needed to avoid a curb or something, because her backward motion ceased for a second, then her foot slewed to the side. Faith gathered her breath for a last try at a scream. The pressure on her ankle ratcheted up, and bursts of pain made her realize that he hadn't broken the skin until now. Thank God for thick leather. She whimpered.

Having realigned them, the wolf jerked her back another couple feet, then another, like a dog with a heavy toy. Gravel abraded Faith's forearms and cheek, and she couldn't help but put all her effort simply into trying to twist up enough to put her weight onto her hips and belly, covered by her clothing. She couldn't hear cars passing on the road at this moment anyway.

Someone must have opened the door for the wolf, because Faith bumped over the threshold to carpet. The pain in her ankle ceased for a glorious second as the teeth disappeared and then rushed back in as the skin could bleed and swell properly. Faith pushed to her hands, then to her knees, and when she'd gotten her angle right to look all around her, Amak was standing behind her, naked. Uncircumcised, which, of course, when she thought about it, and also why the fuck was she thinking about it?

That was what had given her the illusion of a head start, she realized. The pause for him to change into a wolf. She hadn't been anywhere near reaching help, not really. Fuck.

Chuck circled in, still fully clothed at least, to stand between her and the door, and Amak snarled at her. "How in the Lady's name did you manage to make yourself sick on purpose? It better not be life threatening, because if it is, you're going to just have to die in your cage now."

When Amak grabbed Faith's arm again to manhandle her back downstairs, she snapped her teeth in his face, because it seemed like a canine thing to do, even if it was a useless gesture. They were going to get out of here. Somehow. She wasn't giving up, even if, with a throbbing ankle and wobbling guts, she felt like one solid mass of misery.

Once the door had slammed closed on her downstairs, Faith would have sat down on the floor where she was, but Laurence caught her with a strong grip across her shoulders like she would faint. "How badly did they hurt you?"

She concentrated on not crying instead of pushing him away. Reaction was compounding the hollow feeling throwing up had left behind, leaving her weak and shaky. She examined her arms, and found not as much road rash as she'd feared, then pulled away to sit down and peel off her boot. The teeth punctures were shallow and already scabbing over, but the skin around them looked like it would be a mess of bruising, and her boot was toast.

"Fucking hell. All that for nothing," she said. Laurence had no answer for that—which was fair, she couldn't think of one either—and continued to hover, expression crumpled with concern. This time she was actually glad of it. She held her hand up to him. "I have to wash it so it doesn't get infected."

Laurence bent, and swooped her into his arms. She'd meant he should pull her up and then maybe lend her a shoulder to walk over. But this was…okay. Better than okay. She could perfectly well get there on her own, but just this time she'd relax and enjoy the feeling of secure support.

9

Faith was dozing on the table, back to back with Laurence for warmth, when the sound of the door's locks jerked her awake. Laurence must have been properly asleep, because despite his awesome hearing, he jerked sitting at the same time as her.

The door cracked open, and Amak's broad face appeared briefly around it. "So you're free to go, apparently. Hurry up."

And then he pulled his head back and disappeared. Faith stared at the inviting crack in the door. "Is this a trick?"

"Don't question an abandoned fresh kill." Laurence hopped to the floor and boosted her down so she wouldn't land on her ankle. Which wasn't great, wrapped round and round with toilet paper inside her perforated boot, but it would certainly hold her weight. As soon as he set her on her feet, he took a good grip on her hand and dragged her out of the room at a jog.

Outside an empty hallway greeted them, with no evidence of the goons. Laurence kept turning his head and sniffing like he expected to find them hiding somewhere, but they made it to the front doors unopposed.

Outside, Amak was waiting alone. He shoved a phone at Laurence the moment he pushed open the doors. "You're supposed to talk to your alpha. Forgive us if we run like fuck because our friend is abandoning us, so we're not planning to be the only ones in reach when her husband hears." He nodded at Faith, then sprinted off. It wasn't quite Mikhail's "being in one place and then suddenly being in another" thing, but he was at the SUV and peeling out faster than her mind said he should have been.

"Roanoke?" Laurence said, hesitant, into the phone. "Yeah, they're driving off right now. They escorted us outside and then shoved my phone at me. Why isn't this one of the numbers in my address book?" That all came quickly, then Laurence seemed to collect himself. "Roanoke Silver. It's just you there? Yes. The Alaskans are gone. We're free...wherever this is." He listened for a moment, and then the person on the other end must have hung up, because he took the phone from his ear and grimaced at it. She could see the screen had gone blank from lack of battery.

And they were alone. Outside. Faith wanted to whoop, or possibly burst into tears. Laurence seemed to have run out of forward momentum as well. He shoved his phone in his pocket and paced around as if checking for enemies, while Faith took in their surroundings more generally.

Behind them, slumped on the concrete beside the door was a purse—her purse. She darted for it and found all her possessions inside, along with a few others. It must have been Laurence's phone Amak handed him, and she separated out his wallet too, but didn't go diving for his keys jangling with hers at the bottom just yet. "Thank God. We can call a taxi or something."

"I don't think we're near Seattle." Laurence tipped his nose high. "Might have to be a taxi to an airport."

"You can what, smell a map?" Relief made Faith punchy, and she laughed at her own joke more than he did.

"Different places smell different, so I mostly know this isn't somewhere I've been before. I mean, it's the same thing as if you looked around and didn't recognize a place." Laurence peered across the street at a block of modest, one-story houses in generous yards.

Faith pulled up her phone's map and told it to locate them. It did with a sullen clunk of its own low-battery noise. "You're fucking kidding me. Anchorage?" She looked all around again. It didn't *not* look like Alaska, she supposed. She'd never been there before.

"They must have come up by plane. Wouldn't have thought that either of them would have their license, but I suppose living up here..." Laurence trailed off into thoughts of his own, maybe to do with planes because he muttered a couple model names she recognized.

Faith shivered. It wasn't really that cold out here, but it certainly didn't feel like July and she had no coat. And they'd stopped moving, too. It suddenly struck her that Laurence was standing there completely shirtless. And looking delicious with his muscles and his silly blond peach fuzz, both on his jaw and a line below his navel that promised to lead lower. But that wasn't the point. They couldn't catch a flight back with him looking like that. The blood on his jeans only looked like some mysterious dark stain, but it was still a mysterious dark stain.

She coaxed just a little more out of her phone's battery and found a store within walking distance. "We need clothes." She oriented herself, pointed, and let her phone go huffily dark.

Laurence looked down at himself and finally laughed properly, just as punchy as she'd been earlier. "Okay." He flung an arm across her shoulders and drew in close—for warmth, of course.

The store had an attached soulless corporate coffeeshop, so Faith warned Laurence to sit down and relax if he had to wait for her. Which he probably would have to—Faith didn't care if she was going to wear them for only a day to get home; she wasn't going to buy jeans without trying them on. She didn't really need new clothes the way Laurence did, but she reveled in picking new everything anyway. After this experience, she relished the thought of tossing the clothes she'd lived in for days straight in the garbage rather than trying to wash them.

The store may have been soulless and corporate too, but the familiar logos and brands made Faith start to feel like she was living in the real world again, a place where no one she knew was kidnapped and werewolves didn't exist. More than once she caught herself flipping through a rack of shirts or coats, not seeing any of them but just listening to the *shunk* of metal hanger along metal bar, and feeling the crisp, clean sensation of new fabric.

Finally she had a basket of everything she needed, including bandages and antiseptic for her ankle, a phone charger, and a whole handful of chocolate bars. Laurence was lurking in front of the cash registers, exactly where she'd told him he didn't have to be. Guilt gripped her. How long had she spent flipping through clothes, again? He'd at least used the time to hit the restroom with his purchases, because he looked as normal as the store surrounding him in trendy T-shirt, light jacket, and jeans. He must have tossed his dirty jeans in the trash just as she'd thought of doing, because his plastic bag showed only the shapes of what looked like some snacks.

He smoothly joined her at the register and opened his wallet before she could say anything. He chose not the card on top, but one from several slots below. "Pack money," he explained, low-voiced. Faith didn't even consider arguing with him. The werewolves could pay for her new clothes and her flight home, too. It was only fair.

"No flights until tomorrow morning. I booked us a hotel room." As they collected themselves in front of the store's doors, Laurence tried to show Faith his phone screen. She waved him away. She didn't care what hotel he'd picked, as long as the room had beds and wasn't in a basement. And they weren't locked in.

They picked up take-out before they called a cab to the hotel, but Faith ignored the food and went straight for the shower the moment they entered the room. The need to be clean trumped hunger, hands down.

And the water was wonderful. Hedonistic. Faith let it flow and flow, inexcusably wasteful, while practical concerns slowly nibbled their way into her thoughts. She should call home. Work. Make sure no one had missed her. Faith was a little surprised to realize that she'd already decided not to call the police, but what would she tell them? The werewolf black hats were all long gone, and all she had to show for it were some bruises and a dog bite on her ankle. And maybe for no reason at all, she trusted that Laurence would make sure his fellow supernatural beasties policed their own and took care of it.

Finally she wrapped herself in a towel and ceded the hot water to Laurence. A groan of pleasure from the bathroom made her grin, and also made her acutely aware of the somewhat rough terrycloth texture against her nipples. Down, girl. It was just…reaction to the relief, of being free.

She dressed in the new, clean clothes, and tried to find her earlier simple pleasure in that sensation instead. She was sitting cross-legged on one of the two beds, prodding at the container of teriyaki with a fork when the water turned off.

She looked up, only to have Laurence walk out completely naked, using the towel on his hair. She stared. She couldn't help herself. No amount of "down girl"-ing herself was going to help now. No six-pack, but that didn't matter because his stomach was absolutely flat and those *hipbones*...

Laurence looked apologetic and grabbed at least his jeans and pulled them on. "Sorry. Nudity taboos, I know." Then his face changed—maybe he'd caught her scent, as corny as that sounded, and damn it sounded corny—and he grinned. "Here?"

It took Faith a moment of digging to remember what he meant. She wasn't very verbal right now. *Not here*, she'd said when they were locked up. She loved that he'd remembered her exact words. Of course he had.

She licked her lips. Yes. But first she glanced reluctantly toward the door. "We should see if the little hotel store has—"

Laurence rummaged in his shopping bag—his opaque shopping bag—and came up with box of condoms. "These?" The grin got wider.

"Jackass." Faith grinned too, and as she stood, she pulled off the shirt she'd so recently pulled on. Laurence tossed the condoms onto the bed and met her halfway, kissing her, and he was just the right height after all, the *perfect* height for her. She pushed against him, deepening the kiss as he nudged her backward.

The back of her knees hit the bed before both of them expected it and she sat down and he tumbled onto her, both of them laughing. He knelt between her knees and urged her to the very edge of the bed. Faith knew where this was going, and it was very classy of him, but—"There's something I like even more," she said, working to make it come out as sexy as possible. "If you're willing…"

Laurence sat back on his heels, face lighting up. "Show me."

Faith stood and scooted out from between him and the bed, and pushed him to sit down in her place with an imperious hand on his chest. She shucked off her jeans but left her panties. She climbed up to straddle his lap and put her hand on his shoulder to balance. She needed just the right angle…

There. She caught the lump of the button of his jeans and fabric around it and ground it against just the right spot. Her body lit up, climbing with each stroke. She leaned back to check Laurence's face, to make sure he was into it too, but she could tell from his wicked smile that he was feeling friction as well, which was why she liked this position so much.

He undid her bra and pressed a hand against her back so her nipples were at the right height to take into his mouth. He sucked and Faith made an encouraging noise. "Harder," she urged. "Teeth." He obliged with the merest light brush.

"You can be rougher." Faith settled her weight back again, sitting more over his thighs. "Like, really rough. If you want." Maybe he didn't want, and it was just her own baseless assumptions that had made her initially dismiss the possibility that a werewolf could be the vanillaest of vanilla. She didn't usually roll this out until the second time with a guy.

"I'd love to. But I could hurt you." Laurence's smile twisted darker, and more self-deprecating. "I'm stronger than a normal guy…"

"Tell you what." Faith scrubbed the heel of her palm absently against her nipple to keep arousal from dropping down to nothing while they worked the important stuff out. "If it hurts or you go too far or I'm at all worried, I'll say—" A good safe word escaped her for a second, and then inspiration struck and she had to laugh. "Silver bullet."

Laurence returned a laughing groan worthy of the worst pun and dragged her back close to him again. "Show me how rough," he demanded, and she dipped down to grind against his jeans again and then did. His hair was just long enough she could get a good grip, and she jerked his head back and kissed him only to get his lower lip in her teeth and bite, hard. He groaned, a wonderful groan, and his fingers dug deep into her back. When she let him go to catch her breath, he tangled his fingers up in her damp hair and took a punishing, delightful grip and renewed the kiss.

It didn't take long at all before she could feel she was close enough that this was the right moment. She leaned over and shook out the condom box, tore one of the foil packets. She tried to push him to lie back on the bed, but he resisted, and growled low and strangely, alluringly, canine beside her ear. "Got an idea."

He guided her to stand and wiggled out of his jeans carefully, since he was rock hard and ready. He rolled on a condom while she got rid of her panties, then just picked her up, so easy, and bumped her back against the wall that divided the main room from the bathroom. Probably better for the neighbors that way. Faith did her best to help, taking some of her weight on her hands across the back of his neck, but he got a good grip under her thighs and seemed to know what he was doing. He slammed home in one smooth thrust once he got lined up.

Faith groaned herself. So good. "Hard," she urged, and he did, and bit at the side of her neck, where it met her shoulder. Faith passed the point where she knew what she was saying, just "yes" or "hard," maybe, with every climbing, grinding stroke and bite, and when he shuddered and pressed against her, panting, all she had to do was free fingertips to grind a last couple times and she crested up and shuddered too.

He let her down carefully to her feet, and she found herself without words once more. "Thanks," she settled on, after a moment, diffident but emphatic. Maybe it was just the high of celebrating their freedom layered on top, but that was the best sex she remembered ever having.

Laurence pressed a gentle kiss to her temple. "No, thank you."

He cuddled exactly like a dog of her friend's, Faith discovered, curled up together in bed after their second showers. Normally when guys tried to hold her in their arms, she started feeling confined and banished them to their own side of the bed to sleep. But Laurence kept his hands to himself and tucked up against her, as close as he could get, but not trying to wrap her up. The only odd thing was the way he kept trying to tuck his forehead against her shoulder too, but Faith was so fulfilled and also exhausted she started drifting off even with him right there.

An unfamiliar ringtone jerked her out of pleasant floating. Laurence hissed a curse and rolled away to grab his phone. "John? Yeah, they let us go. No, I'm in a hotel." He froze suddenly, muscles twanging with tension, and climbed deliberately off the bed. "The human?"

He waved for Faith's attention, and didn't continue speaking until she was looking straight at him in confusion. "I gave her a choice whether to…to just walk away. We all know she didn't get a choice about whether to get dragged into our world in the first place—and get hurt because of it—and I thought she deserved the chance to forget about all of this and go back to a normal life. I mean, no one's seen her but a couple dumb Alaskans and some Russian who's gone now, right?"

Faith stopped halfway through the motion of sitting up. He was right. She could just walk away.

And she needed to. She'd known it in the store, she realized, though she hadn't admitted it to herself. Laurence's world wasn't hers, and they'd shared something dangerous, and something really fun together, but that wasn't love or even really friendship. They weren't bound by anything more than circumstance, and better to admit she needed her normal world now, before they *became* bound. What happens in Anchorage stays in Anchorage? Something like that. Enjoy—well, that was a strong word—endure the adventure, go home, treasure the memories.

She swallowed, nodded, and got up to pull on the rest of her clothes and grab her purse and charged phone.

Another man's voice came indistinctly through the phone, shouting. Chewing Laurence out for letting her go, clearly. "I don't know what flight she's taking. We separated at the door of the building they were keeping us in."

Her phone showed an email with the e-ticket he'd bought her earlier in the evening, with the pack money again. Faith dumped Laurence's keys on the bed near the door and started rummaging for anything else of his.

Laurence gulped and that kicked-dog look came back into his body language as he told whoever he was talking to the name of their hotel. "Twenty minutes away? Roanoke Silver said you were coming, but I didn't realize you were so close—Yeah. Okay. Great."

That was hardly long enough to get a cab to the airport before the werewolves arrived. Faith had to leave *right now*. She still hesitated in the doorway. When Laurence looked so low like that, she wanted to at least hug him goodbye, but there was no time. And she wasn't leaving him behind; she was accepting a gift of the protection of a normal life he was offering her. Wasn't that worth something as well?

She shut the door and jogged down the hallway for the elevator. Maybe it was for the best.

10

It wasn't until Faith was transferring various possessions from her purse into her pockets and field bag ready to go out in the field about a week later that she noticed the extra clinking weight at the bottom. Rather than leave the usual litter of receipts in the bottom for next time, she dumped her whole purse out on the kitchen counter.

Pocket change clunked and rolled around. Not hers, because the purse had a zippered pocket she always used instead. It must be Laurence's, and they'd dumped the complete contents of his pockets into her purse. She brushed away the receipts and counted. That was a dollar eighty-six he was never going to see again, she supposed.

But she wasn't going to think about that, because she wasn't thinking about anything that had happened. She'd make sure her field bag was ready, catch a *CSI* rerun or something, and then get an early night so she could be at the office for 6 a.m. tomorrow.

Among the coins was another object, of roughly the same diameter but not the same thickness. Faith picked it up and examined it. It looked like one of those glass aquarium rocks that she'd seen used as counters or in plant pots but never actually in an aquarium. It was bigger than most, mostly flat on the bottom and rounded on the top, and a translucent shimmery white color. She turned it over and discovered the flat side had been painted black, though the glass was too smooth and the paint was steadily wearing away. Something to do with the moon, no doubt.

Without thinking, Faith settled the glass stone with the rounded surface against her cupped first two fingers, and stroked the flat surface with her thumb. It felt right that way, like it had been shaped specifically to be a worry stone. Of course, she considered that kind of thinking to be highly unprofessional and unscientific in other techs: this naturally shaped rock fits perfectly in my hand, so obviously some ancient person felt the same way! No, not necessarily. Any *evidence* it had ever been used?

She supposed in this case, the paint was evidence. She twisted the stone in the light, trying to see if there was less paint in the middle, where a thumb would likely touch most often. Hard to tell. It could have been worn off against the inside of a pocket easily enough.

Faith set the stone aside, swept the change into her purse's zippered pocket, and went back to packing her equipment and then making her lunch for tomorrow. The stone waited there, patient, until she came by later that night during a commercial break and picked it up again for no particular reason other than it was smooth and pretty.

She let it settle into her fingers, where it did feel absolutely right, and stroked the back without looking as she watched TV, until the glass warmed to her body temperature.

Maybe she'd keep it in her pocket too, as Laurence had.

Back a Winner

This story is set before the events of SILVER. Both alphas, John and Michelle, go on to play important roles in the Roanoke pack hierarchy, but Pierce himself also appears throughout the series, helping out in the middle ranks.

Pierce winced as his alpha put a hand on their guest's back to direct her to the stand selling race programs. Emerald Downs swarmed with crowds down from Seattle, but here at the entrance they weren't thick enough to justify John's touch. Michelle didn't need help parting the crowd, either: she was a short woman, but that only concentrated her intensity. Today, she wore her mass of dark hair loose, and the light brown of her skin glowed even in the cloudy brightness.

Michelle's scent soured with frustration and she increased her pace to pull away from John's hand. If Pierce could smell that from over here, he didn't see how his alpha could miss it right next to her.

"Would you grab programs for us too?" Pierce jogged a few steps to catch up to Michelle and offered her a twenty before putting himself squarely in his alpha's path. John stopped, frowning, and Michelle accepted the opportunity to put a little more distance between them.

Being on the receiving end of his alpha's frown was rather intimidating. John wasn't much taller than Pierce, but he was much more solidly built. Pierce put a hand on John's elbow anyway and leaned in as Michelle spoke to the program salesperson. "Ease up with Portland, would you? I know she's hot, but if you flirt any more overtly, you'll piss her off, and we'll lose our nice, quiet border with her pack."

John stared at him with an expression of such confusion that Pierce wanted to growl. John was fine with other women. Pierce supposed it was Michelle's high rank that made her so attractive that John's social skills turned to jelly and his nose turned off. Even beyond wanting to keep the advantages of an amicable border, Pierce hated to see his friend embarrass himself this way. He was usually such a stable, competent leader.

"Relax." John shook his head, apparently just discarding his confusion. "This isn't a territory negotiation or something. I'm just showing a fellow alpha the local sights." He stepped around Pierce and ran fingers through his short brown hair, which just encouraged the cowlick.

Pierce moved right back into his path. "Seattle—" He hoped using the title would lend more weight to his advice than casual teasing between friends, but John frowned again.

"If you're this worried about politics, you should accept my offer to be beta. Otherwise, leave it to me." John pushed Pierce out of his way and strode to join Michelle. His fingers clumsily lingered on hers as he took his program from her.

Pierce gritted his teeth. Well, that had backfired. Rather

than compound his mistake, he let John and Michelle move off alone. Eventually he realized he was blocking traffic, so he let the stream of people carry him into the building. He drifted out of the flow into a clear area near the food court and stood with his hands shoved into his pockets as the announcer pattered about the next race in an Australian accent.

He wasn't sure he was cut out to be beta, that was the problem. He wished John could understand that. Just because Pierce was friends with the alpha didn't mean he was suited to take on the responsibility of watching over everyone in the pack as well as backing up the alpha. And Pierce wanted to *be* sure before he made his decision. If he took that responsibility on, he couldn't in good conscience abandon it if it proved too much for him.

A blond college student pushed by and Pierce sidestepped to avoid a slosh of beer from one of the two large plastic cups filling the man's hands. Too damn crowded. At least this outing had been carefully planned to coincide with the new moon. Being jostled in crowds of humans set most Were on edge at the best of times. It was much easier to remain calm when the need to run on four feet wasn't itching underneath your skin.

But he still clearly needed to stop standing around brooding with this many people trying to crash into him. John wanted privacy to dig himself deeper, so Pierce supposed he might as well try to have some fun at the races on his own.

He slipped out through the open side of the building to stand among the bleachers at the edge of the track. On a board in the center of the track, brightly lit numbers updated odds and counted down minutes to the race. With the odds in mind, Pierce followed his nose to the paddock area. John swore it was possible to make some serious cash if you smelled out the winners. Maybe he could sniff out a hot tip and use that as an excuse to go back and distract Michelle. John hadn't said he couldn't talk to her, and Pierce really didn't want her going away angry. An amicable border meant the Seattle pack could take business trips or even vacations to Oregon. And more importantly, it meant he and the pack's other fighters didn't have to be constantly on their guard near the border, waiting for some of Portland's bored fighters to jump them because they felt like a skirmish.

Behind a black-painted railing, the horses were being led between short walls in the suggestion of stalls to get their saddles and colors. Once saddled, grooms wearing bright vests with the horses' numbers walked them around the outside of the paddock. Chattering humans pushed to the railing, pointing to the horses as they passed. The number two horse suddenly kicked up its heels, drawing a general laugh of surprise. Pierce edged closer to the rail and captured a spot as a bored teen left. He drew in deep breaths, trying to tease apart the different horses' scents in the confined space. What did a winner smell like, anyway? John hadn't mentioned that.

The next horse to approach in its circle snorted and pulled toward him with marked curiosity. Pierce's heart sped as he waited for any of the surrounding humans to react. But the groom dragged the horse back on track and the next one seemed too focused to muster curiosity. Pierce snorted mentally at himself. Of course no one had noticed. The horse could hardly shout, "That doesn't smell like a human!" Animals reacted to all kinds of things in their environment, and while it was best to avoid the dog park, there was no need to freak out.

A few of the following horses smelled tired, or bored, or angry. One smelled joyful. Pierce smiled as it passed. That one had the enthusiasm needed to win, he suspected. He checked the smaller odds board at the side of the paddock and grimaced. It was the favorite. Of course. Not much money to be made there. He lingered at the rail, hoping to find a candidate for one of the other categories—place or show, his vague memory of the informational signs out front prompted him—but none of the other horses stood out except as very bad bets.

A good-looking woman battled her way to the rail a few rowdy children down from him. Her fingers on the rail were bare and she wore an ice-blue top sewn to look as if the fabric was gathered in a knot just below her generous chest. Tight above, it floated loosely over her stomach below.

A moment later, Pierce's nose broke into his appreciation to explain the reason for that. She was pregnant. Far enough along she needed the shirt to disguise it, but early enough the trick should work on those who couldn't smell her. Even if he'd felt like flirting with John's terrible example on his mind, he wouldn't want to pester this woman.

The rowdy children climbed up on the concrete step the rail was set into, pressing themselves against the rail to keep their balance. The oldest boy shoved his neighbor and they all tumbled off, shrieking. They crashed into the woman and she stumbled back into the crowd, eyes wide with surprise. Pierce lost sight of her, but he was certain any moment he'd hear the skidding thump of her impact. What if the fall hurt the baby?

Pierce shoved several people roughly aside, desperate to get to the woman. He couldn't let the baby get hurt!

When he reached the edge of the paddock crowd, he found the woman still on her feet. She stood slightly bent, hands on her knees as she collected herself. Something about the posture raised a flash of memory: his mother, standing that way, panting harshly, smelling of sweat and fear and desperation.

Pierce shook himself out of the memory and strode over.

This woman was breathing just fine and smelled merely startled. He hovered a hand near her elbow. "Are you all right?"
He frowned at her belly. If something had gone wrong with the
baby, would he be able to smell it? Her scent didn't seem any
different.

The woman straightened with a breathy laugh. "Oh, fine.
Just lost my balance for a second." Her eyes flicked to his face
and she seemed to note the angle of his gaze.

"Well, give yourself a minute." Pierce nudged her across the
paved area beside the paddock until they were well away from
the crowd.

The woman's smile suggested she was humoring him. "You
noticed, didn't you?" She smoothed the fabric of her shirt over
her slight bump, then fluffed it up again. "Trust me, I'm fine."
She offered her hand. "Thanks, though. I'm Terry."

"Pierce." He shook her hand. He could see from her expression that any more concern would be unwelcome, so he
tried to make normal conversation. "Got a bet on any of them?"
He nodded toward the horses. The crowds by the paddock dispersed as jockeys guided the horses away and music over the
loudspeakers trumpeted that the race was about to start.

Terry shrugged. "I'll bet the next race. My friends and I got
here too late to study the program for this one."

Pierce assumed she wanted to get back to her friends now,
so he stepped back and looked her over a final time. "Are you
certain you're all right? I'm sure the track has a medic."

"Yes, Jesus. It take a lot more than a stumble to cause a mis-
carriage." Terry pulled a face, then grew thoughtful. "Did you
have a girlfriend or someone who…?"

Pierce shook his head automatically. No, it had been his
mother who'd lost the baby. Babies. His parents had wanted
more children so badly, but his mother was one of those who

couldn't shift even once after conception or she'd lose the child. He'd been fifteen the last time they tried.

He'd been out with the hunt. His mother had been back at the house, watching the kids while the baby, six months along, kept her in human anyway. They'd returned to the stink of sweat and panic, and sobbing, frightened children gathered around his mother in the nursery. His mother's hair straggled over her forehead, stuck down with sweat from the effort of holding herself in human. She stood bent, hands on knees, shaking all over and panting harshly.

"Laura!" Pierce's father shoved through the pack gathered in the doorway and strode to her.

She stopped him a step away, one hand thrust out, still shaking. "I can smell the trees on all of you. I just want to run—"

A few urgent hand motions, arms held out for children who were happy to flee the confusing storm of emotions, and the rest of the pack faded away. Pierce remained huddled in the doorway, clinging to the jamb. He should do something, everything in him screamed that he must help, must *do* something, but he had no idea what. His father would help, he told himself. He could relax. His fear didn't listen, squeezing like tight fingers around his throat.

"Laura." His father's face twisted with anguish. "You can do this. You're so strong. Were woman are stronger than Were men, to be able to hold back for nine months in a row. You've done it before. The Lady's with you. Believe in yourself."

"The Lady's the one calling me." Pierce's mother gasped and cupped one arm around her belly. "I was so worried, and the more I worried, the closer the shift got—I can't, it's too close now, I can't think of anything else…"

His mother's body began to twist. Pierce whirled and set his back against the wall beside the doorway so he didn't have to see. Why couldn't his father stop it? He could hardly breathe through the tightness of his throat but he could still smell it. Smell the slow seep of blood as the human-form child was crushed and cut off from nutrients from the alien body suddenly surrounding it.

Pierce fled before he could smell anything else.

"—Pierce?" Terry's tone suggested she'd repeated his name at least once already. He must have missed all the race calling, too, because the announcer was now listing the winners in the background. Terry frowned at him, lip caught in her teeth with concern. "I didn't mean to dig up bad memories."

Pierce waved away her apology. "My mother had a genetic condition. She lost several, when I was young. It's a long time ago now." He didn't realize he was going to tell a version of the truth until he heard the words.

He scrubbed at his eyes. A decade and a half later, and the memory still twisted him up. He wanted to pant through his mouth to stop smelling that blood, feeling the burn of knowing nothing he or his father could do would stop what was happening. Even knowing his mother had recovered, moved on with her life, didn't blunt his emotions. His parents had never tried for a child again.

Terry looked at the ground. "I'm sorry," she said, tone turning it from apology to sympathy. "From what I've read since it's been on my mind, miscarriages are much more common than anyone talks about."

"I'm sure *you'll* be fine." Pierce summoned a smile that grew more natural when Terry returned it. "Nothing to worry about." The overwhelming smell of horse chased away anything else in his mind, and a waft from the food court added fried food to the mix.

"I think I'm far enough along now. And my sister had really easy labor with her two. I'm free to worry about things like what I'm going to do when it gets here." Terry laughed. "It scares the shit out of me sometimes. Having a whole human being who's completely dependent on you, and one day they won't be dependent, and you have to hope to God you didn't screw it up early, because by that point you can't do a thing about it." She stepped to the side to get a more direct view to the track and pointed. "Like the trainers for those horses. When the race starts, they're just like everyone else, cheering because they can't do anything to help. Only they can feel guilty about the outcome. But isn't that life? Do your best, then step back and see what happens."

Pierce exhaled in amusement at the aptness of the metaphor. He froze as a realization gripped him. His father hadn't been able to reach out and help his mother keep control. In that moment, he had only been able to offer words and his presence. Pierce would have moments like that if he became a beta.

Moments cheering his alpha and packmates on.

Grooms trickled in, readying for the next race's horses. Pierce banked the spark of his epiphany and returned with Terry to the railing, securing a spot before many fans arrived. The horses' arrival gave them something lighter to discuss than miscarriages and raising children, but Pierce only gave half his attention to the conversation.

Now he knew why something deep in him had held him back from being beta. He never wanted to feel that way again, trapped with no way to help. But what about everything you could do beforehand? As Terry had said, that was life. You prepared as best you could, and didn't beat yourself up when something unexpected went wrong.

He could be beta. More than that, he *should* be beta. He should accept the position so he didn't let a failure to help his mother that wasn't his—or anyone's—fault haunt him for the rest of his life.

He and Terry fell silent as the last of the seven horses for this race circled to its stall area. Absently, Pierce smelled each as it passed. Only three horses smelled like they planned to even try and he remembered his earlier plan to construct a hot tip. Picking all three winners in the right order gave a large payout, even if some were favorites.

Pierce glanced at Terry and her bright interest in the horses. If he thanked her now, she'd probably ask what for. He couldn't really explain how she'd made him realize what decision he needed to make. He lowered his voice, turning the conspiratorial volume into a joke. "You should bet on the two, six, and four. In that order." He grinned and stepped away from the rail. "It was good to meet you."

Terry waved a bemused farewell. No telling if she'd use the tip, but Pierce felt better having offered it.

He couldn't track his alpha with so many humans around, but he doubted John and Michelle would stay in the stands between races, and the building wasn't that big. He spotted them at the food court before too long, and paused while he was still unobserved to check the situation.

Michelle was still speaking to John, though she held her shoulders stiffly, arms crossed. Pierce strode up into a discussion of different food options involving much pointing to the large, bright boards at food court stations. "Portland, Seattle," he said, and dipped his head respectfully. John stilled, probably expecting Pierce to try to speak to him alone again, but Pierce ignored him.

Michelle grunted in acknowledgment. "Win anything on the last race?"

"Didn't bet." Pierce shrugged and glanced at his alpha. Hopefully John wouldn't be *too* annoyed by this method of accepting his offer… "While you're here, I actually wondered if you could give me some advice since I'm such a new beta. I know you share some of your eastern border with Billings, and I wondered how you have your beta and patrols handle it when his young pack members cross to cause trouble?"

Michelle must have liked the implied compliment that Pierce respected her handling of Billings enough to want to emulate it because she relaxed visibly. "Why don't I tell you over a drink?" she said, and strode to the counter to order her own rather than give John the chance to awkwardly offer to buy it for her. The race calling started in the background.

John hung back without Pierce having to do anything. "New beta? As of when?" He smelled amused, Pierce noted with relief. Thank the Lady. But his friend had been trying to talk him into it for some time now, so why shouldn't he be happy?

Pierce made a show of checking his watch. "Seven minutes ago."

"What changed your mind?" John's eyes narrowed as a thought seemed to occur to him. "Because of the flirting? I am not that bad!"

Pierce clapped him on the back. "As your beta, I feel it's my duty to tell you that you're *worse*." He paused to listen as the announcer listed the winners: two, six, four. He grinned. "Come on, we shouldn't keep Seattle waiting. But try not to touch her, all right?"

John growled, low and grumpy, but he followed Pierce's suggestion this time.

Temper

This story is set near the end of REFLECTED. Tom—and his relationship with Felicia—matures over the course of the whole series and here he's the first to discover evidence of a lost piece of Were history.

Tom turned off the highway, such as it was, following the lead of the car ahead of him. They both bumped over a set of railroad tracks that cut a thin line of scrub between green, irrigated fields. Their goal stood out against the same fields, the cemetery's stones barely visible among a tangle of golden, dead grass. Green rose farther back, trees probably gathered around some creek bed, perhaps dry at the moment. Tom found himself sniffing for Were through the open window, which was stupid. Even if the photograph he'd seen turned out to be legit, that gravestone would have been carved by Were who lived more than a century ago.

The car pulled onto the shoulder, but the ditch veered so close to the road immediately before and after that spot Tom had to go about a hundred yards farther to park his battered pickup. Clearly, no one had conceived of more than one visitor to the cemetery at once. The young human woman waited by her car as he crunched down the road to join her. Tricia looked even more out of place now than when he'd first met her in the coffee shop in town. He'd asked about her photographs, displayed on the walls in the usual "local artist for sale" style, and the barista had offered to call in the photographer herself. Most of the customers had been stylish enough in a battered-jeans rural farming town sort of way, but Tricia had walked in with store-weathered jeans and very expensive sunglasses.

Even those must not have been enough now against the low, early evening sun, because she shaded her eyes as she examined the little cemetery. "They don't get much vandalism out here, fortunately. Overgrown as all hell, but so many of the little family plots are. When the owners don't try to cart off the stones in the night like that will make it all right for them to build on it."

Tom set his worries aside long enough to crack a smile, stuck his hands in his pockets, and ambled after Tricia. Who'd have thought someone could be so interested in cemeteries? Not something normal like genealogy research with the names from the stones, but documenting their locations and conditions, and helping to restore them. In the coffee shop, she'd called it a hobby. Cemetery hobby. Crazy.

"And the one in the photograph? Where's that?" Listening to a hot woman talk about something she was passionate about was one thing, but it wasn't idle curiosity that had brought him here.

"This way." Tricia pointed and strode out confidently. Expensive sunglasses aside, she wore sturdy hiking boots. "You're lucky I was around when Mare—Mary—called. I live in Spokane, but I'm here often enough visiting my aunt and uncle that they suggested the display. Then again, you probably don't need me to direct you. There are a number of stones with those motifs in this plot. Some kind of family thing, clearly, but I can't figure out what. I've never seen it anywhere else."

Tom sure hoped not. He paused and tore at grass obscuring a stone beside his path. It was clearly one of the ones Tricia had mentioned. Lady damn it. Moon phases framing the name, running wolves along the bottom—how *could* they? How could any sane Were carve a stone like this and leave it for humans to find?

Tom took a deep breath. He couldn't read the Cyrillic characters, but the years were recognizable. If humans had managed to overlook these stones for a century and a half, they couldn't be the end of the world now. "Do you know what it says?"

Tricia backtracked and leaned over the stone. She absently fit her thumb into the circle of the Lady at full and brushed some blown soil from the bottom edge. "I keep meaning to send my photographs to someone who speaks Russian for a translation, but I haven't yet."

Small mercies. Tom gave her his best smile. "You know— I'm kind of wandering at the moment, but the reason I wandered this direction is I was trying to trace where my family came from. No one's mentioned any Russian immigrants before, but I could be related to some. I know my ancestry's a mixture of various pioneers who headed out West. And my family breeds dogs, maybe…"

Just when the damage control story Tom was spinning seemed to be going well, his phone rang. He cursed under his breath and checked the screen without answering. Felicia. Of course it was. Lady damn her to the void, when was she going to get the message that he *didn't want to talk to her*? Some things you couldn't apologize for that easily. He sent the call straight to voicemail, to join the probably thirty-seven other ones that had accumulated by now, and shoved the phone back in his pocket.

"Anyway." Tom cleared his throat. Damage control. That's what he was doing. Not thinking about Felicia. "Breeding dogs. Maybe that's what this is about." He pointed to the wolf silhouettes. And Lady, didn't he hope that if she did get the stone translated, it wouldn't be a prayer to the Lady or something. He wouldn't have thought any Were could be that stupid, but he also wouldn't have believed any Were could be so stupid as to carve wolves on their gravestones.

Rather than giving the beep of a voicemail recorded, his phone started ringing again. Tom rejected that call too and shoved the phone away before he could crush it. He knew he'd regret the loss later. But it would be so *satisfying* to crush it into dust. Why wouldn't Felicia *stop*?

Tricia grimaced in vague sympathy. "Forget to call your mother often enough while 'wandering'?" She wasn't mocking, but Tom could hear the quotes in her tone that made "wandering" into "unemployed and needing to get out of parental hair for a while."

Tom bristled, barely keeping a too-canine growl to a vaguely human rumble in his chest. What was she, two years older than him? Certainly not more than twenty-six. She wasn't far enough from her own irresponsible early twenties to look down on him, and besides. Irresponsibility wasn't his fucking problem, it was Felicia's. He was perfectly capable of finding a job the moment he felt ready to go back and face Seattle again.

"For your information, it was a bad break-up, and she's in denial, okay? I don't want to even *see* her, not after she chose her bully of a childhood sweetheart, or whatever he was, over—"

That came out all in one breath and only a need for air let Tom wrestle himself back under control. What in the Lady's name was he doing, blowing up at strangers? And not just any stranger, but one he was trying to charm so she didn't think too hard about wolves on gravestones. He took a deep breath, but no charming words entered his mind with it. All he could think of was what he'd say to Felicia if he did answer one of these times. Flay her voice with his, he would.

Tricia's expression twisted with embarrassment. "I'm sorry." She looked at his pocket with the phone, lips parting to add something, then she pressed them together before changing the subject with unnecessary brightness. "Come to think of it, I've seen that moon motif somewhere else, maybe with the dog connection too." Her voice trailed into a questioning intonation, checking if he was interested before she continued.

Tom dredged up an encouraging smile. Concentrate. Focus on solving this immediate problem. Moon emblems were nowhere near as bad as those of wolves—or the combination of the two—so he wasn't too worried about whatever lunar connection she was making. Tricia relaxed. "It's in the car, actually." She jogged off. Tom followed more slowly, meeting her on the way back.

He'd expected her to have her camera, to show him something in the memory, but instead she held something small enough to close her fingers over. "I found this in an antique store in the next town over. It's the same design, look." Tricia opened her fingers, revealing a large pocket watch of tarnished brass. She traced her finger over the arc of the Lady's faces there, then traced it in the air before the stone they'd been examining.

Tom's heart picked up with anxiety instead of anger, as it had when he'd happened to glance at the photograph in the coffee shop, Were symbols in artful black and white. She was right, that was remarkably similar. What in the Lady's name—?

"The best part is inside. Like a proper eighteenth-century miniature." Tricia pressed a knob to pop the watch's lid. The hinges must have needed cleaning because it stopped about halfway up. Tom took it and nudged the lid the rest of the way.

He stopped breathing for a second. The painting was exquisitely, delicately done, colors preserved inside the watch case, but what it showed...a white wolf walked beside a lean, black-haired man, his hands lifted as if in some comfortable conversational gesture. It must be—but it *couldn't* be—the Lady—but that was *blasphemous*. The Lady and Death were trapped in human and wolf, respectively, and to show their other forms was simply—

"What's wrong?" Tricia's incredulous stare brought Tom back to the cemetery, the golden dead grass, the low sunlight. He'd been properly growling, he realized, and cut the sound off immediately.

"Just concentrating. There's a lot of detail." Tom almost couldn't bear to keep seeing the image, but he pretended to examine it more closely. He focused his eyes on the wrong distance, and it settled into a safer blur. "I wonder if that's my ancestor. Family stories say we used to be known for our white dogs, but that bloodline died out. Like white German Shepherds, you know?"

She held out her hand, but he couldn't—he couldn't relinquish the watch. "How much did you pay for it? I'll give you double. My parents and everyone would be delighted to get it back into the family." Even if it was expensive, Tom knew the Roanokes would pay him back. This kind of artifact needed to be out of human hands yesterday.

Tricia pulled it away from him. She grimaced in vague apology, but did it anyway. Tom didn't think he should make this into a physical struggle, even if he was sure to win. "I'm sorry, it's not for sale."

Deep breath. Tom usually considered himself fairly good with words—though he couldn't line his kills beside those of the Roanokes—but they seemed to have deserted him once more, even without his anger at Felicia tangling his thoughts. "Are you sure? You could name your price—"

A bark echoed from downwind, beyond the line of creek-fed trees. Tom figured Tricia would assume it was a dog—most humans weren't aware wolves could do more than howl—but he knew a wolf bark when he heard one, especially when said wolf was one of a pair being jackasses and sneaking up on him. He'd *told* Mark and his brother Sean that he wanted to roam alone for a while. At least they weren't howling.

"That's probably my cousins now." Tom maneuvered as if to get a better view, in reality trying to separate their scents, so the fact he was with a human would stand out better to the jackasses. "I knew they were camping somewhere out here. I was supposed to meet up with them." Mark was twenty, his brother seventeen, both part of the Billings pack, and Tom had thought at least Mark might be mature enough to be fun to run with, but apparently even three years was too big a difference given Tom's experiences. Their juvenile humor had grated before a week had passed. He hadn't thought they'd be so hard up for entertainment as to follow him.

No more barks sounded, and no one appeared, in human or wolf, so Tom dared to hope they'd gotten the message of the human scent. He still had a job to do. Maybe he could soften Tricia up by getting her talking about her hobby again, then bring up the watch once more when she'd relaxed. "How do you find these old cemeteries?"

"Oh, through a variety of methods. Talking to people in town, old maps. Those can be a lot of fun, though they're often inaccurate—"

A furry blur barreled into the back of Tom's legs. He could have saved his balance—if he'd *wanted* to—but a human would have tumbled back onto his ass in the grass, so Tom let it happen. And then Sean licked his face. Lady bright. The *morons*. Tom slapped away Sean's muzzle.

Mark strolled up a moment later, hands in his pockets and thumbs in his belt loops, probably to keep his jeans secure since he'd forgotten his belt in his quick change. Though the boys had the same parents, the same mixture of ancestry, Mark had inherited his human Native grandfather's features, where Sean had the coloration.

"This is my cousin Mark." Maybe Tom could salvage this yet. "I was just telling Tricia how our family has a history of breeding dogs." He got a good grip in Sean's ruff and stood. The boy was colored dark with a bit more brown than people probably expected for gray wolves. He had completely the wrong build for a domesticated dog, too narrow in the chest, but hopefully cemetery research didn't leave any time for canine biology.

Of course, rather than playing along, Mark just stared at him. "What?"

Sean tore out of Tom's grip and romped around Tricia. Tom could see the trick coming a mile away. "Bear, you damn—" He swallowed a too-Were curse and practically choked on it. He was only lucky one of the dog names used for Were in wolf came so automatically. Sean stuck his nose right in Tricia's crotch. She only laughed and pushed him away. He yielded good-naturedly, but Tom grabbed his ruff again anyway. He clenched his fingers very close to Sean's throat so he'd feel the strength of Tom's embarrassment on his behalf. Just because a human didn't know any different didn't mean you did something like *that*.

Mark would probably much rather have flirted with Tom than Tricia, so he snorted, ignored Tom's lead about breeding dogs, and wandered off, thumbs in belt loops, to stare at a stone. Tom crouched. If he chewed Sean out in a whisper right next to his ear, Tricia shouldn't hear anything. Before he could start, though, he could have sworn he *heard* Mark's eyes widen. Lady, that was just what he needed, Subtlety Personified and Subtlety Personified's younger brother blundering into that situation.

"What's this?" Mark demanded.

Luckily, Tricia seemed amused by his reaction. Maybe she figured Mark couldn't imagine why Tom was interested in cemeteries. "Tom was telling me he thinks these might be his ancestors. The stones with the moon and canine motifs. There's a bunch of them."

So now Mark knew not only that there was a pattern of Were secrets on display, but that a human had noticed it. Great. His idea of damage control would probably be to come back at night and steal all the stones, like no one would notice that. "*I* am taking care of this," Tom hissed into Sean's ear, then released him with a shove to his flank. "Get the *hell* out of here, both of you." He kept himself from shouting, but Mark's shocked expression as he whirled to face Tom suggested it hadn't been enough. Tom didn't care. As long as they got. Mark wiggled fingers beside his hip and Sean slunk over and leaned his ruff into the touch. "I guess we can talk later, Tom." Mark's tone slipped from meaningful almost into threat. Fine. When Tom had taken care of the problem with the gravestones, he would be sure to let Mark know.

Tom took a deep breath as he watched their backs recede over the long-shadowed scrub. The scent of Tricia's surprise reminded him he'd added a whole new layer of damage control to the situation. Okay. Okay, he could do this. "Sorry. Bear's trained much better than that, if Mark didn't let him run wild."

"He was just being friendly." Tricia dusted her knees, dislodging a guard hair or two. "No worries. I love dogs."

Tom stalled a beat longer by shading his eyes and frowning in the direction the boys had disappeared. He pulled his thoughts together with an effort. The watch was the priority. The gravestones were bad, but one point of strangeness was just one point. Two points of strangeness made a line. The watch was so much more specific, as well. It was clearly no good coming at that head-on, though. He needed to get to know Tricia better so he could figure out what might motivate her to sell.

He pulled out his phone to check the time. "I don't know if you have plans for tonight already, but I was thinking about grabbing some dinner..." He only let the words lift into a question at the last second.

Tricia looked him over and raised her brows. "Rebound?"

"No, dinner." Lame as the joke was, Tom smiled at her, trying fill the expression with simple friendliness. Even if it was somewhat exhausted friendliness. After a beat, she reflected it back, and Tom felt almost like his old self for a second. Things weren't so bad if you could smile about them.

As they stepped out of the diner into warm twilight, Tricia laughed, and Tom judged it the right time to mention the watch again. "Do you think I could take a picture of that watch to send to my folks? Maybe they could tell you more about it and the graves." He wasn't absolutely sure, but he thought maybe Tricia might trade the watch for information.

Bars and other restaurants had filled the closest city parking lot, so both of them had parked in another, a couple blocks away. It served stores, now all closed for the night, leaving the lot surprisingly quiet. Small towns: desolation falls at six p.m. sharp. Tom didn't suppose she noticed it, but Tricia walked closer to him, unconsciously defensive in the way many humans, especially women, were after dark.

Tricia sighed after a moment. "Just a picture?"

"Promise." The streetlights were old and deeply orange, so Tom had steer them right under one before he judged that a human would be able to see the small mechanism to open the watch. He popped it open while leaving it on Tricia's extended palm.

Only a whiff of scent warned him, because they'd come up from downwind again. Both of the boys were in wolf, and running so fast that there was little time to think. Tom stepped between them and Tricia, she closed her hand over the watch, then the boys were on them.

Mark leaped and slammed into Tom, a dove-gray missile at that stole his breath and folded him over. Payback...? But why would he do that in front of the human?

Oh, Lady. It came to Tom all at once, hearing Mark's snarl and smelling him intimately as they both tumbled to the pavement. He smelled like frustration Tom was in the way, not anger. He and his brother were trying to take care of Tricia directly. Kill the human who'd seen something revealing, then vanish that something. Far too simple a solution for this situation. A wild dog attack might hunt very slightly better out here than in suburban Seattle, but that didn't mean it would hunt well.

"Gonna have to get through me first," Tom spat, rage rolling up to fill him. His voice went almost too tight to speak. Mark had him on his back, and he risked a look to see Sean landing from a jump that had snatched Tricia's phone out of her hand. He crunched it with a proud air, so thoroughly that Tom could tell he was stalling. He didn't want to kill Tricia. This had been Mark's idea.

Mark's teeth came right for his face and Tom barely got his forearm up in time. Mark chewed on it, pinpoints of pain joining into one solid wad of agony. That fire burned and dribbled and flowed into the massive inferno around his voice and he got a grip on Mark's leg.

He hauled. Hauled with everything he had, and Mark's shoulder crunched and squished right out of the socket. Lovely sound. Mark yelped, as close as a canine could get to a sob. He stumbled off Tom, back, nearly falling before he got the hang of three legs. Sean had Tricia backed up against the bricks of the nearest building. He glanced over, clearly torn about wanting to help, but he continued to menace Tricia, preventing her escape without making a real move to hurt her.

Tom shoved to his feet and advanced on Mark, who got himself braced and snarled. Tom kicked him right in the good shoulder and he went down. That would heal too fast, though.

He needed to *break* something, if Mark was going to hurt enough to realize Tom meant business. He stood over Mark and kicked. His belly, again and again, giving him so much to heal that he'd run out of energy, then stomp on his jaw. *Crack.* Yes. "Fuck you." Tom wasn't sure if he was shouting or not. His throat felt like he was screaming. "Fuck you!" Mark, Felicia, Felicia's Spanish boyfriend, the universe? He wasn't sure.

Mark whimpered, and the sound finally made it through to Tom. Mark stopped trying to get up and lay there. Surrender. Tom backed up, panting. What was he doing? Sean rushed up, whining, and helped his brother up, dragging at his ruff and then standing firm to lean against. The two of them vanished back into the night as fast as they could go, though from his limping gait, the speed must have been agonizing for Mark.

"Oh my God. Where's your phone? We need to call—" Tricia crossed to Tom. It took him a moment to realize she was reaching for his arm because it was all gory with blood.

His anger drained away to a level that at least let him think, but left him a bit shaky with reaction. His arm was bloody with no wound underneath. Healing was long finished and he felt no hint of pain. Hiding that was one of the things he could do on autopilot, though. He hunched over his arm, careful not to smear away any of the camouflaging blood. "It's not actually that deep. By the time anyone gets here, I could have driven to the ER twice."

Tricia looked wildly around, checking for additional threats. "I can't believe they just attacked you…"

She thought the attack had been aimed at Tom. Good. His head felt fuzzy, but he could work with that. "Told you my cousin's dogs weren't well behaved. They probably thought they were playing." He dredged up an awkward laugh and Tricia looked like she didn't quite believe him. Lady grant that she'd been too focused on Sean to notice him laying into Mark. That especially didn't fit the story. What in the Lady's name had he been thinking? Disgust with himself started to congeal into nausea. Mark hadn't deserved that, no matter how much of a purse dog he was being.

"Don't worry, I'll get it bandaged up." Tom cradled the "injured" limb against his chest with his other hand, but Tricia keep hovering close.

"No, I'll drive you." Tricia's face set into stubborn lines, so Tom didn't try to fight her.

"Let me get my stuff." He headed for his truck, and pointed to the crunched remains of her phone. "Don't forget your SIM card." He grabbed his jacket while she leaned over the phone, picking up all the pieces to avoid littering, he supposed. Good of her.

There wasn't much town to drive across, so they reached the ER in only minutes. Tom hopped out, frowning at the entrance. Well-lit, small…it would make his job harder. "Thanks. See you," he muttered to Tricia, frowning at the doors ahead.

"Call me—give me your number. I'll call you tomorrow, make sure everything's okay." Tricia gave him an embarrassed smile, lips pressed together. "And I'll send the pictures." She rustled around and came up with a pen and gas receipt while Tom was still hesitating. A lot of him wanted to walk away, but he really should have prompted this next move himself. He still needed the watch, even if he managed to figure out what to do about the brothers. He rattled off the number.

Tom took his jacket and walked up to the hospital's well-lit sliding doors, with the reception desk right there. He bundled the jacket over his arm and rummaged in his pocket with his off hand. People forgave a lot when they thought people were checking important messages. He stepped inside and looked from his phone to the receptionist. "Has Mark Milton come in?" It was honestly the first name that occurred to him, but reminded of Mark, Tom couldn't help but catalog all of his injuries. If he'd been human, he definitely would have been here. Tom didn't even hear the receptionist's reply, he was too busy pushing Mark to the back of his mind and watching Tricia out of the corner of his eye. She got into her car. Thank the Lady.

Tom nodded to the receptionist. "Thanks." He frowned at his phone and turned aside as if to read a new message. Now the hard part. Second hard part. Tom angled his body away from the receptionist and the waiting room beyond and tried to think boring thoughts at her. He was just some asshole checking his phone. No need to look at his arm as he shook out his coat and pulled it on, right arm first.

She didn't yell at him. Tom drew one breath, then another. He wanted to be somewhere private before he started drowning in guilt. He checked for Tricia in the parking lot, then strode out. At least he'd survived the night. Tomorrow was another day for dealing with problems he'd caused himself. And for making apologies.

The day wasn't done with him, though. Tom made it to his truck, parked it on the shoulder of a rural side road, and collapsed on his back in the bed. He lay there for a while, glaring at the grimy ceiling of the canopy, without getting out his sleeping bag. It wasn't that he'd enjoyed Mark's pain, he'd just been so angry he hadn't cared about it. He didn't—didn't understand how he could have felt that way, even though he remembered taking those actions in crisp detail. He'd wanted to—what? Expend the anger until it was gone? That sure hadn't worked. Or maybe he'd just wanted to burn away the remembered helplessness of getting his ass beat by Felicia's Spanish boyfriend. He hadn't been helpless with Mark.

Mark had been.

His phone rang and Tom immediately felt an almost overwhelming urge to smash the phone against the metal of the truck bed lip above the liner. Hadn't Felicia set all this in motion, by inviting her Spanish boyfriend to stay in Seattle? But Tom knew better than that. This anger wasn't him. He wasn't like that.

It wasn't Felicia anyway. It was worse. Tom stared at the ROANOKE DARE on the screen and then answered before he lost his nerve. "Alpha?" He flopped one arm across his eyes.

"I'm in a quandary, Tom. On one hand, I have Billings, howling to me about one of his roamers being viciously attacked and beaten half to death, and on the other, I have a pack member I've never known to even sprain someone's wrist. It doesn't match up."

Tom fought the urge to curl into low-ranked body language. Roanoke Dare wasn't here to see it anyway. "He attacked first. I stopped beating him when he surrendered. Then they ran off. That's all."

A sigh carried over the phone's speakers. Tom supposed he should keep explaining, but he didn't want to hear his mistakes stated out loud, stark and incontrovertible. "Why?" Roanoke Dare prompted, and didn't sound pleased about the fact he'd had to.

"Why were we fighting?" Tom checked, then winced. Enough stalling. He knew what his alpha meant. Once he started talking, all of it tumbled out, more or less in order: the cemetery, the watch, Mark and Sean's apparent plans for Tricia. When he was finished, Roanoke Dare was silent once more, this time wielding it like a weapon.

Tom couldn't stand it any longer and filled it with the essential truth of all of this. "I was angry."

Thoughtful silence, this time. "That isn't like you."

Tom clenched his free hand. "No fucking shit." He coughed. "Sorry, Alpha."

Roanoke Dare laughed rather than getting annoyed at the language. "Only you can fix that, though. Not even my daughter can. She told me that you've been avoiding all of her apologies."

"I'm not ready to—deal with that yet. Thinking about it makes me angry. And then I act without thinking to get rid of the anger, that doesn't work. It only makes things worse." Tom cleared his throat. He didn't want this to turn into a bunch of excuses. "That's the past. I guess the situation here isn't as bad as it could be. No one shifted in front of the human. There's room to shove things along the backtrail yet."

"There is nothing either good or bad, but thinking makes it so. Don't think about my daughter for a while." Roanoke Dare's voice warmed, giving the vaguely familiar words extra weight. "And your punishment will be to deal with the situation there. Walk it back. Calmly."

Tom noted his alpha's choice of words: calm, not peaceful. And he could add one of his own: not so *serious*. He'd do his best. He mumbled his goodbyes and started thinking—not about the past, or Felicia, but what about he was going to do next. Here.

———

The barbeque Tom had bought was cold by the time Sean showed up at the truck's open tailgate, but that wasn't the point. The brothers couldn't get any warmer food of their own, not with even the bars closed this far past midnight. Tom opened one box of the three and nudged it out onto the gate. Though he was in human, Sean's ears practically perked up, under glossy black hair that blended into the dark sky behind him. The cold food must not have been giving off much scent as the boy approached.

"Mark's fucking pissed." Sean paused a few feet short of Tom and shifted his weight skittishly.

"He has a right to be." Tom looked at the other two takeout containers. "He's got to be hungry, after all that healing. I just want to apologize to him. Do you think you can talk him into coming out?" He scanned the horizon, downwind, but didn't see anything move. Mark wouldn't be letting Sean wander around all alone, though.

Sean considered that for a bit and slid his hands into his pockets. "That was all his idea, you know. I didn't want to kill her. She seemed nice enough."

"I don't think we have to. I just need your help. And Mark's." Tom grimaced. "Kind of a challenge. Do you think he'd go for it?" Tom explained his plan, and when Sean laughed, he knew he'd crafted it right. Now it all depended on whether he could apologize well enough that Mark accepted it. He was willing to sacrifice any appearance of rank, and his pride, but he didn't know if those would weigh against physical pain for Mark.

Tom extended the open box to Sean, who dug with his fingers. "Mm," he said, raising his voice pointedly. "Maybe I'll just keep Mark's share for myself, so he can keep sulking."

"Shut up." Mark spoke softly, and walked up delicately. He showed nervousness, of all things, in the way he kept rubbing knuckles along the side of his jaw. Tom couldn't catch his scent to confirm his mood.

Tom held out the two boxes atop each other. Mark should start eating while he talked, but it appeared Mark didn't want to come any closer yet. "I'm sorry," Tom offered. "You shouldn't have tried to deal with the human that way—I'm sure your sub-alpha already told you that—but I shouldn't have beat you like that." He paused. Nothing from Mark. Now for the pride-swallowing part. "Ever since I got my ass handed to me by Felicia's Spanish boyfriend, I've been wanting to do that to *him*." The admission sounded even more pathetic out loud. First he was too weak to defend himself, and then he took it out on others. But it was true.

Sean looked up from stuffing his face. "Were you really *with* Felicia? The Roanoke's daughter?" The words were indistinct until he swallowed properly.

All right. Time to practice not getting angry. Tom tried to answer without thinking about all the complexities involved. Sean didn't care about those. "Sort of. Briefly."

Sean rocked forward on his toes. "She's only a year older than me, isn't she? What's she like?"

Tom was silent a moment, finding that he didn't want to call her any of the names he'd used before in his head, not out loud to people who didn't know her. "Intense." That was true enough.

"And she's single now?" Sean grinned, like he was considering hopping a bus for Seattle the next morning.

"By the Lady's name, don't you dare—"

"Oh, Lady, no, don't—" Tom's warning overlapped Mark's

threat. For a moment, their eyes met, sharing a certain protective exasperation. Then they broke the gaze to avoid measuring dominance. A feeling of empathy lingered, though, at least on Tom's side. He still couldn't tell what Mark was feeling. Mark had been trying to be mature and protective by dealing with the human as well, Tom supposed. The very same things Tom had felt when he saw the gravestone photograph in the coffee shop.

"Anyway. Felicia's not evil." Tom didn't realize he meant it until he said it. "She's just got so much shit of her own to deal with, it's almost guaranteed to splash out and burn you, Sean."

Sean shrugged philosophically. "I was kidding." Or so he claimed now, anyway.

Tom jumped off the tailgate to set Mark's food on neutral ground, but Mark finally met him to take it from his hands. "So what is it we're doing about the human?"

When Tricia called, Tom asked her to meet him in the same parking lot where he'd been "attacked." The breeze was right—partially because Tom had scouted where the buildings funneled it—and the three of them smelled Tricia approaching. The day hadn't warmed completely yet, and the breeze's chill made it feel even more capricious when it danced over the skin.

Tom and Mark straightened from leaning against the side of the truck and Sean picked up the end of his leash in his mouth and offered it to his brother. "Okay, down." Tom sidestepped to give their tableau a little more room to play out on the asphalt behind the truck. He gave an exaggerated hand gesture which Sean just stared at. "Mark, you say it, then pull him down."

Mark glanced at Tricia, but pulled his attention back pretty quickly. "Down," he said, without any conviction, and tugged on the leash slightly.

"You have to mean it, or he'll run wild again." Tom judged Tricia had gotten close enough, so he glanced over and gave her an apologetic grimace. "You'll get arrested and Bear put down or something," he concluded, ostensibly still speaking to Mark.

Tricia grimaced back. She halted well clear of all of them, but stood her ground when Tom ambled over without Sean making any threatening moves. "How's your arm?" she asked.

Tom showed her the bandage, which he'd wrapped this morning himself. He thought it looked fairly professional, if he did say so himself. "No stitches. Some antibiotics to take, in case he'd been eating road kill."

Mark tossed Tom a dirty look for the implication about his hygiene, like he didn't eat road kill all the time in wolf, same as any other roamer. Sean, on the other hand, waved his tail a few times for Tricia. Tom knew wagging didn't feel particularly natural without practice, so he nodded in appreciation of the effort.

"Well, good." Tricia glanced at Sean once more, then rubbed her hands together awkwardly. "You'll forgive me if I don't scratch his ears."

Tom allowed himself a trickle of relief. That was one layer of their problems peeled away, at least. Now they were just left with the gravestones and watch. And he had at least one plan to try for that last layer. A calm plan.

He pulled the sheets he'd composed and printed at the library from his back pocket and unrolled them. "I took photos at the cemetery this morning and got my parents to ask around. I guess my great uncle recognized the writing. It's some lines of poetry." Not the greatest poetry, composed by Tom on short notice, but that could be blamed on the translation. He'd made it bland, all about finding peace among rolling hills and flowing streams.

Tricia accepted the sheets and scanned the top two, glancing from the printed photo to the text beside it. She smiled, slowly. "Thank you."

"And..." Tom looked at the ground. He was worried she wouldn't react well to this suggestion. But the translations might not be enough. He had to be sure. "My cousins live out here, and I'm going to be around for a while longer. You talked about cemeteries getting overgrown, and clearing them—I just thought, if you ever need grunts for the heavy labor, we're your guys. It's the least we can do." Mark nodded, not looking at her either. Tom could smell his embarrassment at having even considered killing her.

Tricia looked surprised, then a wide smile suddenly bloomed. "Leave the dogs at home, but—yeah. Okay. I know just the place, actually. It'll take me a week or two to make sure I have the permission I need, but—" She laughed. "That's not an offer I get often. I'm not going to turn it down."

Tom allowed his shoulders to slump in relief. Perfect. With that continued contact, he could keep feeding her safe information, stay on top of the situation. He tipped his head to release Mark, who strode off with plenty of slack in his brother's leash until they were out of sight. Tom only gave half his attention to the task of talking over possible schedules, double-checking contact numbers, and other business-like small talk with Tricia.

"Oh, and here." Suddenly Tricia had the watch out on her hand again, commanding all of Tom's attention. "I thought about it, and you're right, it does belong in your family. I just liked it so much it was hard to let it go. But I took a bunch of pictures for myself. I paid ninety-something with tax, so call it a hundred, and we're good."

Tom wanted to laugh with joy, to swing her around playfully, but that probably wasn't quite appropriate in this situation. Instead he dug out the cash, accepted the watch, and slipped it into his pocket immediately. He wanted it out of human hands, but that didn't mean he particularly wanted to see the painting inside again.

Then he kissed Tricia's cheek, which turned adorably pink. "Rebound," she said, repressively, but with humor glinting beneath.

"No, gratitude." Tom grinned, then headed off after Mark, lifting a hand in farewell.

Lady Ceremony

This story is set between REFLECTED and WOLFSBANE. Where Tom matures over the series, Ginnie truly grows up. A first shift marks when a Were begins to define their adult dominance, separate from their birth path, or in Ginnie's case, her rather infamous father, Rory. The song Rory sings in this version of the story is also available to listen to online in its entirety.

Ginnie's anger at her father kept her running along the rural highway until her back was plastered with sweat. The late evening sun striped the much-mended pavement and she stomped hard on each shadow. She was nearly thirteen, for Lady's sake. Why couldn't she go visit Tom and her other friends in Boston for the summer, instead of being stuck up here in Quebec because her father had screwed—no, fucked—up and got himself exiled? And let himself stay exiled because he was too proud to apologize.

Ginnie heard a car in the distance and slowed to pick her way onto the shoulder without tumbling into a ditch. Sometime in the run, restlessness had relaxed its teeth from her neck. Fine. Maybe she'd sneak off. Take the bus to Boston. If she could get onto another pack's territory fast enough, then her father's pride would be working for her because he wouldn't be able to follow unless he apologized and asked for permission. She clambered up the slope on the other side of the weedy ditch and into the bushes between the trees there, to cut back to the house.

When Ginnie looped around to approach the house from the back, she crossed her father's outgoing trail. She should be grateful he'd left, she supposed, because she'd avoid punishment for their earlier shouting match a little longer. But he'd left in wolf, since it was nearly the full, and that suddenly made her even angrier. She wasn't sure why. She should be having her Lady Ceremony soon enough, but the first shift itself seemed slightly scary to her. What if it hurt more than people said? But her father was off running and having fun in wolf and she was stuck here hot, sticky, and in human.

At least her mom was still home. Her voice drifted through an open window as Ginnie approached the back door. Her mom must be on the phone. Ginnie probably should have gone up and opened the door noisily rather than eavesdropping, but Ginnie couldn't not. What if her mom was angry with her too? You could never tell with her mom, she was so quiet and nice.

"—both of them screaming at each other, and Ginnie didn't even eat her dinner. I'm afraid it's turning out like you warned me, Boston." A pause. "You know I don't have any status any-more…" Ginnie's mom sighed. "Yes, all right. Like you warned me, *Benjamin*. Two alphas squaring off without even other pack members to distract them. He's gone a lot for his job, guiding the hunting and fishing trips, but he doesn't have as many overnights scheduled this year. It's not enough to give them space."

Alpha? Ginnie looked at her hands, like it would be written on her skin somewhere. She didn't feel much like an alpha. And there was no one around who would listen to her if she told them what to do, so how would she even know?

"I'm afraid she pushed him. She wants out as well, now school's finished for the summer." Ginnie's mom laughed, low, and Ginnie relaxed a little. Things couldn't be *that* bad, then. "None of you alphas know how to persuade someone subtly, do you?" She listened for a few seconds. "Well, I'm glad you agree, anyway. I'll see what I can do to convince him slowly."

Convince her father of what? Ginnie crept closer to the house, making sure to keep at least one tree between her and the window, but then a breeze trickled in from behind her. Her mom would smell her in a minute, so Ginnie gave up on eavesdropping and jogged up to the back door as loudly as possible like she'd just gotten there.

Her mom was off the phone when Ginnie opened the door. She sat at the kitchen table where Ginnie's plate of food still waited for her. Probably a little cold by now, but she didn't really mind at this point. Her stomach had remembered it was really hungry. She checked her mom's face and scent. She seemed worried, but better than she must have been while Ginnie and her father were yelling and not paying attention to her at all.

Ginnie felt really bad about that, now she thought about it. So when her mom held out her arms in invitation, she ignored the food to sit on her lap. It was a little silly now she was as old as she was. She was still a little shorter than her mom when standing, but sitting on her lap, she could practically rest her chin on the top of her mom's head. She curled down to at least get her cheek on her mom's shoulder. "Sorry," she muttered. She hoped her mom wouldn't tell her to apologize to her father too. He was still wrong.

"You do have to learn diplomacy, puppy. You can't be disrespectful like that." Her mom hesitated for a moment, then leaned her head so her hair tickled Ginnie's nose. "But maybe not during the full. Your friend Alouette, didn't she invite you to go with her and her family to Montreal this weekend?"

Ginnie sat up straight, pulling away from her mom. Alouette had, and Ginnie hadn't bothered mentioning it to her father, because she hadn't wanted to waste any good mood he had—which apparently wasn't any—on Montreal when she could put it toward Boston. Apparently her mom thought it would be good for her and her father to stay away from each other for a few days.

And how much easier would it be to catch a bus from Montreal? If her mom was suggesting the trip, Ginnie assumed she'd stop her father from showing up and dragging her home immediately, so she wouldn't have to worry about that. She could go to Montreal and have Alouette's family take her to the bus station. And maybe Tom could pick her up at a closer bus stop than Boston—he had his truck to roam in, and they'd only talked about meeting in Boston when Ginnie thought her mom could take her straight there.

She'd love to be able to drive part of the way with Tom. He was *fun*, and she'd missed having him around to act like a big brother, after he moved so far away and then her father got exiled. He could drive her into Boston's territory, and once they were there, her father wouldn't be able to do anything about it, no matter how long she stayed. If he tried to show up to get her without asking for permission, he'd get his ass beaten. And he'd never ask for permission in a million years.

Ginnie felt like jumping off her mom's lap and dancing

around in victory. "Thanks, Mom." She hugged her mom tight instead. Maybe she shouldn't seem too happy, so it wasn't suspicious, though. "Maybe when it's not the full, I could ask Dad—"

Her mom squeezed tight in return, then let go so Ginnie could see her grimace. "We'll see, puppy."

"Okay," Ginnie said, focusing on her disappointment from earlier so hopefully her mom wouldn't smell that it had disappeared now. She was going to get to see Tom after all!

It seemed later to Ginnie that things went wrong right about when she started feeling smug about having gotten away with her plan. She and Alouette had a such great time running around Montreal and shopping and staying up half—well, nearly all—the night, Ginnie almost wanted to stay one more day. But she'd told Alouette's mother that the plan was for her to get the Sunday morning bus to Albany, and she'd texted Tom to meet her at the station there. When she called Boston to get her permission to visit his territory, he didn't ask her any questions, just told her she'd be welcome.

So she took her backpack and got on the bus that stank of humans, but not as bad as she remembered the Metro doing, back when her family still lived in Virginia, and congratulated herself. Her excitement made it hard to sit still, and her stomach felt a little weird too. Maybe all the restaurant food she'd had yesterday. But she really hadn't slept much last night so she finally dozed, secure in the knowledge that by the time her parents would be expecting Alouette's family to drop her off tonight, she'd already be with Tom.

She woke when they went through customs, then again when the bus pulled into the first stop in New York. The first thing she smelled on waking was blood.

That was a little scary, but not that weird, except that it was really close. Ginnie scrubbed at her nose as everyone filed off to go into the station and use the bathroom and buy snacks or whatever if this wasn't their stop.

The smell of blood didn't move, and that was when she realized it was her. She wasted a little time checking her arms and hands for where she'd been scratched, but she knew better than that. As soon as she admitted it to herself, she stood up quickly and checked her pants and the seat. No blood on the seat, thank the Lady, and she couldn't see anything on her jeans either. She'd better get inside to the bathroom before that changed.

In the hurry of digging out quarters and getting the handle to turn on the ancient metal dispenser to get a pad, Ginnie almost managed not to gag at the smell of the bathroom. Public ones were never great, but this was down at the very bottom of ones she'd ever had the misfortune to have to use. And she had to *stand* on the *floor* with her stockinged feet for a couple seconds while she changed to a clean pair of underwear.

But then it was done, and she actually felt a bit proud of herself. She wasn't a child anymore. She could handle getting her period when she was on her own, no sweat. The pad was thick and gross when she sat back down on the bus, just in time, and she smelled blood too much to nap now, but she'd deal with it.

As they pulled away, she started to ache. Not in her belly, like it was cramps, but all over her body. She wished she had a shade to block the sunlight spearing her through the window like an ant under a magnifying glass. She hunched down as far in the seat as she could, leaned against the wall, and tried not to think about running. If she could only work these aches out, stretch and twist and unkink her muscles and run—

That was when she got it. First shift happened after your

period, at the next full, or the one after that, but what about if your period was *on* the full? Shouldn't that mean you had a whole month to wait until the next one? But it was supposed to happen faster for high-ranked Were, and her mom had called her an alpha. Was she going to have her first shift *today*?

That couldn't be right. Ginnie was just worrying too much. But when they got to the next stop, an hour later, she could no longer deny it. She hurt, really bad, and she wanted to—to something. Her mind kept suggesting "stretch," but that wasn't right at all. She wanted to be home and with her mom and dad and not here stuck on a bus full of humans who'd all see her if she shifted. She absolutely couldn't shift here.

What should she do? She didn't know. The moment the bus was empty, she called her father. She almost sobbed when it went to voicemail. That wasn't really that strange. Even if he and her mom weren't in wolf, he was probably out of range. The voicemail beeped and she hadn't even heard it telling her to leave a message. "Daddy—I'm sorry, I'm so sorry, I'm on the bus to Albany and I feel like I'm going to shift—I got my period—and I don't know what to do, should I keep going to meet Tom, or . . . ?" There must be so many other things she should say and she couldn't think of a single one of them, so she ended the message and scrubbed at her tears before they could fall on the phone. She typed a quick text to tell him to check his voicemail, then called Tom.

He did pick up, and that made Ginnie cry so hard she couldn't get any understandable words out. "Ginnie Gin? What's wrong? Did your father change his mind?"

Ginnie choked into something trying to be a laugh. Her father didn't even know she was here. "Tom, I don't know what to do—" A woman with two children clattered noisily up the stairs and Ginnie ended the call in a panic. She'd have to text him so no one would hear. Her fingers were shaking now, and she had to pause to ride out a wave of aching, so she sent the text as the bus was pulling away again.

Tom didn't take long to type his answers, full of typos probably because of his hurry: *get of the bus.* Then, *now. find someway private and text me where you are okay?*

Ginnie stared out the window at the buildings sliding by, getting farther apart and giving over to trees as they headed out of town. She'd made the wrong choice, then. Again. Lady damn it. She clenched up into the smallest ball she could for a minute. She couldn't shift here. She'd have to wait. Wait two hours. She remembered this next stop was farther away. When she could breathe again, even if she still hurt, she typed carefully, putting all her focus into the task. *Can't. Have to wait until the next stop.* She sent that and hung onto her phone like that was her lifeline.

Okay, came back. *I have to drive now, I can't text, but hang on. I'm coming.*

Ginnie clutched her phone to her chest. She thought about checking the map on it, to see how far the next stop was from Albany—or from wherever Tom was now since he hadn't expected to pick her up yet. But she didn't really want to know. She wanted to focus on not letting the ache take over her whole body until she shifted in front of humans. And on praying to the Lady. She'd made some bad choices, but maybe the Lady would still help her get through this. She'd never try to trick her parents again. Ever. She promised with her whole voice.

Ginnie gave a great gasping sob of relief when the bus pulled away from the next little station, a modern brick building that still kind of fit with the old brick buildings in the little downtown. It was bigger than the downtown where she lived now, but nothing compared to where they'd lived in Virginia. Some of the other passengers who'd gotten off here were still loading luggage into their cars so she wasn't alone yet, but she was getting close.

She clenched her hands on the straps of her backpack and the next problem occurred to her. Where was she supposed to be private in a strange town? Not in a bathroom, and someone could always come out to the Dumpster if she tried to hide behind a store or something. She needed woods, but everything here was single trees and decorative plantings.

She took one step, then another, with no thought beyond "away." But it didn't really matter which direction she went, did it? As long as she headed out of town. Walking helped the ache a very little bit, and forward movement was better than nothing, so she moved forward. She'd follow the sidewalk in a straight line until it ran out and then she'd smell for woods because hopefully there would be less car exhaust in the air by then.

She wasn't sure how long she walked. The sun got hotter, but not unbearably so and she did have a water bottle in her backpack. She was probably healing a sunburn, too. But this town was surrounded by *fields* and she couldn't shift in those, someone would be sure to see her. She felt so tired of fighting against the all-consuming need to do something that she didn't even properly understand. Maybe if she got exhausted enough, she wouldn't have to shift yet.

Cars passed her regularly, some giving her plenty of room along the shoulder since the sidewalk had long run out by now, some whooshing right past. She was too miserable to be angry at them. One slowed and she started to get worried, because maybe she was going to get in trouble with the humans for being a girl walking alone, but then it pulled up behind her and the door opened and she smelled Tom.

She ran for him and he grabbed her up in a hug and lifted her feet off the ground to carry her, backpack and all, to the back of his pickup. He set her down to open the canopy and lower the tailgate, so she scrambled up on her own.

"You left a good trail," Tom said, in that voice adults used when they didn't want her to think they were angry at *her*, rather than her situation. He seemed more than a little scared, mixed with the angry. "I could follow it pretty well even from the truck, with the windows open. I'm sorry we couldn't get here sooner."

Ginnie missed the "we" until the passenger door of the truck opened and shut. Felicia set her hand on the side of the canopy and leaned around to give Ginnie a tentative smile. "Hello," she said. Ginnie hadn't seen her in a long time, and now she looked so *adult*. And glamorous, with her long, wavy black hair and big chest. Why did *she* have to be here, and see Ginnie such an aching mess and smelling of humans and that bathroom and blood?

But she was Tom's girlfriend now, wasn't she? Ginnie had heard that, though she'd thought she'd also heard they broke up. Why wouldn't he want to go roaming with his own girlfriend? Ginnie wished she didn't have to be here now, though. "I have to shift," she told Felicia, and climbed farther back into the bed. Felicia made a noise of sympathy—like Ginnie was a pathetic injured child or something—and boosted up to join her.

"I'll keep watch," Tom said, and closed the tailgate and leaned against it. Even not fully enclosed, the space was uncomfortably warm and the light was dimmed by the grime on the windows in the canopy. Ginnie tossed her backpack to the corner to join a spare pair of boots and an old sleeping bag and pointedly ignored Felicia.

Now. Now she could shift. But she didn't . . . know what she was doing. Should she clench up her muscles? Try to relax and let something happen? She didn't think she could relax right now. It felt like she should be doing something, but she still didn't know what.

She wiggled out of her clothes, she knew to do at least that much, but then she leaned her weight on her hands and panted and nothing happened. "How do I do it, Tom?"

Tom glanced back, then grimaced and returned his attention to the road. He scraped his sandy hair out of his face. "You . . . kinda fall into it? It's not really something there are really words for."

"Silver talks about—" Felicia's Spanish accent threaded through her words. "Wild selves. She says kids keep their wild selves behind their eyes. So I guess you have to set it free?" She sounded as confused and worried as Tom, which actually made Ginnie feel a little better. She might be eighteen or nineteen, but she didn't know the right answer to everything either. Ginnie looked at her, kneeling on the plastic of the pickup bed, and noticed the sweat starting to stick down her shirt under her arms and the crinkle where she'd had her hair in a ponytail earlier. Maybe not so glamorous after all. Just normal.

Ginnie tried to fall. Or set something free. She really did. But she had no idea where she was falling to or falling from. Or what she was freeing.

"I could show you?" Tom rolled his shoulders like he was

pretty itchy in the full too, but then he'd had ten years or more to learn to control it. "Do it with you."

"I've seen it before," Ginnie snapped, suddenly angry and then it *hurt* again and she dropped her head to get through it. She'd had twelve years of being around shifts and watching them happen. It wasn't particularly helping.

Tom straightened away from the tailgate with a noise of surprise. "Are you allowed to be—?"

"Move." Her father's voice. Tom did move, and her father stepped into view and opened the tailgate. Felicia knelt up taller, not quite bristling yet, but definitely keeping an eye on him. Ginnie hugged her arms around herself. She hoped he wouldn't be angry right now. She couldn't deal with him being angry right now. If he could wait, for when she'd shifted and they were home . . .

But he was in another pack's territory. She'd never thought he'd unbend enough to apologize and get permission for that. He must be even more angry about having to do that. "I'm sorry," she tried to say, but it came out as a sob. "I'm tired."

"I know, puppy." His voice was gentle. Her father, big and strong and broad-shouldered, climbed up to sit on the open tailgate and opened his arms. When she crawled into them, he embraced her and stroked her hair. "Should have known you'd be a strong one. Surprise us all by shifting early." She hadn't heard him speak so softly since he'd been exiled and became angry all the time.

Though maybe Ginnie had spent so much of that time arguing with him, she hadn't really given him an opportunity for that either. He pulled back to catch her eyes. "Let it take you, all right? Don't fight it. My father used to have a song he'd sing to the cubs in his pack…" He hummed, low and sweet. "*Lady*

*keep me fleet of foot, me keen of eye, my belly full. For I am her
true-born child, and my voice will cry her name.*

"Listen to the song. Let it carry the Lady's light through
you, until you're floating." He measured dominance through
their gaze, and she let him be the stronger, protective one this
time. "Relax." That last was an order, an alpha's order. Ginnie
knew he was trying to help her, so she tried to follow the order,
instead of opposing it because he was so often wrong, like she
usually would have.

And he sang, voice deep. If the Lady's light moved through
her, it was because the song settled low into her skin first.
When she stopped holding on so hard, everything changed. It
was hard getting there, but her muscles twisted and settled and
then that was right, too.

She was on her side now, four legs stretched out, and
her dad ruffled her ears. Tom, leaning in to see her properly,
laughed in slightly giddy relief. "You're almost white! Throw
on a little flour and you could be Virginia Dare for Halloween."

Ginnie wanted to grumble at Tom for dredging up that bit
of childishness—she hadn't wanted to be white like Virginia
Dare for years now—but the words came out as a yip instead.
She examined her flank and found it to be the lightest of grays,
but peppered with flecks of black on the guard hairs. It wasn't
really white at all and it felt exactly right. Felicia grinned at her
and smoothed the fur along her flank. "Lady welcomed," she
said, solemnly.

Tom's phone beeped and he pulled it out and typed a reply
to what was probably a text message. "Boston ended up not
being that far behind me."

Ginnie's dad tried to get his arms under her belly, but she
wiggled away from him. She wanted to stay here and rest for at

least a few more minutes before she walked anywhere, and she wasn't going to let him carry her. She wasn't a baby now. She'd had her first shift.

Ginnie's dad growled. "We have to go, Virginia."

A car pulled up behind them. Tom didn't look surprised this time, so he must have recognized it, but Ginnie didn't relax until Boston got out. He always made her feel centered, somehow, dark-brown skinned and deeply grave. When she looked at her father again, he'd jumped to the ground and was backed up against the tailgate, smelling of fear turning quickly to anger.

He hadn't asked for permission, Ginnie realized with a jolt. When he'd gotten her message, he'd just come straight to her. Maybe he'd hoped he could take her home before he got caught. But now he had been caught. Would the Roanokes have him beat up before he got dragged back to Quebec?

"Rory," Boston said. He stopped about two meters away and waited.

Her dad closed his hands over the edge of the tailgate, barely-suppressed violence seeping into his scent. He couldn't possibly be planning to fight Boston, could he? Her dad was in the wrong here and everyone knew it. He knew it, she could smell that too with her nose newly sharpened.

And if he did hurt Boston, that was so much worse than territory trespass. The Roanokes would have to give him a similarly worse punishment. Would they decide they had to exile him to somewhere different—and terrible—like among all the hostile packs in Europe? He could move to somewhere without many Were instead, like South America, Ginnie supposed, but that seemed worse in another way. At least from Quebec she could visit other packs within a day's drive.

If she went with him. She knew her mom would. Would she have to see her parents only once a year, or even less? Ginnie didn't want *any* of those possibilities.

So she couldn't sit back and let this happen. She had to talk to them, and to talk she had to be in human. She didn't know if going back would be like falling as well, but she did know trying too hard probably wouldn't help. She tried to search for the feeling of herself that had twelve years of weight behind it instead of a few minutes. This was her too, now, but that her was more familiar.

This time, it did feel like stretching. Stretch and then she was back to herself. She didn't really feel any different in human than before she'd been able to shift, which was odd. She would have expected to. "Daddy, please. Can you ask for permission to be on his territory now? Better late than never, right?" It came out breathy, making her realize that she was still so *tired*. She leaned on her palms again.

Her father ignored her completely and pushed away from the tailgate. He flexed his fingers, then they settled into fists.

"You're not allowed to be here, Rory," Boston said, tone sharpening, though he didn't get any louder. Ginnie didn't know how he managed to sound so dangerous while still being so soft.

"What are you going to do, drag me home all by yourself, old man?" Her father's voice was plenty loud, in comparison, laid over a growl. "None of Dare's eager bootlickers are here to help you."

Boston settled into frightening stillness. At least, it frightened Ginnie. It didn't seem to change her father's plans. "I can cause you more pain than you think, Rory. Little as I want to.

And greater pain than that will come later, when the Roanokes hear."

Ginnie took a deep breath, but swallowed anything she might have said. Her father was wrong again and she wanted to shout at him. Apparently nothing had changed with her first shift. Nothing at all. He wasn't even listening to her to shout back this time, he was so focused on Boston.

She groped after her clothes. She had to at least get between him and Boston. She didn't want her dad to get beat up and have to move to South America. She didn't. She got her pants on herself, without underwear, and then Felicia was handing over her shirt and helping her pull it on. "Stop him before he says something worse I can't 'forget' to mention to my father," Felicia whispered.

Ginnie's legs were unsteady, so she didn't make it to the narrowing space between her father and his chosen opponent. Instead, she caught herself against his back, fingers clenched around a handful of fabric. He started like he'd forgotten she was there.

Ginnie should say something, now she finally had his attention, but she had no idea what. He *had* come to help her. He wouldn't swallow his pride now, but he could have let that make him stay home and let Tom and Boston help her instead.

So maybe she could be the one to make a change—she could be happy he'd do that for her, and let go of the fact that he couldn't set his pride aside. If she admitted it to herself, something in her knew that he'd never change that much, at least not anytime soon. She loosened her grip on his shirt to press her hand against his back and made sure not to shout at all. "Would you be willing to go now, Dad? If Boston could pretend not to have seen you . . ."

"I can't do that, I'm afraid." Boston offered Ginnie the smallest of smiles, and grew a little less still. "But I'm sure, if I advise them to, the Roanokes will grant your father a certain latitude due to the extenuating circumstances." Boston turned his attention to her father, gaze tight. "Ginnie deserves better than to have you make this rather traumatic experience worse for her."

Her father twisted to hold her and Ginnie felt like some kind of contest between him and Boston had snapped, so it would no longer escalate. Now it was Boston he pointedly ignored. "We can leave once you feel ready to travel," he allowed. He ushered her back to the truck and she climbed up to get dressed properly.

Ginnie tried to dress as fast as possible, but she ached all over. "I think you have to go *now.*"

"Not without you." Her father leaned in to grab her shoes and socks, and she sat on the tailgate and allowed him to put them on for her.

Another shout bubbled up. *If this is for me, then ask for permission, for my sake!* Ginnie swallowed it too. "Boston, may we have a little more time—" She got tangled up in her words, trying to phrase it diplomatically, like her mom had said. "To let Dad get out of here because he'd too stubborn to give in" wasn't diplomatic.

Boston sighed and rocked his weight back on his heels. "If you promise, as you grow up, to not shield him from the consequences of choices he makes only on his own behalf," he said solemnly.

"Oh, for Lady's sake," her father snarled under his breath.

"Okay," Ginnie agreed, over top of him. She wasn't sure she completely understood what Boston meant, but she'd gotten the gist. Her father was here because he was helping her this time. That might not be true other times.

When her shoes were on, Ginnie pulled on her backpack and held out her arms for her dad. Maybe she was a little bit okay with being carried. This time. "Dad, I want to come back to Boston for the summer in a couple weeks, after we have my Lady Ceremony at home."

Her father considered her, face set. "Why should I reward you for disobeying me and getting yourself into a lot of trouble because of it?"

Ginnie bit her lip. Because he frustrated her but he was a good dad and she wanted this so badly? But she supposed good parents didn't give their kids everything they wanted. They gave their kids what was good for them. But why would he believe her opinion about what was good for her? "Because two alphas yelling at each is making Mom upset," she said finally. "Only until school starts again. Please?"

"I suspect Ginnie has fully reaped the consequences of her actions in this case," Boston put in.

Her father was silent for one more beat. "Fine." He boosted her up and held her tight, head on his shoulder like she was much younger, his touch protective, not angry.

"Thank you, Daddy," she said, because that seemed right. He'd helped her. She did love him.

"Sorry, puppy," he said, so low she wasn't sure she'd heard it. Was he actually apologizing for—no. She wasn't going to prod at it.

She let her head rest on her father's shoulder. Viewed sideways as she climbed out of the truck, Felicia gave Ginnie a nod like maybe she was a little impressed, which felt pretty good. And Tom caught her eye and grinned. He dropped his head over his phone, then hers buzzed. She could guess the message: *See you soon.*

She closed her eyes. So that was her first shift. If she felt different now, it wasn't really due to having a wolf form. And she'd think more about that later when she wasn't so Lady-damned tired.

Lead and Follow

We jump to the future in this story. It is set nearly six decades after the events of the main series. If, as originally intended, this had led to a spin-off novel, a few other characters from the original series would have appeared, though most have died in clashes with humans by this point. A version of this story was originally published in the FITTING IN anthology, from the Mad Scientist Journal.

Fumes from the bus's ancient gasoline engine stung Dana's nose and dust made her eyes water as they jounced over the dirt road. Sagebrush scrub extended as far as she could see, ending only at the broken sides and flat tops of mesas in the distance. The brush cast paltry shadows with the sun so high, but the shadow of the bus's roof writhed on the floor. Sometimes a bump would throw them sideways, and the shadows oozed up the corner of her seat, reaching for her hungrily.

Dana closed her eyes, but not before her heart sped, panicked. Were the shadows getting worse? She only had to last one more week, maybe two, to accomplish her goal. Then it didn't matter if she lost the rest of her mind before she died. She focused on a deep, gasoline-tainted breath. You'd think the government could have afforded to retrofit their vehicles. But maybe the bus was supposed to remind "beasts" like her of their place in this human world. As if they could forget while being transported to the camps.

She opened her eyes when the bus rumbled to a stop at the first of several checkpoints, layers of electrified fences. Dana stared without moving her head, to avoid attracting the attention of the two guards on seats behind and beside her. She couldn't let self-pity distract her from her real purpose here. She would free the prisoners. They'd make it to the enclave in Russia, even if she wouldn't. She counted the guards outside and traced the numbers on her knee to fix them in her mind. It was possible, then. One, two, then four. They smelled overconfident, what she could catch over the dust. If the residents of the camp were lucky, the guards would put too much stock in their silver bullets. The shadow of one guard's sleeve slipped over his gun, caressing it, mocking Dana.

The buildings, once they reached them, seemed so prosaic. She'd never been to this part of the United States, but she'd seen similarly rundown houses driving in, shacks plopped on pieces of desert land that looked no different than all the other square kilometers surrounding them. The camp had about half a dozen buildings arranged haphazardly in a cluster, all single-story and falling to pieces. A two-story building stood in fenced isolation on the other side of the compound, stucco smooth, tile roof unbroken, a broadcast tower sheltered in the middle of its courtyard. The shadows from its roof clung greedily to its walls.

"C'mon, beastgirl. Out." The female guard of the two stood and motioned Dana to precede them out of the bus. The woman hadn't been unkind on the journey. Since she'd let herself be caught, Dana had learned to spot two types of people. The first thought of the Jews, of the Japanese, of all the times before humans said "never again" as they stared at the camps of their age, and then sincerely convinced themselves that beasts were not only inhuman, but dangerous. Were, Dana corrected herself. She was a Were, not a beast. The humans couldn't take what her parents had taught her about herself and her people, that was locked away in her mind.

The second kind of people enjoyed themselves, because each kick or jab they gave her was a blow they gave to their fears.

Dana lifted her hands in acquiescence and rose, silver-cored shackles rattling. Her left foot woke to agony as she put weight on it, but the limping was easy enough to disguise in the gait enforced by the shackles. Shadows sucked at her feet with every step, and Dana tried to ignore them. Not real. Just a symptom of the degradation of her mind caused by the silver poisoning.

She stepped through a patch of comparative cool directly in front of the laboring air conditioner as she exited the bus, then into even worse heat as the sun found her skin without the bus's protection. Even knowing the light kept the shadows at bay, it was hard not to wilt under the glare.

The female guard followed Dana, silver-loaded gun at her back, and directed her into the building in good repair. Dana counted guards again as they processed her in, rousing only to repeat her name. She focused on faces as well, to avoid over-counting the complement when she encountered them in different situations. This far out in the back of beyond, they couldn't change people too often.

The female guard snapped a collar around her neck with a finality that matched its lack of keyhole. Not meant to be removed easily, if at all. Both guards relaxed with that snap. When they finished unlocking her shackles, Dana stood quiet and put her fingers to the collar's cool metal. The stench of silver was ever-present for her, but she still got a shivery sense of the liquid silver nitrate core beneath her fingers. Break the collar, and it ruptured everywhere. A shadow from her fingers slid slippery over her hip and breast and she dropped her hand.

They had her strip and gave her garments like a bikini top and cut-offs, though the fabric was shoddy and thin. Dana held the fabric against her chest and frowned at the female guard who was watching her all the more closely now the male had turned his back. Why hadn't they given her a jumpsuit? She swallowed and pulled the clothes on quickly. It didn't matter. It didn't change her plan, which was flexible anyway, since she didn't know the conditions here. The Were who'd escaped at the beginning hadn't lingered to share their experiences.

Back out into the heat. Dana faked anxiety about the collar to hide her limp this time. The male guard just snorted and prodded her in the back with the muzzle of his gun. "Go on, join the others. Eat a lizard or something, knock yourself out."

Once she'd passed through the gate in the command center's fence, the guards disappeared back into the building. Dana hugged herself and stared at the rundown buildings. Here was another hurdle. Her shadow sneered at her from where it pooled around her feet. What if the other Were betrayed her to the humans? They'd know something was wrong with her. She hadn't been part of a pack, so they had no reason to trust her. Her whole plan could end right there, at the muzzle of a guard's gun. Rumors said they executed the troublemakers for "trying to escape."

As she neared, Dana smelled overlapping Were scents in three of the buildings. She swallowed, gritted her teeth, and headed for the closest, slow and steady in her steps. She wanted to escape this sun as soon as possible, anyway.

The building's interior was as minimal as the outside: a few LED light panels down the center of the ceiling, and a dozen beds without mattresses pushed together to hold a pile of napping Were. There was no fabric to be seen in the whole building. Just the mass of Were cuddled together, women wearing clothes like hers, men wearing just shorts.

Dana's shadow tightened around her ankles like the constriction in her throat. She'd never seen so many Were before. Only her parents. Why would this pack want her, when her whole life had been cowardice? Her parents had abandoned their pack, to save the child soon to be born. She'd abandoned her parents to save herself—they'd begged her to do it, did that excuse it?—and even that hadn't mattered in the end. They'd found her parents, gotten their names before they were accidentally killed. Then her name was on the list of those with beast blood. And she'd run again, to save herself.

But she didn't want to keep running. The Were man who'd found her, he'd told her to get to Siberia, that Were lived there secretly, free. She could have gone alone, healthy, and offered that pack her cowardice. Instead, she'd decided to do something more than run. To make a sacrifice to save those who hadn't been lucky enough to stand at the end of a long line of sacrifices, as she had. And here she was, to save them, and the sight of so many Were was almost terrifying. Were her unrealized good intentions enough for them to accept her?

But she had little to lose now. She'd never make it to Russia before she died, so this was her last chance at anything like a pack. Dana took a step forward.

A long-limbed dark-brown-skinned woman at the edge of the platform they'd created from the beds lifted herself to her elbows. "C'mon in, new girl. We can do introductions after siesta." She settled down again.

Dana hesitated a breath longer, then climbed onto the platform. She settled on her side, separate, but a broad-shouldered man turned over and flung an arm over her hip to draw her in. "Edmond," he murmured, and Dana returned the introduction in the same low voice.

She felt him inhale, then his muscles went rigid. "Silver," he breathed. Dana curled up as tightly as she could, praying that he wouldn't scream for the guards. An image of her parents' Lady didn't come easily to her mind, but she prayed to something. Close enough.

"We should talk, later." Edmond drew closer and spoke into her neck. "After siesta."

Dana nodded with a jerk and waited. Nothing happened. No one demanded she defend her right to sleep among them. Edmond's breathing returned to the rhythm of a doze, and the stress of the day sucked her under before too long. She drifted off, feeling something she thought might be contentment, even as she watched the shadow puddle under the bed platform ooze bigger.

As the heat eased toward evening, the Were pile slowly separated into individuals, stretching and pushing to their feet. Dana sat on the edge of a bed and watched them. Here and there she spotted silver scars, hinting at everyone's journey here through a world of humans eager to check for beasts among them.

A shriek sounded from outside and two kids, perhaps six and eight, pelted in, chasing each other. The woman who had greeted Dana scooped the younger one up, held him out of reach while the girl jumped impotently, and twisted to set him down again, giving him a new lead. They screamed with laughter and slammed outside again.

Dana stared after them. She hadn't expected children. She hadn't imagined anyone could bear to bring them into a world with camps, but she rubbed the warm spot on her hip where she could still imagine Edmond's arm and the feeling of cuddling up against everyone. Maybe it wasn't a bad childhood, growing up with a pack.

She'd have to add time to her estimate for the escape. Children couldn't run as fast, and they'd have trouble sitting still for her to get rid of their collars. She'd have to warn parents to carry them, when the time came. What to do about the collars she didn't know yet.

Edmond returned from what Dana suspected was the building with the bathrooms. He seemed to make a point to touch everyone he passed on his way to her, a hand on a shoulder or arm. "The alpha asked me to tell you guys to be distracting for about an hour," he murmured here and there and received nods. When he got to Dana, he offered a hand to pull her up from the platform. Seen standing, his rugged frame was most obvious, but Dana saw a touch of what must be his mother in his softer lips, slightly curved now. For a white guy, his hair was dark, but brown beside the black of hers.

"Shall we?" he asked. Dana nodded and accepted the hand.

"The alpha?" Dana asked as they crunched over the dirt

crust between the bushes outside. The volume of the children's shouts had increased, and now adults joined the game, making the concrete paths and courtyard between the buildings seem a hive of activity. Even when it was quiet, she suspected she couldn't feel alone here. "Who's the alpha here?" That was the person she needed to convince first, she knew that much from what her parents had taught her about real Were society.

"The alpha is a polite fiction. The guards watch for leaders, and they get yanked into another camp." Edmond clenched his jaw, and gestured ahead to a dusty empty space beside the path, enough room for two people to sit without getting prodded by dry sticks or sharp rocks. "Everyone knows I'm not really talking to an alpha, but it keeps everyone's instincts quiet if I play my natural beta."

He dropped to sit cross-legged. Dana hesitated before following. The only space left was in his shadow, and no matter how many times she told herself it wasn't real, seeing the thing writhe, she didn't want to sit there. She swallowed and did anyway.

"But I can organize everyone if you have a way to get us out of here." Edmond's eyes were heavy on Dana's and she met them in shock. Was she really that transparent? If she was, the guards had to know too. Maybe they were laughing at her, even now. The longer she locked gazes with him, the more she felt the strangest pressure, like hundreds of people were watching her all at once, waiting for her to break.

Edmond broke the contact first, clasping her shoulders bracingly. "Sorry, didn't mean to measure dominance with you. We're all betas here, huh?" He laughed awkwardly.

Dana shook her head. "What was that? What did you just do?"

Edmond blew out a breath. "You're one of the hidden children, aren't you? Raised after families scattered because packs were too noticeable?"

Dana searched in her memories. Measuring dominance did sound familiar, but her parents had taught her so much, all of it abstract, easy to forget. She smoothed a hand along her forearm, trying to also smooth down panic. In all her worries about a pack accepting her, she'd never considered all the things she might not know. "My father left his pack back in Turkey, when things got bad there, and met my mother in the US. And then her pack broke up, before they had me. How did you grow up, then?" He didn't look old enough to have been born before the humans found the Were.

"I grew up in the Seattle pack. I suppose you're used to how humans age, too. I'm around sixty." He sounded pitying. Jealousy and anger welled up in Dana, mixed, and curdled. He was lucky enough to have been born in a different world, but she was the one who'd injected herself with silver nitrate, to give herself immunity so she could touch silver in the camp and release him. She was the one who'd traded her ability to shift for his freedom.

She kicked at his knee, he *oof*ed, and then, to her surprise, grinned. "Fair enough," he said, dropping his head in respect.

"How did you know why I'm here?" Dana pushed the rest of the questions crowding in on her aside. Were society didn't matter, except for how it helped her get everyone here out. For her, it would be moot soon enough anyway.

Edmond reached out to take her arms one at a time, frowning at the smooth insides of her elbows. "I know what an injected Were smells like. If you were injected, you'd heal at human speed, and you could touch all the silver they've spread everywhere. You could pass all their tests. Unless they've been able to perfect the genetic test since I was tossed in here?"

Dana shook her head. "We're genetically human in human, genetically *Canis lupus* in wolf. They haven't isolated the genes for the trigger to switch between the two."

Edmond nodded. "So if they can't find you, you let yourself be caught. And if you let yourself be caught, you're here for a reason."

Dana folded her arms against her belly. "Because this age has no hero like Silver." She managed a ghost of a laugh at her own joke. Figures of myth never seemed to survive into today's world, when you needed them most.

Edmond gave her the strangest look, almost tangling his gaze with hers again in his distraction. "Silver was my alpha, you realize. She raised me. She was a gifted leader, but I don't know she was..." He seemed to be struggling to match a description to her tone.

"A saint of the Lady?" In Dana's peripheral vision, a bush shadow congealed into a line and twisted like a snake between a couple of small cacti. They were definitely getting worse. She'd never seen a shadow separate from its original object before. What was to stop them ganging up on her from every direction now?

"My parents always talked like she was a real person. But then I did this, to be like her—" Dana lifted her left foot and pulled the toes apart to show the needle mark. She assumed that was what he'd been looking for on her elbows. "And instead of gaining the power to comfort the grief-stricken and heal the sick—or at least touch a guard's keys to get us out of here—I start dying by centimeters. I can feel it!" Her tone grew strident as she tried to forestall the objection she saw on his face. She lowered her voice again, conscious of the guards. "I knew I wouldn't be able to shift afterward. I thought the sacrifice was worth it to free so many. But I didn't know it would hurt so much." She took a deep breath to press that memory down. "I didn't know the muscles would be partially paralyzed so I'd hardly be able to walk. I didn't know I'd start losing my mind. So now I can only pray I can still free you all before it's too late for me."

Edmond cupped her face. "Look at me, Dana. Silver wasn't a saint. She was injected and lived to be almost *ninety*. Not as long as a Were, but long enough. She died of old age before the humans even knew about us. If you're seeing things—well, Silver said she saw Death."

Not—dying? Dana could barely take it in, especially while the shadow under his jaw extended a tendril to curl possessively up over his cheekbone.

Dana heard the crunch of footsteps at the same moment Edmond's head snapped up. He leaned in and slid one of her bikini straps down her shoulder. He spoke in a whisper against the side of her neck. "Forgive me, but they know this is where we come for privacy, since everyone hears and smells it in the dorms. They won't look twice if that's what they think we're doing."

Dana laughed low in her throat, suddenly punchy with relief from his revelation. Not dying. She was hardly going to argue with the act. Edmond was damn good looking, and it had been years since she'd had the time for any of that. And never with a Were before, either. She slid her fingers into Edmond's hair to add verisimilitude, and the footsteps moved off again.

She was here for a reason, though, as he had said. Even if she had more time than she'd realized, she couldn't let herself get distracted. Her plan could still be discovered by the guards.

She sat back. "Anyway, since I can touch silver, I can break everyone's collar and not worry about getting splashed."

Hunger flared up in Edmond's eyes so fiercely he must have been feeling it from the moment he'd realized she'd been injected, and kept it banked until now. "That's why we're all half-naked. In the first couple escapes people popped the collars and used fabric to buffer the worst of the damage. This stuff's so thin, it won't work unless the whole pack goes naked, and they watch the cameras for that." He tilted his head to a flash of a lens mounted on the top of the fenceline.

Dana tugged at her own collar. The damn thing chafed already. "And I can touch any keys, the gates—get you all out, and on the way to Russia. Like—" She searched her memory for the Were man's name. "Tom said."

Edmond's face lit, chasing a shadow down to drip sullenly over his collarbone. "Thank the Lady, he's still alive. And that the Russian enclave is still safe."

While she'd been watching Edmond, a rock's shadow had crept up to her fingers, fouling them with heavy blackness. She felt as if the same thing had happened to her thoughts. She wasn't dying, so she could join them in Russia—but how was she supposed to escape after opening the gates for the others, when she literally couldn't run? She'd be recaptured for sure. And would the Russian pack really want a Were who not only couldn't shift, she could hardly walk and kept staring at what wasn't there?

Dana clenched her teeth. If she was meant to be forever alone, so be it. She would free the others first. She was no coward. "Shall I do your collar first?" She was impressed with how even she kept her voice.

His hungry look returned and he nodded, unable to speak past it. She leaned into him and slid a few fingers into the space between skin and metal. "You have to promise you won't shift and take off. I need time to do everyone's collar, and the camp looks set up to hold wolf forms best, anyway. Better to go out the front gate in human."

"Don't worry, I'm not stupid." Edmond reached up and caught her wrists, his grip shakily tight. "Are you sure—?"

Dana nodded. "Crack it, once I'm ready…" She wormed her hand up so her palm was beneath the collar. No need to mention this was all theory she'd concocted after reading about the collars in the media. There was no reason it shouldn't work. "We want it to drip out at first."

Edmond's throat muscles worked under her hand, then he reached up. He tested the strength of the metal first, fingers on either side of her hand. Then he grunted and the internal latch cracked. Silver nitrate leaked onto Dana's palm.

Shadows skittered toward her along the ground from every direction, bush shadows and lizard shadows and the heavy smothering weight of a building shadow that made it hard for her to breathe the moment she saw it.

Dana bit the inside of her cheek to force her attention away. She wasn't dying. She had a job to do. She angled her hand so the silver nitrate dripped into her other palm. She scattered those drops harmlessly onto the dirt every few seconds. Edmond was shaking visibly, but he kept the movement from more than vibrating against her hands. At last the trickle slowed, then stopped. Dana sat back and rubbed her hands in the dirt, then rolled the dust and silver and sweat into little balls between them. She brushed those away and lifted her hands to sniff them. They smelled safe to touch other Were. The shadows boiled over the spatters of silver on the earth and seeped into them, leaving Dana alone.

"You can take it off," she told Edmond when she noticed he still hadn't touched the metal. She opened the collar and shook it over the dirt to get rid of any drops lingering inside.

Edmond drew in a shuddering breath. "Lady above. Do you know how long I've been here, with that on?" His muscles twisted and his back started to arch.

Dana snapped the collar back on, keeping her hands there as an extra reminder. A wolf neck was too thick for the collar, that was the point of the things, to keep Were from shifting forms. Even empty, it should remind him. "You can't. They'll see." She bit her lower lip. Maybe should have given him more time to prepare, warned him better. She'd remember that for the next Were she freed.

"You're right." Edmond checked the collar to make sure the ends were seated firmly together. He stood. "Thank you. I wish there was something more than just words I could offer you."

Dana started to wave that off, but then an impulse took hold of her. She stood too and kissed him. He kissed back, leaning into her. She closed her eyes and sensation reached down deep into her core and took firm hold. She pulled away first. Too much left to do. She needed to count how many Were this camp had, how long it would take her to break all the collars without being noticed.

Later, she'd pick up where she'd left off with that kiss. She promised herself that.

"They'll be serving dinner," Edmond commented as he followed her back to the buildings. He looked a little disappointed, but the suppressed excitement of knowing his collar was a dummy remained in his scent. Dana savored that scent. If the others felt as he did, she could be part of his pack for a while, before they escaped and left her behind in the humans' hands. Maybe that would be enough.

The more collars Dana broke, the bolder the shadows got. By the time she'd finished forty of the approximately fifty residents, the shadows dogged her footsteps in a roiling carpet that extended chill tendrils up her ankles whenever she stopped moving. It was as if the shadows were reminding her that soon, she'd be dragged away from the bone-deep feeling of security she'd discovered in this pack. Though she knew even that feeling had a falseness to it. Here, no one else could shift either. Here, there was little enough room to run. Outside of this prison, things would be different. But for now, she had the other Were. She had a few stolen hours with Edmond.

Things all went wrong the morning of her fifth day at the camp.

They fed the Were two vegetarian meals each day, morning and evening. The guards had no wish to stand out in the midday sun either, handing out lunch. Breakfast today smelled like macaroni and cheese, but Dana caught a whiff of something else as she approached the cart in the control building's gateway. The shadow of the cart's upper level shrank down to single-foil wrapped tray on the lower shelf and oozed over it as if searching for a way in.

The woman Dana had met first, Lizzie, was directly in front of Dana in line, her son pressed against her hip. When it was Lizzie's turn, the female guard glanced at the child and reached for the tray the shadows loved. As she offered it, the shadows sprang for the boy, covered him so only him face showed.

Dana jerked a step forward and cut off her protest. The food didn't smell like poison, it smelled like fried chicken. And the female guard's expression held only concern for a child who looked plenty human enough to stir her protective instincts. The second guard, a red-haired man, frowned at his partner and shoved Dana's tray at her without looking. "What are you—?"

Dana jerked her tray from his hands. Had he noticed something wrong? She needed to distract him. "I'm fucking hungry, here," she said, but he still didn't look at her. He nodded for the third guard to move closer, covering them all with his gun, and then strode to the boy and jerked him around.

The boy clutched the tray and screamed when the redhaired guard tried to take it away. The sound shattered the shadows. They formed wolves on the ground, running wolves, dappling the dirt as far as Dana could see. Frozen.

Then the shadows moved again. One surged up to the catch the broken collar Lizzie tossed aside. She shifted, leapt, and tore out the red-haired guard's throat in a gout of red and choking stink of blood.

No. No, Lady, no! Dana dropped her food and herself on top of it, because the third guard was shooting. Someone shrieked, the sound full of the rage of someone who lived on, and someone else gurgled, all too final.

But growls grew and Dana lifted her head to see the female guard go down. The shooter was already hidden beneath a pile of wolf shapes, like Dana's shadows but painted with color and warmth.

"It's all on the cameras, they'll already be coming with more guns. Everyone who can shift, to the command building." Edmond was still in human at least. He didn't sound confident enough, without the power of the imaginary alpha behind him, but apparently he didn't need to. More collars thumped into the roiling surface of the shadows and more wolves streamed toward the building.

Dana shoved herself up and looked around wildly. Who was left? Could she possibly open their collars before the guards arrived and shot them all?

No, no time for that. She needed to open the gates. "Go, go!" she directed those she saw still in human, but they were already running. Probably hadn't even heard her.

The shadows licked at the dead guards sluggishly like fire at wet wood, so she could still see what she needed, keys on the red-haired guard's belt. Real, mechanical silver keys, because humans had found that with beasts, silver and simple, strong bars were better than any electronic locks. Dana clenched her hand around the keys with a fierce pleasure that they didn't hurt her. Perhaps the price she'd paid for that immunity had been too high, but she'd paid it all the same. She tried to breathe through her mouth so she didn't smell what she wasn't looking at: the ruin of the guard's throat.

She tried to at least jog for the series of gates leading out of the compound, but the shadows made her footing seem treacherous, and her bad foot kept turning under her. Shots rang out in the command building, shots and screams. Dana couldn't do anything about that, though. She had to get to the gate.

Her focus narrowed, ignoring the wolves, ignoring the shadows, all her attention on the lock she needed, glinting in the sunlight. Then pain, shocking enough to gray out her thoughts and her vision. Her leg collapsed—too much pain, too high. Blood.

She'd been shot. Dana rolled to clamp her hands over the

wound, keys growing slick with red because she wouldn't drop them, not when lives had been lost to get them. She sacrificed her top to make a pad to clamp over the entry wound—no exit, but she couldn't think about anything more than getting up and making it to the locks, now.

She made it sitting, then to her good knee, and then someone scooped her up and held her standing, so her vision grayed into sparkles from the pain once more. "Dana." Edmond's voice. "You can make it."

She could make it, damn it. She wasn't going to die of silver poisoning, and she wasn't going to die of a Lady-damned bullet. Dana staggered forward, got the key into the first gate's lock. Edmond got her to the next. The third and last seemed so far, just a short jouncing ride in the bus, but an eternity walking as her leg bled. She held the pad as best she could and prayed to whatever kind powers existed in the universe.

The shadows were everywhere, raging around her ankles like the sea and splashing up to paint the horizon. Only she and Edmond and the lock remained. Then wolves began to collect behind them. Another Were in human supported her other side, and the lock loomed up. Dana couldn't match the key with the hole at first, but she pressed until it scraped along and slotted home.

She pushed the gate as much as she could, and the wolves streamed out, disappearing into the desert of shadows. No, that wasn't how it was supposed to work. "Wait!" she called, voice too weak to convince even herself. "They'll hunt from aircraft, you have to leave as humans, in uniforms, confuse them—"

No one listened, even when Edmond raised his voice to repeat her points. Just a couple of betas, shouting at the tide not to go out. Dana's second prop disappeared after the others and she slumped down to the ground before Edmond could rebalance her.

"We're fast, faster than they realize. We have time before backup arrives," Edmond said. He tried to pull her up. Dana couldn't muster the strength to help him.

This was it, then. She'd done what she could. "Go, hurry up," she told Edmond, and dredged up a smile for him.

The shadows on Edmond's face were all metaphorical, born of worry. Her shadows left him bare and thus the only bright spot in her vision. "Dana, no. Get up."

Dana tangled her fingers in his to squeeze, and stop him pulling at her. "I couldn't run anywhere, even before I was shot. It's all right. I succeeded. I got you out."

"No!" Edmond clung to her hands. "Promise me, Dana, that you'll follow us when you can. At your own speed. You'll follow us to Russia, no matter what you have to do. Promise me!"

Dana laughed weakly, tears welling in her eyes. They refracted Edmond's brightness onto the shadows. Hysterical humor took hold of her. "You're no alpha, to make me."

"Promise!" Edmond's voice grew desperate.

He needed to run if he was going to. "Promise," Dana said, because that's what he needed to let her go. He eased her down. She turned her head to watch as his collar thumped down and four wolf feet ran away.

She drifted for a while, slumped on her side, watching the shadows and holding the pad clamped to her leg. Alone. Slowly, the sunlight drained most of the shadows away, beat hot and hotter against her skin. The remaining shadows pooled beneath her, pillowing her head.

The shadow of her own body stretched itself across the sand, formed her standing silhouette, a wolf beside it. The wolf wavered and disappeared, leaving her alone.

She supposed she was. Just human, no wolf left.

And there was her answer, in the sheer irony of it. To save the other Were, she'd become too human, and now being too human would save her as well. And she didn't have to run anywhere.

Energy flooded into Dana, hope kindling a fire that pushed strength into her remaining limbs. But she hoarded the energy, saving it. She lay there, skin burning to red banked beneath the brown as the day dragged on, until the clean-up crew arrived. From her angle, he couldn't see if they'd gathered any Were bodies, and she didn't try. She lay still, only breathing, until one of the medics bent over her, checking for life.

Dana turned her head slowly, eyes searching much faster. There, at the neck of the woman's uniform. Dana lifted her hand and pulled at the loop of chain, dragged the silver cross out from under the shirt. She clung to it like it was her lifeline.

Which it was, she supposed. "Human!" she gasped, letting tears free into her voice. "I'm human, there was a mistake, the beasts forced me to...I'm human!"

The medic made a soothing noise and carefully pried Dana's hand off the cross to see her unblemished skin. "Don't worry. You'll be just fine."

She would be, Dana agreed silently. She would heal, and she would follow the other Were to Russia. Follow as a human, to finally find her Were pack.

Contested History

We end with lost history found. This novella is set around ten months after DEATH-TOUCHED. Faith's talents as an archaeologist are put to good use, and she pulls together the threads of Were we've met along the way: Pierce, Tom, Felicia, and others.

1

Faith's heart about stopped when the werewolf appeared up on a ridgeline. She and three others—two other archaeological field techs and the crew chief—had just finished doing shovel probes along a fairly flat, fallow field, but topography picked up out past an irrigation ditch, on someone else's parcel. She was deeply familiar with wolves in silhouette, given how much she'd read and watched about them over the past ten months, which meant she was pretty sure she knew a werewolf when she saw one: heavier through the shoulders, bigger than a husky but smaller than a Newfie.

She'd spotted it while the crew was loading the company truck, one person up under the canopy to accept shovels and screens for stacking. Faith leaned hers against the tailgate and backed up toward the truck's cab, wary. Cyrena, the crew chief, noticed her and shaded her eyes against the low afternoon sun to pick out the wolf herself. "Some farmer's dog," she guessed.

And damned if the werewolf didn't start moving like a dog. The fact that it was an act was painfully clear to Faith, but the others seemed soothed by the way the canid bounded over the low, brushy weeds of the field, tongue hanging out and tail waving. So if it was someone coming for her, it clearly meant to lull the humans into a false sense of security so it could get close to her. But it had been ten months, with nothing. Why come after her now?

She could come up with no answer before the wolf was close enough for her to recognize that shade of gray, fading to white over the belly. More of a bluish gray, rather than the tan, sandy shade she'd seen on the majority of gray wolves she'd watched clips of. She knew this werewolf.

His name was Laurence.

She stepped forward without meaning to, and then he'd reached her. He threw himself at her feet and went into an ecstasy of canine writhing, belly ready for scritches. Faith noticed the rest of the crew relaxing subliminally, and wondered if Laurence had done that on purpose. Most big dogs, when they got this excited, started jumping to try to lick your face, but that was a lot more threatening from a strange dog with no owner in sight.

"He likes you," Cyrena said, expression growing bemused. The others went back to packing the truck, but Cyrena leaned on the tailgate, watching, no doubt in case the friendly dog turned less so, and she had to intervene. She was tall and extremely lean, but that hid considerable strength. And she probably didn't want to write up a safety incident report, either.

Faith crouched and manhandled Laurence upright, making a show of checking for a collar as she spoke. "This is my ex's dog. So he knows me." That was even almost true. Her fingers found a leather cord and she traced it around to a couple official county registration tags and a name tag, the kind you could get engraved in front of you at the machine in the pet store. It was in the shape of a bone and said LAURENCE.

On finding that, Faith couldn't force herself to remain wary any longer. Scary violent werewolves still might be coming for her later, but this one had made a dog tag with his *own name.* "Oh my God, you're a dork," she muttered, and then realized she better start watching her pronouns, so she didn't slip up on something that couldn't apply to both man and "dog."

"I didn't know you had an ex out here on the east side of the state." Annalisa returned from dumping her personal pack in the back of the cab. The other tech on this project Faith didn't know that well, but she and Annalisa had been on a lot of projects together, and done a lot of drinking in the evenings. You couldn't help collecting ex stories over time.

"I don't. He lives—lived?—in, hell, Virginia, I think? I met him when he was visiting family in Seattle." Faith settled the cord back into the fur of Laurence's ruff and ended with her fingers buried there. Unless he hadn't been real, and she'd imagined it all. It seemed that way sometimes. "Not really an ex, I guess. A fling."

"You mean Wedding Hookup Guy?" Annalisa's Mexican heritage had granted her the most enthusiastic dark brown curls, only slightly smushed now even after having been ruthlessly corralled back in a tail for the day. Annalisa had released her hair at the same time she ditched her field hat, and the curls tumbled forward over her shoulders now as she crouched over the "dog" too, giving Laurence's fur a ruffle, but really leaning in for a little privacy with Faith. "Kinda stalkery, isn't it? I mean, I know you're completely not over him."

Privacy with Laurence *right there,* looking from one to the other with a singularly gormless expression. "What are you talking about, not over him? It's been ten months of utter silence. And *he* was the one who suggested we completely cut contact. Since his family is crazytown." Faith aimed that squarely at Laurence, who stared at her, panting. *I am a happy dog! More petting!*

Annalisa made a finger gun at Faith and clicked her tongue. "You're still counting the months. Not over him."

Cyrena called their names out the driver's window, and Faith jerked to her feet. She didn't need to hold everyone up with her paranormal life problems. "Give him the benefit of the doubt," she told Annalisa, to tell Laurence. "Maybe he was going to text me to meet somewhere and actually talk about this, but his dog got away from him and caught my scent or something." Or he turned into a wolf specifically to bloodhound his way to her. One of the two. "I guess he can meet us at the EconoLodge."

Laurence was off like a shot, dog on a mission. Annalisa laughed as she circled the truck to get into the back seat on the other side. "He's gonna bark it like Timmy down the well, huh?"

"I'll text him in a minute." Faith was busy for the moment, shoving everyone's personal packs out of the way. At least there were only two people sitting on the back seat for this job, not three, but she'd inherited her Thai grandmother's height, if not many of her features, and everyone thought she should have to have the extra crap in her footwell. She was already behind the driver's seat, so it wasn't like she had much of a footwell to begin with.

Buckled up, she pretended to type as they bumped their way back to the dirt access road, though of course she didn't have Laurence's number. The drive was only going to be about half an hour today, one of the closer parcels in their current discontinuous project area, but it still felt like the longest thirty minutes of her life. Why was Laurence here? What did he want?

What did *she* want? To order him to get out and leave her alone for good this time? Wouldn't that be the smart thing, not to get sucked into his world, with the kidnappings and the violent beatings and whatever else she hadn't experienced yet and probably didn't want to?

Was it really that obvious she wasn't over him?

2

No Laurence waited for them when they pulled into the hotel parking lot, but Faith supposed even a werewolf couldn't outrun a truck. He'd have had the interval on four feet to get back to his car, wherever that was, and then the drive in from there. She delayed as long as she could, lifting out people's packs for them, helping Cyrena check the locks on the canopy to make sure the equipment would be safe overnight. Everyone but Annalisa scattered in urgent search of showers. She lingered beside Faith, ass hitched on the bumper while Faith paced restlessly, trying to watch both parking lot entrances simultaneously. "Want backup?" Annalisa asked.

Faith grimaced apologetically at her coworker. "At least until I see if he can explain what he's doing out here. Anyway, if he's not here in the next five minutes, he can wait in the lobby until I've finished showering." She checked the time on her phone.

A car pulled up four minutes later, very sedately. She wasn't sure what model she'd have expected for Laurence, but this wasn't quite it—it was older, though impeccably maintained, and clearly had originally been intended to be as sporty as your budget could afford until fashion marched on and left it dated. *So* early 2000s. Which was an absurd thing to think.

Laurence must have seen the company trucks, parked at the back of the lot where they wouldn't crowd anyone, but he pulled neatly up next in line near the lobby. He got out and ambled over, hands in the pockets of his jeans, and he was exactly the way Faith remembered him. In human form, that was. She'd remembered his wolf form better than she'd expected as well.

He wasn't too much taller than her, slight but athletic. His blond hair might have been shorter than she last remembered it, not buzzed but certainly too short to screw around with product, and as ever, he could have been growing a beard for days and she'd never have been able to tell without putting her hand on his cheek.

Which she caught herself leaned onto her toes, planning to do, before she sternly shut down the idea. She'd walked away then, and it might be that she'd have to walk away now, depending on what he said. But if she so much as touched him, or worse, let him *hold* her...

Laurence stopped about five feet away from her. "Hey, Faith," he said. His hands stayed in his pockets, still casual, but having been around him when he was deeply frightened, she could see the ghost of tension through his shoulders. She wondered if the opposite applied. She'd certainly been terrified nearly out of her wits several times when *his* werewolf enemies kidnapped the both of them by mistake.

"You came back," Faith's mouth said without any sort of consultation with her brain.

"I had to." Laurence offered a lopsided smile, looked down at his feet. "I couldn't get you out of my head. But this time, if you say you want me gone, I'm gone for good. I just—I wanted you to have a real choice, with time to think about it, instead of having to run out the door."

Faith caught herself on her toes again. Two steps, and she'd feel his arms around her, that strength against her skin, and she was not *allowing* herself that. She needed to be clear-headed. "You said with your…crazy family—" She glanced at Annalisa. Laurence probably didn't need the reminder of the amused audience, but she found she did. "I was better off not getting involved with you. So a choice without time pressure is great and all, but what changed?"

"I have to admit my…family is still in play, but I'm in therapy." The last part came out all in a rush, like it had shouldered its way past something much more poetic and rehearsed. Laurence laughed at himself, though, and rather than turn self-hating, it stopped at self-deprecating, definitely a change since she'd last seen him. "Have been for a while. Trying to get my shit together to do a relationship properly, you know? My family, they only put me in unhealthy situations if I let them. If you're willing to—to try, with me, I promise to absolutely stay on top of it, making sure I'm not falling into bad habits with them."

"I don't know about you, but that answer gets a thumbs-up from me," Annalisa said, and pushed herself off the bumper. Faith waved permission to go ahead. That was a hell of an answer, utterly unexpected. She gave up the fight and threw herself into Laurence's arms.

It was everything she'd been missing for ten months, such stability in the clasp of his arms around her waist. His smile lit up his whole face. "God, I'm covered in dirt," she protested, seeing the fabric of her field shirt against his white T-shirt. "You probably shouldn't kiss me."

"I want a little credit for the fact that I restrained myself and didn't lick your face when I had the perfect opportunity," Laurence said, low voiced just for her, and then kissed her anyway. He was such a perfect height for it and Faith could actually taste some of the dirt herself and she didn't care because she also tasted the memory of the last time his lips had been on hers, and everywhere else on her body, and his hands too.

A whoop startled Faith into coming up for air. Annalisa waved a hand from over by the side door of the hotel, then disappeared inside. "Just listened in while my coworker spilled everything." She poked him in the stomach, and he made an exaggerated *oof* sound and looked not even a little bit sorry. "I have to admit, you do good derp."

"It's a skill. I practice. Timmy's stuck down the well!" Laurence changed his grip suddenly, hands on her waist to whirl her around effortlessly, startling a shriek of laughter out of her. God, she was acting like some lovesick fifteen-year-old, making those kind of noises in public. "Wedding Hookup Guy, though? Really?"

Faith sobered, pulled away when her feet hit the ground again. She let Laurence keep one of her hands, though, to lace their fingers together. "Yeah, don't you remember? You had won two tickets to this mountain getaway cabin in Anchorage and were pathetically single, so we blew off the end of your friends' wedding and went and had a fling for three days, barely any cell phone service at all. Makes a great story. Explains why I was kinda distracted when I got back to work."

"Yeah." Laurence matched and surpassed her tension with his own. He looked down at their joined hands as he spoke. "So, before we go any further, I have to warn you there's another reason I'm showing up now, instead of later. My bosses will be contacting you soon, and I wanted to warn you about that, even though I'm not supposed to be talking to you yet. So you have your time to decide, before they show up."

Faith jerked her hand out of his clasp, exactly as he'd been expecting, she realized a beat later, as he slipped both his hands awkwardly into his hip pockets. "Contacting me? Why?" They'd let her go this long without interference, hadn't they?

Laurence smiled, thin and fairly twisted. "They need an archaeologist, so they'd like to hire you. I'll explain properly, if we can go somewhere private."

It took Faith a moment to backtrack and realize even with Annalisa gone, he'd said "bosses," not "alphas," as she had mentally filled in. Better than her by far at not blabbing secrets in the open air. "My room," she said, grabbed her pack, and strode for the nearest side door rather than the lobby.

Down the bland hallway, Faith felt Laurence's presence behind her like a heavy, radiating source of warmth on a more than merely physical level. *Hire her?* She'd imagined plenty of versions of her next meeting with a werewolf, good and bad, and not one had included something like that.

Laurence strode a few steps into the room ahead of her when she'd unlocked the door, turned when he'd reached the end of the farther bed. "I didn't actually understand all the details of the archaeology part, but we're worried about Were artifacts being found so we want someone trained in archaeology who already knows about the Were. And since you fit those criteria…"

He rebalanced his weight, as if about to pace, then settled again. "I want you to know, though, that they're separate things. The job, and…me. If you decide you need the money—I assume it could take months, and I'll know they'll be generous in the rate they offer—and you want me to stay away, I absolutely will."

Of course Faith needed the money—archaeology at the field tech level in this area was a patchwork of projects lasting a day to a couple of weeks, and there weren't any multi-week ones on the horizon yet this summer. That had been why she used to rely on her catering job to fill in the gaps, but she'd quit that after the kidnapping and hadn't yet replaced it.

If she knew nothing else, she knew her response to that part of Laurence's offer, though. She stopped hovering just inside the door, and stepped up to him though she didn't allow herself his touch again just yet. "No. You're not the problem. It's the other werewolves I'm not sure I want to face."

Laurence shook his head emphatically, a breath of canine about the motion. "I know I told you it might be better to walk away, but I was wrong. In the end, it took them only a month or two to find you, but they only kept an eye out to make sure the Russians didn't bother you. If not for the Were artifacts being found, they'd have left you completely alone, and I'd still be trying to get up my courage to contact you. You absolutely don't have to fear anyone in the Roanoke pack. I promise."

Laurence sealed the promise with an odd gesture, fingers curled up, thumb pressed to his forehead. He caught her look and shook his hand open again as if the gesture was liquid to be flicked away. "On the Lady, that's what that is."

It was funny, no matter how often Faith chanted *werewolf, werewolf, werewolf* at herself, and reminded herself that the "dog" had been just as much him as this man was, not some kind of passive animal vehicle that the man had listened in through, it was this small hint of culture that punched her in the gut.

"I need time to take this all in," she admitted. Maybe given that time she'd start being freaked out by the fact that the werewolves knew who and where she was. Then again, she'd been imagining that they might know for so long, confirmation didn't change much at the moment.

She realized she was still standing around in all of her dirt, pack over her shoulder. She stepped away to drop the pack on the bathroom floor where the dirt would be easier for the maids to sweep up, and returned to where Laurence was waiting. The lack of a complete negative in her answer seemed to have diffused his tension at least enough for him to achieve stillness in his stance.

"Maybe we can back up a little. Will you—and tell me if it's rude or whatever—will you let me watch—God, that doesn't sound right—" Faith pressed the heels of her hands to her cheeks, like that would hold back the heat of embarrassment. "Can I see you turn into a wolf? At this point, it doesn't seem really *real* anymore."

And Laurence was blushing too, she realized. He coughed and turned away to cover the worst of it. "It's not rude. It's more like—I mean, the answer is of course you can, but I know you're curious about the underlying logic of stuff—it's like whether I can watch you shower. Putting aside anything sexual, it's really intimate because—" His face cleared as he found the word he wanted. "Of the vulnerability."

He pulled his T-shirt over his head while Faith was still processing all that. "I am? Curious? I mean, of course I am, I just hadn't realized it was so obvious."

"It's great, I love it," Laurence assured her. Adorably, he was still wearing the dog tag around his human neck. He pulled off shoes and socks next, sitting on the end of the bed, then stood and popped the button on his jeans, very matter-of-fact about the nudity parts of it, which she remembered from before. "So. It's about a week until full, so it'll take a bit longer than it would at the full. And I already did it twice today. That doesn't mean it's painful, it's just—more work, you know? Climbing a steeper hill."

Faith nodded jerkily. She realized she'd not only twisted her fingers together, she was clenching them hard enough to leave nail marks in oddly angled places on the skin of her hands. When he was fully nude, he crouched, one hand on a knee, then...started to change.

The best comparison she could find to make was a set of Cirque du Soleil contortionists she'd seen when her parents took her to Vegas as a teen. Their costumes had all been the same color, so when the lights came up, you couldn't quite find the human bodies in the knot—clearly a combination of living beings, but the eye couldn't follow them, couldn't pick them out. And then one arm stretched free and then a leg and finally all three stood separate and recognizably human once more.

This was like that in reverse. Her eye couldn't pick out human or wolf, confused by ambiguous lines, and then it all snapped into focus and Laurence stretched, muzzle and ruff and tail and recognizably wolf. He immediately flaked out on his side, clearly exhausted by the effort.

Faith petted his flank, wonderingly. That had been pretty fucking real. Then a ridiculous thought occurred to her. "Shit. Don't shed too much. The office admin will flip out if a pet cleaning charge shows up on the hotel bill."

Laurence lifted his head to eye her, then let his head down again with a whuff of exasperation. At least, that's how he sounded to her.

"I gotta shower, anyway." Faith pushed up and hesitated at the bathroom door. It was only *fair*, after all. After struggling with herself for a couple seconds, she left it open. She was relieved not to see any canine silhouettes through the frosted plastic of the curtain, though. When she came back out wrapped in a towel to retrieve her clean clothes, he was human and dressed again, seated on the end of the bed and scrolling patiently through his phone. She ducked back out of his line of sight to dress as quickly as she could.

"So how did your alphas—the Roanokes?" Faith paused for his nod that she'd remembered correctly. "How did they find me?" She hesitated for a breath over her choice of seat, then took the other bed so they could face each other. Laurence dumped his phone to the side on the comforter and leaned back on his hands. The nonchalance was overdone, but she didn't call him on it. She understood the impulse.

"It wasn't too hard, once we found out your name, but a lot of the process happened before then." Laurence smiled lopsidedly. "Look, I'm just going to do a blanket apology now for the fact that I helped them, okay? They would have gotten there eventually on their own, and I wanted to see you again myself."

Faith waved away the apology. She couldn't fault him for that when the obvious strength of his wanting made her stomach flutter. "I guess Faith isn't that unusual a name."

Laurence shook his head, expression going even more embarrassed. "You misunderstand me. I didn't know any of your name. We never got to introductions before those cat's bastards snatched us, remember? And then you were pretending to be Susan, so it seemed safer to me that I didn't know."

"Oh, God." Faith pressed her fingertips to her lips. Had she really never—? "But I knew yours—because the guy said it." She remembered now. He was absolutely right. "How *did* you find me, then?"

"Obviously the catering company wasn't going to be very productive. My friend Tom has a friend—a human friend—who records cemeteries as a hobby. I guess she friend-of-friend links to contract archaeologists via…local historical societies? Half of these terms might be wrong, but that got us to your first name, given your physical description as one of the…field workers?"

"Techs," Faith supplied, then shut up so he could continue. Even knowing how it turned out, she was getting invested in the story. It was like the last act of a TV procedural, in a way.

"Once I knew they were going to offer you the job, I could have showed up at your office, I guess." Laurence finally gave up on leaning on his hands so he could fidget with his dog tag. "That's probably where the Roanokes will contact you. But one of the other techs was on social media, posting about a restaurant out here, so I thought I'd come and follow my nose." He shrugged. "So."

"I don't spend a ton of time at the office anyway. Drop off gear, fill out the timecard software." Faith edged forward on her bed until she could grab and still his hands. "Since…then, I've been doing more of exactly what I was doing before. What about *you*? And the alphas and the Russians and—all that."

Laurence looked down at the floor, or perhaps their joined hands instead. "Roanoke Silver and then Roanoke Dare went to Russia and deposed the alpha, helped put a better one in his place. The new one's still neck-deep in assassins trained by the old regime who are whiny about not having enough to do, or so says the gossip in the lower ranks, but she's hanging on. That's why you don't have to worry about anything like…what happened, happening again."

"Lower ranks?" Faith offered when he ran out of steam. He'd been smarting over no longer being a sub-alpha, when she met him, she remembered that pretty clearly. Hard not to remember, given how tangled it was with his account of how a former alpha used to abuse him.

"Well, mid-ranks. I haven't asked for my sub-pack back. I've been staying in the pack guest house as part of the 'misfits who need the alphas' attention' contingent of the Roanoke home pack. Which is not on the same level as a sub-pack; Dare calls it their White House staff." Laurence paused to check for comprehension. Faith nodded even though she was mostly taking this all in and filing it away to correlate at length later. "Seattle's pretty nice. I picked up my pilot's license again. At the moment, I'm running some lessons, which about covers my fees for my own flight time, so I break even. I'm looking into maybe trying to get a job with one of the companies that do tours, but the alphas haven't been growling under their breaths about me being a drain on pack finances. And now there's all the archaeology stuff to arrange."

Faith's phone broke the moment with a buzz. She wiggled it out of her pocket, but she already knew what the content of the text message would be: was she coming to dinner or what? You could certainly save your food allowance if you bought something at the grocery store and ate in your room, but in a random town where you didn't know anyone, what else were you going to do for the evening besides go out with people you at least knew?

She dismissed the message and stood, groping after a decision, or at least a direction for the immediate future. "You know your alphas probably don't want me doing their archaeology. I'm not even a field supervisor. But this is too damn much to handle on an empty stomach. Come to dinner." She dragged

Laurence up by one of his hands. "I'll show off my sexy pilot... friend." She'd almost tripped and said "boyfriend," which was absurd, considering they stood at...zero dates.

Laurence tucked his dog tag under his shirt and squeezed her hand. "Only fair, if I get to show off my sexy archaeologist friend later," he teased. Faith laughed, and clung to his hand as they left the room, like if she let him get out of sight, he'd cease to exist, since he was a werewolf and those didn't exist.

But he had to exist, because he'd found her. He'd *come back.* Dragging all the implications of his supernatural world with him, of course, but it seemed even those weren't enough to get her to send him away again. Unless she came to her senses. Any time now.

But how could she when he'd come back *for her?*

3

Laurence was relatively quiet over dinner, but he never seemed impatient with the shop talk and Faith had a hard time keeping herself to her firm press of hip and knee against his under the table. Unfortunately, the more the realization settled into her chest that she did want to be with him, to see where things went, the more the tangled state of her thoughts about all the other werewolves became clear.

Laurence must have gathered an impression of her thoughts, perhaps from her scent, because he maintained a diffident distance from her as they walked back to the hotel from the restaurant. Inside the room, she hovered while he took his earlier seat on the bed. "What if I say no to the job? Could we still date?" The words tumbled out before Faith caught what an assumption she was making. "I mean. That's what I want. If that's what you want—"

"Yes," Laurence said, lopsided smile returning, then flickering away again. "To both."

"So would I have to meet any other werewolves in that case?" Faith had twisted her fingers together again, but she didn't release them while she waited for the answer.

"We usually say Were," Laurence told her, before he addressed the rest to the carpet. "One's the species, the other is more the…cultural group." He cleared his throat. "So. Yeah. There's honestly no way I'd be able to keep something like that secret, long term. And I wouldn't want to. Being a member of a pack…it's part of who I am."

He looked up suddenly, face so pleading she took an involuntary step toward him. "I *want* them to know about you. Sex with humans—everyone does it, and everyone makes sure they don't find out, and it's not serious. I'd like to be serious. Because you're worth it."

Faith scrubbed the heel of her hand along one of her burning cheeks. "You don't even know me that well to know I'm worth it." She didn't doubt he was sincere, though. Which was scaring her, in a way, because she needed to earn that and maybe she felt the same way about him already and she didn't really know him either.

Laurence shook his head, instant dismissal of that. "So if other Were are a deal breaker, kick me out now." He paused, and Faith completely failed to kick him out or even identify all of her emotions at the moment. "We'll need to kind of gloss over the fact that I came to find you early, since that's explicitly against orders on my part, of course. After that, I can't promise everyone will understand the concept of being serious about a human, but the good thing is, Susan is a firm precedent."

The human the kidnappers had mistaken Faith for, but more than that, if Faith remembered correctly. "She's the…beta's wife? Right?"

"Practically a beta in her own right. And I'm sure she'd stand in front of any attack for you. Metaphorically," he added hurriedly. Faith must have looked worried. "We can work this out however you're most comfortable."

His rhythm indicated he'd planned further reassurances, but his phone rang first. He jerked it free of his pocket, then relaxed slightly when he saw the screen. "It's my friend Tom, the one I mentioned earlier. He is literally the nicest guy I know. Literally." He punched the button to answer on speakerphone and held the phone out between them.

"So'd you find her?" Tom's voice held laughter. Faith wasn't particularly good at imagining people from voices, but he sounded easygoing without being bro-y.

"Yes, I found her. Tom, Faith. Faith, Tom."

"Hi," Faith offered. She wasn't sure what else she was supposed to say.

"Hi, Faith! Congratulations on not being the type to run screaming. Romeo here assured me you wouldn't be, but his judgment might be suspect. Just a smidge." Tom's teasing could have been edged, but instead his tone on the last addition was so deadpan Faith couldn't help but laugh too.

Laurence made an exasperated noise, trending toward a growl. "Did you want something?"

"Yeah, actually. Keep your nose to the wind, Roanoke Dare spotted I was bullshitting when I covered for you about where you are right now. He didn't call me on it, but he had his 'I'm trusting you on the condition that the actual explanation is forthcoming sooner rather than later' look."

So much for glossing over their meeting so Laurence wouldn't get in trouble. Faith caught herself glowering at the phone, as if Tom could see her. Or Roanoke Dare, to be fair about where she directed her frustration. "Is it really the alpha's business where you are for one day? What does he think you are, twelve?"

"For me, it is kind of his business," Laurence said. The twisted quality of his tone brought her attention up to his face, and he looked away, avoiding her eyes. "You met me at the end of a…dark time, I guess. Dare feels guilty for not noticing that was happening earlier. As supportive as the Roanokes have been, I don't begrudge him some hovering."

Faith pressed a hand over her mouth, as if that could reach back in time and make her shut up before she said anything. She had no wish to disparage anything Laurence was doing for his emotional health. "I'm sorry."

Laurence shook his head. "You couldn't know."

"Keep asking questions, though," Tom said, lightly. "That'll get you everywhere in this pack. Anyway, upshot is, Laurence, text Roanoke Dare your iron-clad excuse that I'm sure you've already come up with, and then tell me when you'll be back in Seattle so we can have dinner. I want to meet her!"

Faith didn't realize she'd backed away from the phone until she saw Laurence wince. Another decision point, sooner than she'd expected. She needed to tell Laurence to *leave*, or accept the consequences of her choices and get it into her head that she was going to have to meet and deal with these werewolves eventually. Tom was supposed to be the nicest one, what better place to start?

But.

But their captors had gutted Laurence, slammed his head into the wall multiple times, broken his arm—besides the abuse from a former alpha that had led to Laurence's dark time. Those were different werewolves, bad mean ones, but she couldn't convince her fight or flight reflexes of that, with only Laurence to balance the other side.

"Tom, help," Laurence begged. Faith couldn't figure out what he was referring to.

"I'm not there, I can't read her," Tom said in exasperation. "Faith? Not up to meeting anyone yet? You can wait for the Roanokes to show up officially, if you prefer."

Faith hiccupped a ragged laugh. "I don't think that would be any better. It could be just you, right?" One new Were at a time was better than the alternative.

Hope slipped into Laurence's expression, displacing some of the panic she belatedly realized she'd created when she stepped back. "Of course. Tom's the only one in on the fact that I'm not following orders, anyway. We wouldn't be able to talk at a restaurant, but we could get takeout and go to the townhouse instead. It used to be Susan's place, but now people use it if they need a place to seem normal to someone. Living with like twenty other adults and their kids across two houses being, you know, not that normal." He cut himself off at the end, seeming to realize he'd been talking a bit fast.

"Yeah, I don't think anyone's using it at the moment," Tom chimed in. After a few more moments spent on the logistics of arranging a time the next evening, he hung up with a cheery goodbye.

When Laurence had put his phone away, he sat frozen, so Faith realized she'd have to make the first move to show she wasn't angry. Well, she was frustrated, but not with him. With her own hypocrisy, wanting something without paying the price. She settled herself on the bed beside him, hip to hip once more.

"Knowing I'm going to be meeting a bunch of Were, now

or later, I kinda just want to know—I mean, of course I know, but I guess it might help to hear it out loud—if anyone tries to physically hurt me, I can count on you to—"

Laurence turned into her and squeezed her too tight for her to even finish. "I swear on the Lady, may Death cast my voice to the void if I don't do everything in my power to protect you, Faith. I can also promise no one in the Roanoke pack would dare give you a bruise, but you're right. Better to say it out loud."

Faith shoved her hands against his chest only long enough to remind him to loosen his grip. So. There was that to rely on. "Anyway, meeting Tom is much less scary than meeting the alphas, which I assume is why he suggested it."

Laurence tucked his cheek against her hair, one of his gestures that said "canine" to her, though she wasn't entirely sure why. Dogs tucked their muzzle against your leg, but then humans had similar gestures too. "Or he's just dying of curiosity. You never can tell, with him. He's not stupid, by any means. He's the master who taught me everything I know about derp. And he knows more about the archaeologist stuff than I do. He can probably give you more details on that over dinner."

A huge yawn broke into Faith's circling train of thought. Deep emotional quandaries had apparently sapped any energy she'd had left after a full day of digging and screening shovel probes. She edged back to cover her mouth. "Sorry. Nothing to do with you, I promise."

She checked his face, but found only amused understanding there. "Can we just watch TV together for a while? I mean, knowing that anything more is off the table—" She was going to say something mature about sex and emotional involvement—as soon as she came up with it—but instead another yawn broke free.

Laurence grinned and released her to kick off his shoes and shove up to the headboard of the bed he was seated on. Faith pulled off her own shoes, he retrieved the remote out of the nightstand, and handed it to her with playful formality when she climbed up next to him. She paged through the guide channel and settled on the end of some episode of *NCIS*. The reveal of the killer would mean pretty much nothing when she didn't even know the crime they were accused of, but it wasn't like she was really watching.

Faith tucked along Laurence's side, head on his shoulder. He curled that arm around her. She felt so aware of each point where her body was touching Laurence's, even through the haze of her sleepiness. In fact, rather than being arousing, his warmth made her even sleepier, the sheer security of it. He come to find *her*, strange as that thought sat in her mind, and he was here now and *holding* her. The sex had been amazing, but the times he'd held her, carried her, those anchored all her memories of him.

Faith had closed her eyes for a moment, but then the TV was suddenly quiet and she lifted her head to realize that she must have dozed. More than dozed, the clock radio on the nightstand had jumped by an hour. "Hey," Laurence said, low and amused. "I wondered if turning it off might wake you, but figured you probably wanted to brush your teeth and whatever, anyway."

"And you won't be pinned down as a pillow all night, too," Faith said apologetically. She scrubbed at her cheek, where she undoubtedly had red lines in the shape of wrinkles in his shirt.

"On the contrary. That," Laurence said, "is pretty much my life goal." His smile went all lopsided. "You felt safe, right? You wouldn't have fallen asleep otherwise?"

Faith had been considering a quick kiss before leaving the bed for the bathroom, but she sat back now instead, leaving space between them, because this seemed important somehow. "Of course I feel safe with you." She made it as emphatic as she could, because it was the truth. Whatever she felt about the werewolves he came attached to.

Laurence leaned in, closed the kiss soft and sweet, then pushed himself up. He pulled on his shoes, clearly getting ready to go, and Faith was hit by burst of denial. She couldn't let him go. Of course he'd come back, but she—couldn't somehow. "You know it's stupid, you paying for another room. My bosses won't care if someone else stays here, it's all the same price on the company's bill."

Laurence grinned and shoved his hands into his pockets, apparently so happy his body language reverted to the awkwardness she remembered from first meeting him. "I'll go get my bag from the car," he said, after a beat, and then slipped out like he thought she'd withdraw the offer.

Faith finally headed for the bathroom. Little did he realize, she was pretty sure it was much too late for her to do anything of the sort.

4

Faith gave far more consideration than she should have to the idea of letting her ex's "dog" come with them on their last day of survey the next day—which was to say, any consideration at all—but in the end she gave him directions to the office so he could meet her there. Their work day was purposely planned shorter, in any case, to ensure their longer drive home didn't come during rush hour. She had her own car, but Cyrena had picked her up at home in the work truck at the beginning of the survey, so it was just as easy to catch a ride with Laurence as it was to get one with Cyrena, as she would have normally.

Having de-grimed a little in the office's bathroom, Faith didn't feel quite as bad about all the making out they did, Laurence's ass against the door of his car. She kept it to only five minutes—or at the most, ten—before she reluctantly disengaged. She couldn't enjoy it properly with the meeting with Tom hovering at the back of her mind, anyway.

Of course, the drive to the townhouse fell squarely into rush hour, stretching companionable silence to awkward by the end. When they arrived, the townhouse proved to be one of those with the garage entrance at the back. Laurence pulled up, waited barely a beat, then the door opened as if by magic, sans any sign of an opener. "Tom heard us," Laurence explained as he pulled in. Despite that, the guy himself was not in evidence as Laurence led the way in through a door that was also unlocked.

Inside, the townhouse reminded Faith of a house or condo still occupied, but staged for sale. Not a new one, still real-estate-magazine pretty; one with the scuffs of life lived, but with three-quarters of its contents removed or packed away, leaving it full of elegantly decorated space but ultimately soulless. "Thanks for leaving us the garage," Laurence remarked in a normal, conversational tone, to the empty entryway.

Tom arrived from deeper in the house, demonstrating more of his werewolf hearing, Faith supposed. "Figured I'd give you the option of staying longer," he said, and grinned. He had a face made for grinning, under sandy hair that wasn't even that long, but still managed to be shaggy. In Faith's two "categories of tallness"—taller than her, and freakishly tall—he managed to stay on the right side of freakish.

And compared to what she realized was the picture in her head of "werewolf not Laurence" he was so *mild*. Lankier than the two thug types who'd done the actual kidnapping, but then again Mikhail, the Were giving the orders for the operation, hadn't been musclebound either. But where Mikhail had given off a lethal wariness, Tom exuded only friendly enthusiasm.

He strode up to her, looked her over, and then threw open his arms for a hug she could have dodged but cautiously accepted. "You have no idea how glad I am to finally meet you. Especially since Romeo wouldn't shut up about how amazing you are."

"Can we style ourselves on a couple from different backgrounds who didn't come to a bad end?" Faith said, humor coming out uneven.

"Erik Wolf-Born and Astrid," Tom suggested, bouncing back from her. Laurence speared him with an exasperated look, and Faith made a mental note to ask him to tell her that story later. She hoped it didn't have other worrying associations.

Laurence slipped down the hall a ways, tipping his chin up as his expression went abstracted. Reading the scents, Faith supposed. Was he checking they were the only ones here now, or could he read who'd been here before? How far back?

Tom was watching her watch Laurence, she realized abruptly. She ducked her head. Tom only shoved his hands into his pockets, grin turning to good-natured amusement. "Alluringly concentrated curiosity, is a phrase that was used, I believe."

"Shut up," Laurence rumbled, and waited pointedly for Tom to precede them into the hall, which opened onto the combined living room and kitchen area. Faith took Laurence's hand and checked his face from up close to make sure he wasn't angry, but found he was...blushing? She felt close to it herself. That phrase had been really poetic.

Tom bounded over to takeout containers on the counter and started opening them, cornbread and beans and enough ribs for the entirety of a frat house barbeque. "Guess it's a good thing I'm not a vegetarian," Faith joked. She hunted around for plates and serving spoons among the cupboards while Tom seized a couple ribs right out of the containers.

"Yeah, we won't have to kick you out, then," Tom teased, then dodged a smack from Laurence.

"Real ass tonight, aren't you?"

"Sorry, I meant to be dour and tightly wound, but you sucked all of it right out of the room." Tom hunched in his shoulders, apparently in an impression of Laurence. "Your dietary choices are yours, of course, Faith," he intoned. "We would never be so disrespectful as to—" His "dour" tone ended in a yelp as Laurence swiped one of his ribs, clamped it between his teeth, and went for the other one.

The two men tussled over the ribs—two of literally dozens sitting right there on the counter, which Faith realized was in no way the point. Tom got a grip on Laurence's elbow to stiff-arm him back and Faith's stomach snapped down into a hard knot. She could see it all in her mind's eye: Laurence being grabbed, slammed into the wall, the back of his head making a thud like—

But that wasn't happening. Instead what she heard was Laurence's laughter as he grabbed a handful of Tom's shirt at his side to reel him in close enough to regain control of the ribs. Faith drew in a breath and held it until she knew the next would be smooth, not shaky. The kidnapping had been then, this was now, and now was different. And Laurence seemed so relaxed, she figured she should take her cue from him. She concentrated on calm so he wouldn't notice anything in her scent—she hoped—when he and Tom finished roughhousing.

When they did part a few moments later, both panting and laughing, they had a rib each, which they promptly stripped. Faith pulled a plate from the stash she'd located before she got distracted, and held it out for them to drop the bones on. When she collected her own plate of food, neither of them menaced it. She chose a seat at the kitchen table and dug in quickly to give her calm a full stomach to anchor it firmly. "So, Tom, Laurence says you know what you guys need an archaeologist for?"

Tom set his food down across from her, leaving the seat beside her for Laurence, then considered and made a second trip to ferry both a container of additional ribs and the bone plate to the center of the table. Thus provisioned for at least the next five minutes or so, he flumped into his chosen seat and grinned at her. "I think I have a fairly decent grasp of the kind of archaeology we're talking about, but do you want to make sure he's here for the start of the hunt too?" He tipped his head to Laurence.

"As in, the kind of archaeology that has nothing to do with Egypt?" Faith had to smile. She licked her thumb to swipe away sauce along the corner of her lips as long as she'd paused eating for the moment. Forget werewolves, *this* was familiar. "We talked about it a little bit before—" Before they'd been kidnapped. She couldn't honestly remember much about that conversation, washed out as it was by the memory of seeing Laurence *gutted* in front of her.

She cleared her throat. "So I work for a contract archaeology company. You could call it compliance archaeology—basically, if there's development that involves federal or state money or permits, the law says the developer or agency has to hire us to make sure they're not going to damage anything—archaeological sites, historic buildings, places of cultural importance to Tribes, stuff like that. It's much more than digging—there's background research, to find out what historical sources or maps suggest might be there, to ask the Tribes if they know anything about that location, and to check what other archaeologists have found nearby. Even recent land use is important to know. Like the current manager says, yeah, they wanted a flat sports field in the park, so they trucked in a foot of fill at one end. There won't be anything in that fill. Then there's survey, which could involve digging shovel probes, or it could mean walking transects looking for surface artifacts or aboveground structures.

"And a lot more of our job than people realize involves writing up negative results. We research, we survey, the investigation turns up nothing, and the project can go forward, everyone's happy. If we do find something, often the project can use a different alternative or route around. Or if we're not sure something's there, but we think it's likely, we can do what's called monitoring and send an archaeologist to be around when construction starts to spot and then record anything they might uncover. And less often, we excavate, to get all the data about a site before it has to be destroyed. I'm a lowly field tech, so I get to do the digging and the monitoring."

She collected nods from both men. Tom kicked back in his chair, comfortable. "So here's the story on our possible site: back in the nineteenth century sometime, apparently some Russian Were migrated down from Alaska and ended up in Washington. When I was traveling a few years back, I happened on someone who had found their little cemetery, out toward Spokane."

"Your friend who records cemeteries as a hobby?" Faith interrupted as the connection sparked.

Tom nodded. "Yeah. Anyway, the Russians actually make art and stuff, which is really worrisome to the rest of us trying to keep our own secrets, but no one had freaked out about wolves and the Lady's phases on the tombstones in the past century-plus, so we sort of left it. But when I got back in contact with my friend to find you, she mentioned that she thought she'd linked the original owners of the cemetery to some other parcels from the same land claim. And lo and behold, someone was digging a foundation for an outbuilding on that farm some decades back and came across a bunch of artifacts. Broken bottles and plates and such. Donated them to the historical society. I went out and took a look."

"Yeah?" Faith prompted. So far, she wasn't seeing how she could help any more than the historical society staff could, in interpreting the artifacts.

"They had moon stones." Tom grimaced. "Not the gem. Like—"

"Like this?" Faith dug hers out from among the random pennies in her hip pocket and set it on the table. Well, it had been Laurence's, originally. It was just a clear aquarium rock, with some fading black paint on the back where there had once been a half-phase moon. The dip there was just the right size to rub your thumb along, like a worry stone.

At Tom's raised brows, she explained. "It got mixed with my stuff after Laurence and I…met, so I kept it."

"Did you?" Tom broke into a laugh. "And you just happen to carry it around on your person? Lady above, you're just as crazy about him as he is about you." He gestured an apology for any embarrassment when she covered the stone with her hand and pulled it to her a little too quickly. "Anyway, we don't want more artifacts like that found. Fortunately for us, the owner of the farm was getting up in years, and his children were uninterested in taking over, so he accepted the Roanoke pack's offer for the land. But that's a big chunk of the pack's assets tied up in land none of us wants to farm either. Better to find out what might be there, excavate it, and then sell the land again."

Faith shook her head. She wished she'd understood better what they'd wanted ahead of time, so she hadn't gotten their hopes up. "I can't help you, I don't have my Master's, just my Bachelor's. If you're going to knowingly excavate in an archaeo-

logical site, you need a permit from the Department of Archaeology and Historic Preservation and to apply for one of those,
you need a Master's. Did the historical society record those artifacts as coming from a site already?"

Disappointment flickered over Tom's expression but didn't
take. "I don't think so. The information they had about where
they came from on the land was really imprecise. Does that
mean you could still—?"

Faith shook her head. "I could survey—do shovel probes or
whatever, to see what's there over a wide area—but as soon as
I found any signs of a site, I'd need to record it. Which, again,
I'd need to have a Master's to do. And then to continue into
excavation, I'd need a permit. Anything else would be against
the law."

Tom and Laurence traded a look, filled with meaning she
couldn't read, but could guess at. Tom confirmed that guess a
moment later. "To stay safe, there's unfortunately a number of
situations in which the Were have to work outside the law."

Like dealing with crimes themselves rather than reporting
them to the police, Faith suspected. Like, say, a kidnapping. "If
you're talking about breaking the law anyway, you could go out
there tomorrow yourself, with a bunch of shovels." That came
out more accusatory than Faith had intended, because it felt
like chewing foil to say the words. Logically, she should be
more angry about unreported violent crimes, but the idea of
the lost scientific information punched her right in the gut.

"Over my dead body." Laurence pressed a hand to her back
in sympathy, over her shoulder blade. Faith summoned a weak
smile for him, in gratitude for the hyperbole.

Tom leaned in, carried once more by his enthusiasm. "Or
we could get an archaeologist to guide us, even if she doesn't
have the right piece of paper yet, and excavate properly. That

way, we might be able to learn something about Were history. If we found out the descendants of that Russian pack ended up joining a North American one, that would be a good thing politically at the moment, as well. Since we're trying to strengthen that truce."

Laurence cupped a hand behind his ear. "Tom, I swear I saw your lips moving, but I heard Dare's voice just now."

Tom spared Laurence a growl. "Anyway, you can see why we can't hire an archaeology company normally..."

Faith freed her moon stone, tipped it so the more rounded side was down, and wobbled it back and forth with her fingertip. She didn't know what she wanted to do. It seemed a hell of a choice: run an excavation without any help from colleagues and possibly make mistakes that would lose information...or let that information get destroyed completely. "It's not just the piece of paper, it's the training and also the experience. I'm not a crew chief, never mind a principal investigator. I wouldn't know where to start, formulating research questions."

Tom held up a finger. "But you know that you should have some, which is more than I was aware of, coming into this."

"And I can do sort of...basic glass and ceramics, but nothing really detailed, and given it would be a historical site, if we found a trash pit or privy—which was basically used for the same thing—there would be a lot of information in the faunal—" Tom was frowning, so she translated again on the fly. "Animal bone. And I definitely can't do that analysis."

"Aren't there specialists for that?" Tom seized a clean rib bone and rotated it as if to find the secrets it was hiding from him.

Faith grimaced. "Yeah, and where do we tell them it came from? They can't do their job properly without context."

Laurence fanned his fingers wider, smoothing across her

back from shoulder to opposite hip. "Would you know where to look it up, though? Remember, anything you can do is better than what we could. And if you're not comfortable overseeing the excavation, I'll do it. You can teach me, and I'll teach them."

Faith pushed down too hard on one side of the moon stone and it skittered away to be caught handily by Laurence. She flexed her hands on the tabletop. No, she didn't like that idea either, but she'd have to pick one of the options, wouldn't she? Walk away, teach someone, or do it herself.

Or maybe those weren't the only options. She needed to expand her perspective a little. "Wait a minute, though. We're assuming a site still exists. It might not. The construction of whatever outbuilding resulted in the original artifacts being found could have destroyed the rest of the site. Not to mention whatever other disturbance has occurred on the property since the nineteenth century. Roads, other buildings, plowing…the artifacts at the historical society might have been all that was left. I could lead a survey, and then we'd actually know what we're dealing with."

She managed a thin smile for Laurence, gaining confidence as it settled in that she'd made a decision. "That way, you guys can make decisions properly. If there is a Were site—well, we can cross that bridge when we come to it."

Tom grinned, clearly delighted but sitting on any other expression of it. Faith imagined he assumed there would be a site and she was just working herself up to agreeing to excavate. The more she thought about it, on the other hand, the more she relaxed into the idea that there probably wasn't one.

Laurence slipped the moon stone back under her hands, then set his on top. "Thanks," he murmured.

"I was only keeping this to give back to you, you know." Faith tried to extricate her hands and moon stone both, but Laurence didn't let her.

"I want you to have it." Laurence's voice dipped low, the same as his chin as he ducked his head with a brush of embarrassment of his own. Tom laughed at them once more, as he rose to switch out empty for full takeout boxes, but it was a warm sound, inviting them all to share in it.

5

Tom gave Faith his number and then excused himself to head home soon after they'd cleaned up the remains of dinner, leaving Laurence and Faith to retire to the living room and sip their found-at-the-back-of-the-fridge beers. "We could stay here for the night," Laurence remarked, a few minutes after their store of small talk had run dry, leaving them in charged silence.

"This is the spot for human hookups, isn't it?" Faith considered pretending even to herself that this was another decision point, but honestly it wasn't. She'd had a shorter day working, and while meeting another Were would undoubtedly leave her with a burden of emotional exhaustion later, for the moment she was still wound up.

"I wasn't trying to bring you here just for that," Laurence said, but his tone lost some of its concern at the end when he must have read her body language—or scent—as she thumped her beer on the table.

"Too bad, that's what you're getting," she told him, and he gave his dorky grin. The next second he swept her up so unexpectedly she shrieked and then gave in to giggles. He slung her over his shoulder like a caveman cartoon and headed for the stairs, which she appreciated in theory, but was hard on her stomach. She squirmed and he let her down immediately.

"How about this?" She positioned herself to ride piggyback and he caught on quickly, hoisting her up securely. She took a second to make sure her hold across his shoulders and neck wasn't strangling him, then bounced. "Mush!"

"You're very lucky you're so hot, making sled dog jokes, missy." Laurence carried them up the stairs and shouldered open the door to the master bedroom. It had a modest double-sized bed, with a dark gray, down comforter that *whumph*ed expressively when he turned and dumped her off onto her ass on it.

He considered her for a beat, one thumb hooking behind the button of his jeans, and Faith used the opportunity to imagine the muscles beneath the shirt, the line of hip and collarbone. She posed for him, back on her elbows to show off her chest. "You remember the safe word?" she asked, voice coming out involuntarily breathy with anticipation. Maybe if they were starting over with dating properly, they should be starting with vanilla, but last time doing it rough with him had been so *good*.

"Silver bullet," Laurence verified. "There's something I wondered if we could add…"

Faith sat up from her pose, the anticipation pooling lower. "Tell me."

"If you could pretend to run away…not like you're scared, but like I have to *earn* it." Laurence's expression grew so vulnerable in its longing. "Like a chase."

Faith remembered something about fucking being called chasing—or playing chase?—which she supposed only made sense for a wolf. Wolf-based person. "You know there's no possible way I could be fast enough to prevent you catching me, though, right?" As a human. Which was a buzzkill for sure, thinking about what another Were might be able to give him.

The moment that thought entered her expression, or scent, Laurence was there, knees between hers on the edge of the bed, to touch her, hand cupping the side of her neck. "I don't want to hurt you either," he said. He tangled his fingers in her hair, curled them in tight until the pressure stung and she panted a breath as anticipation returned and burst between her legs. "But it's fun to play."

Well, then. Faith gathered herself, then pushed at his chest. He rocked back, releasing his hold on her hair at that merest nudge. She sprang away, out the door, swinging herself on the frame, then down the stairs. His footsteps stayed a steady two paces behind her the whole time, until she got the couch between them in the living room. As she feinted to first one side and then the other, she could see his face, how it was completely lit up, someone having the time of their life.

She made a break for it, finally, and that's when he caught her. He carried her like a bride this time, all the way up the stairs. She saved extravagant struggles for when he had her over the bed so she could get "free" to fall into the embrace of the down once more. "Hold me down," she begged, and he *did*, his weight straddling her hips and his hands on her wrists. When she struggled this time, she literally couldn't get free, and that was amazing in its own way. She could let *go* and jerk her body against his and each motion ground her clit against his groin through multiple layers of fabric, which was exactly how it worked best for her.

All through it, his weight didn't waver, holding her down, only redistributing a little as he got a grip in her hair again, and nipped at the side of her neck. Then she was concentrating, losing track a little because she was almost, almost—one last thrash and she was there, arching into pleasure and then subsiding, panting.

Still fully clothed. She had to laugh at herself, and Laurence stepped off and away to let her shrug out of her clothes as he did the same. She subsided when nude, flinging her arms wide with abandon. "I think you've caught me." She tilted her head so she could watch his skin revealed, the shapes of the strength she'd felt holding her down just so delicious.

When he'd rolled on a condom and climbed back on the bed, he was gentler at first, to which Faith had no objection. Soft kisses up from her breasts to neck to lips, getting lined up, sliding in. But once he'd found his angle, his next stroke was more of a slam, and then far faster than she'd expected, so she groaned with delight at the roughness of it after all. The grinding must have taken him right to the line himself, because he lasted maybe half a minute before he gasped, slammed home a last time. Finally, he let himself down beside her, sweat-slicked skin against skin.

They cleaned up, but Faith didn't bother with pajamas—those were in her suitcase still out in the trunk of Laurence's car, and it was nearly summer after all. Nearly summer, with the warmth of a sated Were tucked up against her side. Somehow the way he slept, all curled up while smashed against her side, was one of the most canine things she'd noticed about him when he was in human form.

"I think you've caught *me*," he murmured, just as they were both drifting off to sleep.

6

"Shit, we gotta get dressed." Laurence was suddenly gone from beside Faith, rousing her from the half-awake state she'd been drifting in since the time she'd normally have been waking up for field work.

She groaned and groped after more blankets with his body heat gone. "Why?" That was when she heard the footsteps on the stairs herself. The front door must have awakened and warned Laurence. Her heartrate jolted to full speed and beyond, dragging her into full alertness. "You didn't text an excuse, did you?" she said, as her thoughts jolted into motion. She grimaced in apology, in case that had sounded like a complaint instead of a deduction, but Laurence's head was down as he pulled on his jeans.

And she was naked. Faith clutched the blankets to her chest like every stupid rom-com heroine as a man arrived in the doorway. A Were, she assumed. He looked athletic and solid—maybe more in a fireman calendar way, rather than a sports star one. He was dressed casually enough, with hair that clearly wasn't going to abandon its cowlick for anything less than a greaser's worth of gel. "Laurence," he said, voice hard, and set the side of his fist against the doorjamb. "For the Lady's sake, you have *got* to be kidding me here."

Past the point of alertness, Faith found herself in the slightly shaking state of maximum adrenaline. He wasn't going to hurt Laurence, was he? What if Laurence let fear make him attack first? But Laurence was standing loose—head hanging, yes, but apparently with no anticipation of this turning physical.

The man looked to her properly then, and frowned in something like apology. "I'll wait downstairs," he said, turned, and left them alone.

Laurence groaned and ran hands through his hair, though it was too short to be badly mussed. "Well, shit. I'm sorry, that wasn't how I'd planned for you to meet one of the betas, that's for sure. That was John." Laurence dredged up a smile, in an obvious effort at reassurance. "At his most charming."

"Laurence…" Faith wasn't sure what her objection was going to be even when she started making it, so she had to trail off. She threw off the covers. "Wait for me."

"I'm in for a chewing out, that's all." Laurence offered her quick kiss, which she accepted, but she noticed he did linger while she pulled her own clothes on.

Downstairs, John was seated at the kitchen table. Seeing him in a new light, now she knew Laurence was perfectly safe, Faith mostly found it deeply weird to think he was married to the woman Faith had been mistaken for. "You had *orders*, Laurence. Not to approach her until after the alphas did. If they did, which, may I remind you, hasn't been decided yet."

While Faith hovered in the doorway, Laurence took a seat across the table from him, sitting upright and tense. "We both know they were going to."

John slammed a hand down on the table top, flat-palmed.

The only thing on the surface was a forgotten plastic fork from last night, which skittered a few centimeters, but the wood resounded with a thud that made Faith flinch. "You can't just do whatever you feel like, Laurence, not when it affects the safety of the whole group." His voice, though soft, vibrated with an intensity near a growl. "How much have you blabbed to her already? The alphas were going to be careful about how much information they burdened her with."

He softened his expression with an effort. "We're truly sorry for what you went through, Faith. And for the fact that you're getting caught up in this now, but Laurence didn't go about this the right way."

"Look, I didn't tell her about us in the first place." Laurence couldn't manage the same intensity in his tone, but he leaned forward to make up for it. "Not like you did with Susan, if you recall!"

"Yeah, you just sought her out afterwards when you'd been explicitly told not to." John fixed his frown firmly on Laurence. "Or have you been playing chase with her the whole time since you were released? Was all that business about how you didn't know her name a false trail?"

"No, I only saw him again two days ago…" Faith's voice dried up in her mouth when John turned that frown on her. Every word completely left her head under that look, until he transferred his attention back to Laurence again.

"And yes, I fucked up with Susan. It could have gone very wrong. We're not asking people for a little *basic caution* and communication with the alphas—and following the alpha's orders, for Lady's sake!—for no reason."

Laurence hunched his shoulders, apparently settling in to endure. "Faith? Do you want to get coffee or something?" He wiggled his car keys out of his pocket, offered them out.

Faith hesitated, but he truly didn't seem frightened of violence, and if he didn't want her watching while he got chewed out, she respected that. She accepted the keys, and was halfway up the stairs to get her purse when the idea occurred to her. Laurence was right, it was better that he'd approached her first, alone, rather than the intimidating alphas showing up out of the blue. It wasn't fair he should get in trouble for that when he'd done it for her sake. Not that she was brave enough to go back down and offer herself in his place, but maybe—

Maybe she could help by presenting her and Laurence's side of the story to the alphas, before John talked to them. She was a solution to their problem of what to do about the possible Were site, after all. She needed to remember that, and make sure they did too. Speaking to the alphas was a fucking scary thought, one she'd thought she'd have more time to psych herself up for, but what about Susan? Surely she'd understand.

Faith shut herself in the car before she pulled out her phone. When Tom gave it to her, she hadn't realized she'd need his number quite so soon. Fortunately, he answered, even this early. "Hey, it's Faith." She pictured his goofy grin, which propped up her confidence enough for her to continue. "Can you send me Susan's number?"

"Faith—what?"

"You know, the human in the pack that I'm not. I need her number, please." In his silence, Faith could hear Tom's struggle with himself about whether to ask why, but her phone beeped with a text a moment later. "Thanks. I'll explain when this is taken care of, I promise." She ended the call.

All right. Now for the harder part. She didn't have any goofy picture of the beta to rely on. Adrenaline was seeping through Faith's whole body again, but she told her phone to call the number before she could think better of the idea.

Only when it started ringing did she consider that maybe Susan wouldn't answer a number not in her address book. But the Roanoke pack stretched across the country, so Susan wouldn't expect to have everyone's number, would she?

"Hello?" Susan's greeting was pleasant and professional.

"Hi, I'm sorry to bother you. We've never met, but my name is Faith. I got this number from Tom…" Hardly similarly professional, but at least Faith wasn't stuttering.

"Yes? What pack do you belong to?" Susan's voice turned kind, so maybe Faith had sounded young and worried despite her efforts.

"I'm not—it's really complicated—" Deep breath. She needed to not babble. "So I'm a human—specifically, the one mistaken for you like a year ago—and Laurence found me a couple days ago and now he's in deep shit for disobeying orders, but he only did it to make things easier on me. And I thought if maybe I could explain that to the alphas—if that's okay…"

Silence reigned at the other end of the line for long enough that Faith wondered if she'd been entirely incomprehensible. Finally Susan spoke, still utterly collected. "I think the alphas would welcome your perspective. Would you be willing to come to the pack house?"

"Yes," Faith said. "Now? Can I come now?" When Susan agreed, Faith definitely stuttered over her thanks and goodbyes, but those didn't really matter. The beep signalling the text with the pack house address arrived half a minute later.

Faith told her phone to map it, then glanced toward the door into the house. She couldn't take Laurence with her without John following right behind, and she really wanted some time to present her case before he was there with his frown. It wasn't like she was stranding Laurence if she went alone in his car, he could ride with John.

She'd text him when she arrived at the pack house, she decided. The app said that was about a ten-minute drive, which seemed reasonable. She paused long enough to grab her bag from the trunk and carefully brush her hair and check her appearance in the sun visor mirror before she snapped her phone into Laurence's holder and started the engine. Time to go find out if she'd just made things better for her and Laurence, or spectacularly worse.

7

Faith wasn't sure what she'd expected, but certainly not a house as deeply suburban as the one she pulled up in front of. It had a big lot and a three-car garage, with two cars on the driveway in front, and more pulled up along the sidewalk. Faith weighed her options, then parked farther down the street and walked back. She paused on the sidewalk to finish and send her text to Laurence.

Her nerves caught up to as she stood on the doorstep, having pushed the doorbell. What the hell was she doing? But then the door opened on an unremarkable woman with short brown hair in a professional cut, mostly unstyled at the moment. She couldn't be much past her mid-thirties, but she had a definite air of authority, especially when she gave Faith an evaluating look and offered a hand to shake. "Faith? I'm Susan. As you probably guessed. Where's Laurence?"

"I snuck off. But I just texted him, he and your husband should be here before long." Information conveyed, Faith tried to shut up, but the words just kept tumbling out. "Sneaking off was probably a bad idea. This whole thing is probably a bad idea. Is this a bad idea?" She appealed to Susan, then dropped her head to hide a flush. Great job of projecting confidence she was doing.

Susan's lips twitched like she was holding in laughter. "Breathe, puppy," she said, and clasped Faith's shoulders. "Meeting the alphas with fewer Were around *isn't* a bad idea. And don't worry, they won't go all Queen of Hearts if you use the wrong title or something."

It was odd, but somehow the diminutive calmed Faith. Hearing a human use a Were term so easily was reassuring, she supposed. Susan led the way through an entryway more banged up than those in magazines, but with the same sense of scale and underlying graceful lines. No one was around—or at least no one Faith could see—but their path was fairly short, to the dining room. Two people were seated at the end of a huge, long table worthy of a period drama dinner party scene.

Faith recognized one of them, the man. She'd said probably a whole sentence to him at the wedding she'd been kidnapped from. He was dressed more casually now, but he still had the white streaks in his dark hair at either temple, and his keen gaze made her want to squirm in a way she imagined she would if the CEO of her company visited and showed interest in her, a lowly tech. His wife—mate—Faith had also seen at a distance at the wedding, she realized now. Up close, it was clear her hair really was white, not blond, and while her gaze was no less intrigued by the newcomer, she offered a smile of apology for it.

"Roanokes," Faith said, and bowed. That was generally respectful, and they should understand why she wasn't following Were ritual, right? If there was any Were ritual for this sort of thing—they seemed human enough in their body language.

Susan found a seat a little ways down from the alphas, facing Faith. Faith couldn't make herself sit, she was far too restless for that, but no one seemed surprised by that. "Susan said you had something you wanted to tell us? Go ahead," Roanoke Dare invited.

"I don't want Laurence to get in trouble for something he was really doing for me. Being able to take it slow, talk first with a Were I know and trust, it helped a lot. He only found me literally two days ago, and since then he hasn't told me anything more than he did before, when he kind of had to, because the kidnappers shifted in front of me." Faith ran down, and didn't let herself start up again. She'd only repeat herself with minor variations. She needed to see what questions they'd ask.

"You said he tracked you down a few days ago, did you have any contact with him before then? Laurence told us you parted ways immediately after your release," Roanoke Dare said.

Faith couldn't tell if he believed that story or not. It wasn't... entirely true, they'd parted ways after pulling themselves together and then having sex in a hotel room. But that was close enough, right? "Yeah. Right after."

Roanoke Silver's gaze flicked noticeably to the floor, and an ironic smile lifted one corner of her lips. "Indeed." Faith wasn't sure who that word was directed to, but the rest was clearly meant for her. "It bodes well for your relationship with Laurence that you haven't discovered we can smell a lie that clear-cut."

Shit. Faith wanted to spend several more seconds cursing silently, but that kind of delay would only make her look worse. "We got a hotel room, that's all. I mean, we were in freaking Alaska instead of Seattle, and didn't know anyone was coming to get us. And then Laurence got the call that someone was, and we realized that was when I had to decide if I was going to walk away, and I thought that was best—" Still thought it was best, but didn't have the willpower for it. "And he *didn't* contact me after that. For ten months." There. Not a lie.

Of course, there was a bit of omission about what they'd been doing in that hotel room buried in there, so Faith pushed on quickly. "But now I can help you. T—Laurence told me about why you need an archaeologist."

Susan murmured something under her breath, exasperated. "Tom's involved?"

Before Faith could even start to freak out about *that* slip, Roanoke Silver laughed, a friendly sound to draw them together rather than set Faith apart. "Of course Tom's involved. Haven't you seen him and Laurence planning their secret hunts in corners together?"

"Well, Tom told me why you need an archaeologist, that they'd have to keep secret any evidence of Were culture they found, so I'm ideal, because I already know." Faith appealed to both the alphas, but most of all to Roanoke Dare, because his expression was still pleasant, but opaque.

"He told you about the Were homestead?" Roanoke Dare asked. When Faith nodded, he continued. "How would you go about dealing with it?"

It was only then she remembered that she needed to convince them survey might be enough on its own. *Actually I can't give you what you want, but here's why you don't want it anyway.* Great. But would trying to skate past her lack of a Master's read as a lie to their noses? Better to be up front. Briefly, she summarized about site forms and permits for them. "Everyone gets focused on excavation, but there's a lot survey can still tell you. You'll want to see what kind of stuff you can find in the historical record first—lists of land claims, old maps, stuff like that. I can ask the historian at work for suggestions of places to look. Then we'd want to do pedestrian survey—walking transects at regular intervals, looking at the ground for artifacts or features—" This would have been a lot easier if Faith had planned this out ahead of time so she didn't end up with definitions nested four deep. "Features are something that's cohesive, but isn't an individual object. Like a trash pit or a hearth. So pedestrian survey and shovel probes. So you can figure out what's there, and how it might have been laid out."

Roanoke Dare seemed to be following her definitions well enough, however. "And if 'what's there' is the remains of the Were homestead?"

Faith tried to keep her chin confidently high. "If there's been a lot of disturbance or development in an area, sometimes there just isn't that much left to find. At least the survey could tell you if you even need to worry."

Roanoke Dare looked far from convinced. "I think, in this case, it would be better for us to plan as if you will find something. Do you know how to excavate?"

"I have before, yes. But it's against the law for me to…like I said…." She trailed off as his polite attentiveness, despite the fact she was repeating herself, made her feel a little embarrassed.

"Assume for a moment, you found a site and did have your Master's. You fill out and submit a site form, leaving out anything that is clearly related to the Were, I would hope. What about all the rest of the information about the homestead, not clearly related to the Were? It would still be information about Were lives, and thus the beginning of a trail to our secrets, if someone ever thought to follow it." The worst part for Faith was how *patient* he was while arguing his case. It heightened what she was beginning to realize was a leader's particular brand of charisma.

"Site forms aren't publicly available." She was losing to that charisma, though, and she knew it. She'd already committed to keeping Laurence and his people safe through keeping their secrets, and Roanoke Dare wasn't wrong. How could she guarantee knowledge of the very existence of a site in that place from that time, no matter what was written up about it, wouldn't someday make someone wonder?

Roanoke Dare exhaled on an ironic note. "I'd consider professionals the more dangerous ones to be in possession of the knowledge. They'd be more likely to know enough to spot the gaps, and be curious enough to pursue them."

Silence stretched while Faith looked down at her hands, her fingers laced tightly together. "You're right, it is your history. And your secrets. If I find evidence of a Were site, I'll excavate it so we can save the data while making sure it's not found by anyone else." A deep breath. She didn't want to give in *entirely.* "But if we discover other sites in the course of the survey, ones from other time periods that are probably human related, I won't touch those beyond the initial survey, all right?"

"That's more than fair." He inclined his head in gratitude for her agreement. "Do you know how you'd go about the excavation?"

"For data recovery—basically, the site will be destroyed, so you're excavating to save what you can—you still need to come up with research questions. They structure what kind of methods you use, to make sure you get the kind of data that can answer those questions. Like—" Just to pull things straight out of her ass. "If you want to know how the whole homestead is laid out, you might want to do test trenches for longer exposures, looking for foundations of different outbuildings or the house, or window glass and nails. But if you want to know about their everyday life, you probably want to open some one-by-one-meter units over any artifact concentrations in hopes of finding a feature like a privy. Because that's where people threw their trash."

That even sounded like she knew what she was talking about. "I wish there was a way we could send artifacts out for analysis, but at least I can make sure we store them all properly, and then someone could always come back to them. Or even me in a few years, I guess, with more experience and school under my belt."

Now worries about legality had been set aside, she'd started gesturing widely, Faith realized. She dropped her hands, and then noticed the alphas' attention had gone behind her. She turned and squeaked on finding John pretty much right there, having walked up while she was too focused to notice. How pissed at her was he?

Laurence distracted her by ducking out from behind John and embracing her. "Faith!"

"Sorry," she babbled into his shoulder. "I couldn't just stand there and let you get in trouble. And I didn't know about lying…"

Laurence pulled back, probably worried, but Roanoke Dare finally cracked a smile and gestured dismissal of the issue. "Perfectly understandable. Were are much less tangled up about sex, you'll find."

Oh. So her omission hadn't been an actual omission, then. That was good, she supposed, as embarrassing as it was with her own Western attitudes, thanks. And—hell, they'd probably smelled that she'd spent last night with Laurence when she walked in, hadn't they?

"Anyone care to catch me up?" John grumbled from the doorway behind them.

His wife knocked the chair beside her out slightly with her foot in invitation. "I would have thought you, of all people, would know better than to underestimate a young human woman." She was smiling, though, and John sheepishly kissed her hair when he joined her.

The Roanokes shared some kind of look, dense with shorthand communication, and Roanoke Silver nodded a breath later. Roanoke Dare turned back to Faith, and impressed her by speaking straight to her, rather than through Laurence. "You're hired, on the terms you described, survey and only excavation if a site looks like it's from the correct time period. Are you available full time? If you'd be willing to stay in the existing house on the property, that might be the simplest. Tell us what a typical archaeological crew chief with a Master's would make, and we'll make you an offer based on that. If you'd also pull together the list of sources for background research, as you suggested, we'll have Tom and his contacts start with that aspect as soon as possible as well."

"Yes, I am available—uh, thanks." She'd have to tell her regular job she wouldn't be available for however long, but they were used to that. Techs often bounced around to all the local archaeology companies, so a project with one would rule them out with the others for the duration. And, as she'd realized when Laurence first brought up the job, being steadily employed on one project, instead of piecemeal, would give her bank account a much-needed boost. "Thank you," she said again, when nothing more articulate occurred to her.

Roanoke Dare pointed to Laurence. "Now, as for punishment. You. Don't do this again, and we'll call it good." He flicked a glance to John, who acknowledged the ruling with only a slight grimace of exasperation.

"What, don't be kidnapped with a human and fall in love with her? I think I can manage that." Laurence's arms tightened around Faith for a beat. She had to rewind the tape of what she'd just heard in her head. Had he just said—yes, he had.

"Glad to hear it." The two men shared a breath of laughter, then Laurence ducked his head respectfully and ushered Faith back out to the comparative privacy of the entryway. There, she stepped into him and he slipped his arms loosely around her, clasping hands at her lower back. It reminded her again how perfectly the right height he was.

Silence stretched long enough Faith realized Laurence was waiting for her to say something, but she was still too overwhelmed with processing everything that had just happened. He huffed one of his self-deprecating laughs, finally. "I'm sorry, I didn't mean to drop the love thing on you like this. But they can all smell it on me, of course, so I wasn't thinking—"

"I just defended you to the alphas," Faith said, and found a laugh of her own, decidedly punchy. "We'd better be talking love at some point." She pressed her cheek against his shoulder in their embrace, like not seeing the world, and hearing it only muffled, would make it disappear for a bit. It was too early for her to say the word herself, of course—or even think it, if she was honest. But she had the feeling, though she'd never encountered it before, that she could get there in time.

"Do you want to meet any of the rest of the pack while we're here?" Laurence smoothed her hair. He sounded like he already knew the answer, but she appreciated that he was checking, rather than acting like scent told him everything he needed to know.

"Right now, I'd really like to go home and eat some breakfast," she said. And have a little time to adjust to the fact that she'd taken the first step in ensuring her life would never quite be the same again.

She'd taken it, though. Of her own choice. Now to discover what the consequences of that were, good and bad.

8

Faith was no architectural historian, but she found the worn, one-story sprawl of the old-new farmhouse on the property slated for survey decidedly unprepossessing in the late afternoon sunlight. She pulled her car off the two-track driveway onto a stretch of the grassy, gravelly yard that seemed more gravel than grass, and considered the building and the dusty shipping container-turned-shed beside it. The unirrigated and fallow portions of the property they'd seen on driving up were scrubby between hardy pines, not quite the full-blown sagebrush country she'd imagined, but then they were farther east than the real sweep of the Washington Scablands.

"Ugh," Laurence remarked, having climbed out of the passenger side to consider the house too.

Faith held up her finger. "But older than fifty years! As I recall, the county assessor website said it was built in fifty-eight or fifty-nine. Which doesn't mean it's eligible—eligible for the National Register of Historic Places—but it means that if this was a state or federal project and it was going to be torn down, they'd have to at least look to see if it meets any of the criteria."

She left her bag in the car and headed for the front door, Laurence ambling behind. Tom was supposed to be here to meet them with the keys today, but she'd driven straight here without stopping to text a warning first, so she wouldn't blame Tom if he hadn't arrived yet. "What criteria?" Laurence asked.

"Being designed by a famous architect, being one of only a few of its kind left from its time period, being associated with some big social movement—stuff like that. And then it can't have been heavily remodeled, because then it wouldn't really be connected to the history anymore." Faith paused to give the house another glance from close up. "Somehow, I'm not optimistic about this one meeting any of them."

The door opened as they approached, not on Tom, but on a young woman Faith had never met before. She was maybe a little younger than Faith and unfairly gorgeous, with masses of black, wavy hair falling behind her shoulders, to go with her Mediterranean coloring. Were, of course—she had to be, with the athletic strength that filled her every movement. She nodded to Faith, friendly. "Hey, I'm Felicia, Tom's girlfriend. I drove out with him so we could spend the weekend together before I have to go back to classes on Monday."

"Quite the romantic surroundings for it," Laurence said, apparently at ease with Felicia as he murmured a greeting and then slipped past her into the house. Faith followed, peeking into open doors. The grimy linoleum in the kitchen and bathrooms could possibly be original, but the carpet was newer, allowing it to be a deeply Seventies shade of horrific orange.

"I don't know, I'll take hot water and electricity over the camping I had to do for my field school any day," Faith said. She ended her self-guided tour in the kitchen where Tom was investigating the contents of cupboards and papers were spread across the Formica surface of the rickety kitchen table.

"I brought the employment paperwork too," Felicia said, and frowned over the spread, lifting edges here and there. "Tom, what did you do with the pen?"

"A mouse probably ran off with it in retaliation. I told you we missed a couple." Tom came up behind Felicia and settled his hands on her hips, pressing a kiss into her hair behind her ear. "I shall slay it and lay its corpse at your feet, my love."

"Or you could find me a new pen." Felicia grinned, leaning into the embrace for a moment, then pounced on the original pen as it rolled away from her paper shuffling. She pulled up a chair and Faith did the same, across from her. Tom lounged with his hands on the back of Felicia's chair and Laurence took over his earlier cupboard investigations.

Faith accepted the pen and skimmed the first page, finding a rather bland company name there. She tapped it with the capped end. "So this is the...pack?"

"It's a software startup John's building with pack money. It's a convenient way to handle the tax side of things, for you. For the rest of us, the idea is that eventually it will be like in Europe, where the packs each have a company, to employ everyone who wants it." Tom gave a little ironic bow. "Meanwhile, I'm pretty much the only other employee. I do a bit of pretty much everything. Not coding. But administrative whatever."

"And meanwhile everyone bemoans the lack of his employee discount at the movie theater from his last real job." Laurence gave up on tracking mice or counting mismatched plates or whatever he'd been doing and took a chair next to Faith as she carefully printed in little boxes.

She had to smile, head down over her work. She was sure there were plenty of things more prosaic than working as a movie theater usher in your early twenties, but that one was certainly up there.

Tom snorted. "And by everyone, you mean Tracy. She got a good deal out of that for a few years there." He held his arms expansively wide. "You need any movie trivia from the past five years or so, I'm your man."

"He's not kidding." Felicia squeezed his wrist, behind her shoulder. Faith paused long enough to consider their body language covertly. She didn't quite understand how they managed it, but since Felicia had entered the room they'd been able to remain almost continuously touching without it coming off as awkward for observers. She envied them the sheer ease of their affection. "It's probably good you're not feeding Tracy's Chris Pratt obsession, anyway."

"Chris Hemsworth," Tom corrected. Felicia laughed and pulled a face that made it clear movie stars were pretty much all the same in her opinion. "They don't look anything alike!"

"Chris Evans is the most drool-worthy one, anyway," Laurence contributed. Faith prevented herself from snapping a look of surprise to him with a flex of effort. She hadn't realized he was bi, not that it really made a difference to her. But now that she thought about it, that would probably be exactly why he'd mentioned a guy, to let her know in a way that didn't make a big deal out of it.

Tom got bored first, when silence fell as Faith concentrated on what she was writing. He threw his arms around Felicia's neck from behind for a last hug, then bounded to the door out of the kitchen. "I'll go into town and grab dinner."

Felicia murmured her agreement, and Laurence rose, looking from one to the other of them. Worried about Faith being worried about being alone with Felicia, she supposed. She waved away his concern. While she had no illusions she could take Felicia—or any Were—in a fight, she liked the impression she'd gathered so far of the woman. Friendly, not at all intimidating.

"I'll grab the stuff from the car," Laurence said, relaxing.

"I think you and the head archaeologist should have the master suite. Such as it is. Take a look for yourself." Felicia grinned. Laurence had snorted in reply and left by the time Faith noticed the assumption that they'd be sleeping in the same room. Maybe she should have objected, given their perhaps cumulative week or two of time together, but she figured the fact she hadn't noticed meant something.

She and Felicia engaged in benign conversation—no more stilted than some she'd had with significant others of coworkers at summer barbeques—about Felicia's classes after all the paperwork was filled out, shuffled into one neat pile, and slid away into a folder Felicia tucked to the side on the counter. Tom and Laurence arrived together, the former perhaps having collected the latter on the way in.

Tom's stack of takeout containers was a wavering tower worthy of any cartoon pre-pratfall scene of staggering around obstacles. Which was a challenge, apparently, as Laurence, shit-eating grin breaking out, edged up behind Tom and shoved. Tom dodged handily, but the stack wavered even more. "You're eating anything that falls on the floor!" Tom called, his own grin coloring the words.

Faith held her breath, but the stack of food remained safely upright even as the two men tussled over it. Felicia, on the other hand, didn't even seem worried. She watched for a beat, entered the scrum, and emerged victorious with about half the food. "Ha! Mine!"

Tom slid his burden onto the table, then turned the game's target to Felicia, catching her about the waist and twirling her as she held her spoils out of reach. Their laughter was infectious, and as the horseplay spun up, Faith got the strangest feeling she was watching a film strip with frames cut out. Not sped up, precisely, just hitched in places like she'd missed something.

When they'd wound down, all food on the table, and ownership rights settled but not visible to outside observers, Faith turned to Laurence. "Is that—you know, fast thing you do something that takes special effort?"

All three Were stared at her blankly. Faith tried again. "I suspect from that reaction the answer's no. When I was watching you, just now, there was stuff I couldn't—perceive, I think. Like it was too fast."

Laurence assimilated that first. "Were have faster reaction times. I hadn't really thought about what that would look like. I mean, we're not really…moving faster?"

Faith scuffled around in the plastic bag with the cutlery and napkins and came up with a plastic knife. She feinted a throw at Laurence, then launched it at Tom. The next moment he had it in his fingers as easily as if he'd plucked it out of the air from a lazy, underhand toss. That time it didn't seem inhuman, just at the level of a circus performer with skills honed over the years.

"I think we might have to insist Laurence date someone less murderous." Tom thoughtfully reversed the knife to repeatedly stab the air in his best "Psycho" fashion.

"It's just hunger," Faith teased in return. That hunger and her good mood disappeared abruptly when Felicia popped open the first two containers. Enchiladas. Tom was saying something about the place he'd found the food, and how a Mexican-American family ran it together, but the smell—even through her human nose—had reached into her gut and flooded her with nausea.

Enchiladas had been among the food their captor brought them, one night when he'd decided he wanted information. The smell had remained when she had to help Laurence rebreak his arm so it would heal right. She heard the sound in her mind, of that break. A remembered taste coated the inside of her mouth, of the cold food she'd eaten after it had gone bad, so she'd throw up in front of the goons and convince them to take her to the hospital, giving her a chance to escape. An unsuccessful chance, as it turned out.

She'd avoided Mexican food entirely since then, subconsciously, and now the surprise drove a retch up into her throat muscles, though she throttled it down before it could become audible. She sprinted for the bathroom, stood panting with hands on knees over the toilet for a half a minute before her stomach calmed and she wondered what that must have looked like to the others. She'd been too nauseated to check their reactions as she pushed by.

All right. She straightened and cupped her hands at the age-dulled faucet for a mouthful of water. With forewarning, she should be all right with the food, unless all of it was enchiladas. The question was how much of a weird, irrational human the others thought she was.

"Faith? You okay?" Laurence's voice. She hadn't shut the door, just shoved it to, but he remained there until she joined him.

"It reminded me…" She didn't like to put it into words, but Laurence didn't need her to. He pulled her into him, kissed the top of her head then held her for a while as silent comfort seeped into her tight muscles.

"We can go to town and get something else," Laurence murmured.

Faith disengaged to head to the kitchen. How *did* Felicia and Tom manage to stay touching so much of the time? The hall wasn't wide enough for the two of them to walk abreast, so she had to break her contact with Laurence for the moment. "It's all right, I'll eat something else. Tacos or something should be okay." With her hunger gone, she'd only be eating enough for politeness anyway. She and Laurence could see about town for a late-night snack.

"Susan refuses to eat bananas," Felicia offered from her place seated next to Tom at the table, when Faith arrived. Faith noticed that while several of the containers were open, they all displayed items other than enchiladas. "Like, militantly. She says it's because she was eating them to be healthy when she was pregnant with Edmond. So now they're linked to the pregnancy nausea thing humans have?"

The smoothness of how Felicia offered the explanation made Faith go a little limp with relief. And it was even mostly true. "Food poisoning, in my case. It's weird how strong that link can be."

Felicia pulled a teasing face. "You know, that will never not sound terribly dire to me—'poisoning.' Like you survived an assassination attempt."

"Well, it can be serious, but yeah. Not that I'm not still envious that you guys apparently don't have to deal with it." Moment smoothed over, Faith gathered a plate, a taco, and a seat for herself. To hide how slowly she was eating, she decided to follow the Were vs. human line of questioning. She presumed she had full security clearance now, after all. "How old are you guys?"

Tom started to answer, but Felicia squeezed his knee to forestall him and slanted a cautious look over at Laurence. "Thirty-seven," Faith answered for him, to prove she was that much in the know. At least when they'd met, ten months ago. "Thirty-eight?"

"Thirty-eight," Laurence verified. Fourteen years between them, which she supposed was something she should have considered in all of this too. He didn't *act* like he was 38, that was the thing. But divide by two—

"You look like you're doing math in your head, but I can't figure out why." Tom prodded her nearest elbow. "I'm twenty-five, anyway. Felicia's twenty-one. We don't look out of sync until our thirties, usually."

"The rule of thumb for an age gap—I suppose you guys wouldn't have it. Divide by two, add seven. It controls for the fact that a bigger gap gets less weird as you get older." Faith grimaced. "So since I'm twenty-four I could date you like…three, four years from now? By that rule."

"Nah, he still hangs out with us trouble-making roamers," Tom said. There was some kind of scuffle with them kicking each other under the table, which only underscored his point. Faith wondered what part of that Laurence objected to. "And Susan and John are fifteen years apart. I'd say they're pretty Lady-blessed successful."

Which did help, actually. "What's a roamer?"

"North American teens leave their birth packs and travel for a year or two before they settle down." Laurence eyed Tom. "Causing trouble."

"I don't think we count anymore, as the college student and corporate wage slave." Felicia knocked her shoulder into Tom's.

Watching the two of them eat, as the conversation grew more general once more, was interesting as well. Faith would have expected an obnoxiously affectionate couple to be forever eating off each other's plates, but this was the opposite. They inhaled food in similar staggering quantities, but transferred over a choice bite to the other's plate every so often.

After they'd finished, Tom cleared the table while Felicia rummaged in a shoulder bag she'd dumped on the floor off to the side. She exchanged the neat employment paperwork for a folder stuffed full and ragged around the edges. "So this is all the background stuff that's come in so far. I think they're planning to email you the files as well, but this way you can spread it out if you want."

Faith did so, setting aside written summaries for now in favor of maps and photographs. Other than a pile of blow-ups of tombstones, there weren't many of the latter, as she'd expected, but the former looked promising. "Oh, good, you found someone to do the GIS." She traced the red outline that had been digitally overlaid on the historical map, then checked the legend. "Yeah, this is the modern parcel boundary." She dug through the pile to make sure she had all the GIS maps, laid them in a roughly chronological fan. The others crowded in to stare intently as she pointed out features. It was a good thing the GIS person at the company she'd worked for most often was happy to chat with techs who were taking a break from sitting in front of their computer, chained to the stultifying task of cleaning up tables of shovel probe results.

"So basically, they put the historical maps into the computer and tell it to match to modern features—which are usually survey points. The GLO—General Land Office,"—she lifted that, set it uppermost—"maps were surprisingly well surveyed, given they were done in the late nineteenth century." She searched, found what she was looking for. "Here. This one's eighteen-seventy-three. Which isn't to say things are at all exact by modern standards—river courses and streams change constantly, but even road alignments that should still be the same only approximately line up."

She circled her finger over the fat lot of nothing contained in the parcel on the GLO. "Sometimes they'll show cleared fields, or people's cabins, but not always. And there wasn't always something there at that time. Looks like there's a trail a few sections over, that was probably a Native one that European Americans started using too." She widened her next circling of the area to the boundaries of the section. "They surveyed by township—north-south—and range—east-west—so remember the township, range, and section numbers, because that will be listed on homestead patents and stuff that isn't always mapped."

She scanned the other maps, but even not knowing the exact dates they cared about, she doubted that, for example, the Metsker Atlas one from the 1950s would be much use. "It's too bad we're not closer to a city. Spokane itself probably has Sanborn Fire Insurance maps—they're really nifty, they mapped buildings and materials for risk of fire, but they were really accurate about size and placement, and also labeled their uses—and I think there were some USGS topographic maps from the

1900s, 1910s kind of timeframe for urban areas, but those were pretty zoomed out anyway." She pulled the Metsker in front of her. "You'll notice the later atlases show road names and parcel owners, but no actual buildings. So as far as the built environment—meaning all the structures—you can get a real hole where it's just not on any map. In King County, I know there are aerial photographs from the 1930s, but I don't see—" She scuffled around but came up dry. "If it exists, it might have to be something you get from the physical county archives, rather than online, too."

She sat back, but the others stayed silent and rather wide-eyed, passing a couple of the maps back and forth for closer scrutiny. "So I still have to figure out the timeline of when they got the homestead and how long they were on the property, and so on," she offered apologetically. "It's a bit late for me to assimilate all this." She swept a hand to indicate the written summaries that had been shoved to the side.

"No," Felicia protested. "Even this is all so cool!"

Considering she was sitting in a room full of werewolves, Faith decided she'd take the warm glow of satisfaction from having remembered an expert's chatter well enough to bullshit her way into sounding like one herself. Or maybe she did count as an expert, in this situation. Which was a strange thought.

9

Faith had to admit: this was shaping up to be at least a little bit fun. Worry about spoiling data out of ignorance nibbled at the edges of her thoughts, but the more she focused on the details of what she was doing, the more it receded.

She'd spent two days reviewing the maps and historic context and poking around the property by herself—or maybe she could claim it was "opportunistic pedestrian survey." Today her "crew" had assembled, and she was showing the newcomers around while Tom and Laurence organized equipment. The Roanokes had been generous in their budget, so she'd been able to order screens and such for everyone.

Faith crunched out between scrubby pines, away from the house, the two new Were following. Tracy—of the Chris Hemsworth obsession—was probably about nineteen, still lean in that teen way, and deeply enthusiastic, following right on Faith's heels. Pierce was older, probably late twenties, and much more constrained. His dark hair was gelled and his whole appearance pretty in a way where Faith couldn't tell if he was gay or one of those straight guys who was very secure in his masculinity. Or maybe she was reading him completely wrong because he was a Were.

As long as he was aware he'd have to get plenty dirty in the course of excavation. She'd observed enough stunning transformations in the other direction, a coworker she'd only seen sunburned and grime-encrusted arriving washed and dressed up for a social event, she was willing to suspend judgment until she'd seen Pierce in whatever he'd brought for field clothes.

Faith dropped an open hand to indicate the ground. "You might keep your attention around your feet even now when we're walking around casually. I do it anyway—even though there aren't supposed to be rattlesnakes in this part of the state, I keep up the habit. Watch out for anything human-made. Like foundations, gravel paths, depressions from pits, or artifact scatters. Of bottles and rusted cans, stuff like that. I found an isolate yesterday I'll take you by so you know what I'm talking about. We'll do a proper coverage with pedestrian survey when we're all organized, but we might as well keep our eyes open now."

"Pedestrian survey?" Tracy prompted, as Faith had rather suspected she would.

"You walk transects—lines—with a given distance between them, so you get decent coverage of an area. I'm actually used to doing shovel probes at intervals as well, since over on the west side of the state everything's so grown over, there's not much point trying to see the surface. But we can see if we find any evidence of the homestead with pedestrian survey first, and then do shovel probes in the plowed fields and stuff like that. Basically, we know the homestead was somewhere on this parcel, but not precisely where. The artifacts at the historical society were found when constructing 'an outbuilding,' " —Faith made the air quotes, and Tracy giggled—"literally, according to their records. We don't know which one, or if it's even still standing.

"So we can start looking by the buildings that *are* currently standing, but I'm not optimistic that there's anything left of what they found anyway. If it wasn't just an isolated trash pit. There could also be sites from other time periods on the property, and while we're not going to excavate any of those, we'll want to know where they are." Faith winced, internally, thinking about the site forms that wouldn't get written for those hypothetical sites, then pushed it to the back of her mind again. Better to leave them unknown but mostly undisturbed.

"So basically we'll be looking widely first to get a sense of what the property has as far as features of the original homestead or later development, like outbuildings, privies, roads, or whatever."

"If some of us can walk a straight line without haring off after rabbits," Pierce remarked, and his smile snapped into being when Tracy knocked sideways into his shoulder, laughing her protest.

"I asked Laurence—" Faith was aware she was losing even more of her assumed authority in the dip of her head to frown down at the low-brush covered ground, but then again wouldn't it be worse to pretend authority about Were stuff? "About survey in…wolf, but he thinks it wouldn't be much help. Maybe you could smell out the metal of artifacts, but I'm not really expecting many of those from the right time period are going to be right on the surface, so it's better to have the overhead view to see features like pits or paths or whatever?" Dammit, she'd planned to make that a firm statement.

Tracy showed no signs of catastrophic loss of confidence in Faith, however. "Pierce is being a cat, but he's not actually wrong. I'd probably just want to go hunting." She tipped her nose up, gaze going abstracted as she read the wind. "I haven't caught a bunny in forever. They're more fun than squirrels."

While Faith was trying to wrap her mind around the teen with the fashionably bleached hair murderizing fluffy bunnies, Pierce clapped a hand on Tracy's shoulder. "Watch your property boundaries out here, puppy. I'm serious—I know you're used to worrying about cell phone cameras, but out here it's ranchers with rifles. Digging out bullets may be a roamer's rite of passage, but I can assure you, it's not worth it just because you wanted to duck under a fence to follow the bunny a little farther."

Faith slowed. That was an even harder idea to wrap her mind around. She turned a rock over with her toe to provide an excuse for the pause. In her peripheral vision, Tracy gave a grimace worthy of any teen frustrated by smothering older relatives, but Faith noticed she didn't protest that Pierce was wrong this time either. Faith had certainly heard on the news about real wolves shot on the east side of the state. All right, Faith had to ask: "So it was dangerous when Laurence came looking for me in wolf where I was out working nearer Ellensburg…?"

Pierce shrugged, seriousness now gone. "Friendly doggie during daylight hours, I presume? It's a calculated risk. But Laurence isn't a bunny-obsessed cub."

"Neither am I!" Resigned in her exasperation, Tracy surged ahead, then seemed to remember their purpose and turned around to wait for Faith to catch up. "When I catch one tonight, I'm not sharing any of it with you."

Okay, they were definitely not human, but the more Faith talked to these two, the more she found herself relaxing. Tracy was the opposite of scary, and she appreciated Pierce's apparent stability as she mentally started apportioning tasks for the coming survey.

Pierce nudged a potato chip bag with his toe, blown in to snag on the bush that was currently embracing it. "How old is the stuff we're looking for, anyway?"

Right. Archaeology. They were nearing the road, and Faith stepped out of the trees onto a small hill the road cut had sliced into, displaying the columnar basalt beneath her feet. The view was mostly trees, apart from the gravel line of the road in either direction, but it seemed like a good place to do the intro lecture anyway.

"Tom's friends found that the land was a cash sale in the mid-1870s, and the...pack? Family? probably lived there into the mid-1880s. But you need a bit more background than that. So. Spokane history in general: the earliest Europeans in the area were those involved in the fur trade—Spokane House was built in 1810 by the North West Company—and then missionaries. There were also some influxes of miners heading to various gold rushes, but there wasn't much settlement for farming compared to on the west side of the state because irrigation really didn't get going until the 1890s or turn of the century. In the late 1850s into the 1860s, there was unrest in the area with the Army clashing with the local Tribes. So European settlement wasn't a big thing until the 1880s or even the 1890s, meaning the Russian family was there earlier than many. And probably followed the routes of the fur traders down from the Fraser Plateau rather than the Oregon Trail or other routes from the East Coast."

Faith checked her audience for signs of glazing over, but

both were so focused on her, she could imagine canine ears locked on as well. "We're assuming they were ranching, given the irrigation situation, but that's one of our many research questions. It was a cash sale, as I said, rather than under any of the homesteading laws where people could get grants of land in exchange for living on them for a certain period to 'prove up.' But then the land shows up as belonging to someone else, and the best the historian could turn up from the research was that the house and possibly other properties burned down and the land was sold. That fits with the dates on the gravestones in that private graveyard Tom found out about—it may seem a bit far away now, but it was on the other side of the original property. There are a couple earlier years of death, but all the rest are in 1884, possibly related to that one event, the fire. So someone survived to commission the stones and sell the land, but where they went..."

Faith shrugged. "So that's a really interesting question, but not one we can probably actually address even if we do find something from that time period to excavate. I'm hoping to maybe verify the fire and approximate dates they were living here, as well as their level of local ties—were they buying goods from traders in the area, or were they still mostly using Russian goods they'd brought with them? And what kind of markers of...Were culture, did they have, if any?"

"What about North American packs? Whose territory was it out here back then?" Tracy asked Faith the question first. Faith appreciated her blind trust in her ability as an archaeologist to know everything, but she shook her head. Tracy turned her attention to Pierce next.

Pierce shrugged. "Don't look at me. Tom's the one who was tracking that kind of thing down. I know there were some roamers in the early fur trade. I think the first pack in Seattle was fairly early, but Spokane might still have been in the dead zone between that and whatever pack ended up becoming the Billings one, like it is now. I mean, it must have been, if the Russians managed to settle here."

"Unless they were fighting with the local pack." Tracy grimaced. "The Billings roamers are punks."

Pierce snorted his amusement. "Even the ones you haven't met? You forget, we're all Roanoke now."

A laugh escaped Faith despite her best efforts, and she pressed her fingers to her lips. From murdering bunnies to sounding exactly like a college student from a state school casting aspersions on their football rivals. The interplay between culturally familiar and unfamiliar kept catching her off guard.

But they'd been standing here for a while now, and she wasn't wearing sunscreen. She frowned at her forearms, then gestured along the road. "The isolate's this way." As Tracy loped ahead, Faith wondered if perhaps she should have ditched the slight air of mystery. The isolate really wasn't worth it.

When they turned off the road and arrived, Faith seized and snapped away a little more of the dead bush that had eaten the dusty chunk of enigmatic machinery, while Tracy circled to examine it from all angles. "What is it?"

"Fuck if I know," Faith said, offering a lopsided smile. Pierce laughed richly, and Faith relaxed another notch. "Agricultural—or industrial, maybe?—metal, machinery, miscellaneous, if you want to get technical according to one company's artifact coding." She traced the parts. "Those look like brackets for bracing it to...some kind of base? And that's a bolt, and maybe that was—who even knows. I checked it for parts numbers or maker's mark, but no joy."

She straightened, dusting off her fingertips. "There's a lot more largely unidentifiable metal artifacts that not even archaeologists can trace to anything, than people realize. Pulling shit straight out of my ass because we're in an agricultural area, it could have been from a vehicle or something to do with irrigation or…who even knows. It's an isolate because I can't find anything else on the surface to make it a site, but we should definitely come and do cardinal shovel probes—probes in all four directions. And three more around any of those that are positive. Meaning they have artifacts in them. So if it is a site, not an isolate, you can get a rough sense of the boundaries by plotting positive and negative probes."

Tracy was still looking at her with a sort of hopeful patience, as if Faith would declare it all a joke, and reveal the answer with magic archaeology knowledge any moment. "Miscellaneous metal, remember that for when you're cataloging," Faith offered instead, and Tracy finally shook herself and echoed Pierce's earlier laughter.

Faith held out a hand. "Anyway, we should get back so we can sit down with the map and then get dressed to start on the survey this afternoon." She had a bunch of work to do herself as well, to make sure the GPS unit and field forms were ready to go.

Approaching the house from the side, they came first upon the metal shipping container serving as a shed. The door was open at the moment since she and Laurence had been inside yesterday trying to decide if it was worth stringing lights to make it into a lab, or if it would be better to sacrifice some room in the house to that purpose. "I guess they were planning to do some remodeling, so they got this to store equipment and stuff from the house, but then it fell through." Faith gestured at the container as they passed.

Tracy detoured to peer inside, but Pierce stuck with Faith into the front yard of the house, where Laurence met them, having jogged out from the house, phone against his ear. "Yeah, they're just getting back. I think Faith should have a say about any Russian Were as well."

Pierce's expression hardened a little, but Laurence didn't look actively angry, so Faith took her cue from him. A say about Russian Were what? Coming here?

Laurence switched the phone to speaker and held it out in the center of a little huddle soon completed by Tracy's arrival. "My mother and I had previously discussed sending someone," a woman with a Russian accent was saying. "But I had not realized she'd settled on the idea until Alexei called me to say the two of them were arriving. I can personally vouch for Alexei's behavior."

"Though he is more than a little belated in asking permission to enter our territory," came Roanoke Silver's voice, with asperity.

The other woman made an acknowledging noise. "He says he merely wants to observe, since you are uncovering our— their history."

"'Their' history…they're not going to try to assert a claim to this little patch of territory, are they?" Laurence said. "Wouldn't the Russians who came here have severed ties to the greater Russian pack by doing so?"

"No, they have no claim on Roanoke territory," Roanoke Dare rumbled.

The woman with the Russian accent picked up after him. "Practically, any claim they have on territory, or what you dig up, depends mostly on where the survivors of the pack went. Whether they returned home, or joined a North American pack. In the latter case any descendants are here, by their ancestors' choice. And the land incontrovertibly belongs to the Roanoke pack now."

"Well." Faith hadn't meant to break in, but then everyone was silent and she felt like she had to keep going. "The territory, I leave that to you guys, but the artifacts are a whole different thing. I mean, it's a huge question for any archaeologist. Before Europeans and then any Were got here, the land belonged to the Native Americans. But if we find remains of the homestead… It seems straightforward to say the history should belong to the descendants, but what if, like now, you don't know who exactly the descendants are, or if there even are any? The law says the artifacts belong to the people who own the land now, and I signed on to this thinking in terms of Were in general, but really the people who feel it's the history of their specific ancestors, they should be *involved*. In telling the story of it, you know?"

"Well put. For our part, we're willing to allow it if they only observe, as we told Tatiana already, but only if none of you object. We won't be out there dealing with them," Roanoke Dare said.

Laurence looked to her, and Faith shrugged. If the alphas thought these particular Russians could behave themselves, she really did believe it was better to allow them to participate. Laurence collected nods from Pierce and Tracy as well. "No objections here either."

Barely half a minute after Laurence had ended the call, the Were did a pointer dog thing where all their heads came up at once, and Faith heard the car turning off the main road and crunching up the driveway a beat later. So this was the Alexei guy? They hadn't been kidding about him being belated in asking permission to show up.

The car pulled up about a hundred feet down the driveway, and two men got out. One was blond, a solid block of a man who nevertheless had a sympathy to his expression that stopped him looking like a stone-cold thug. The other man… was Mikhail.

Faith flashed on the memory of his hand on her neck, cutting off her air, and she was suddenly at least half a dozen steps back from where she'd been standing, with no memory of having moved. He'd *kidnapped* her and Laurence. He'd had two goons to help, but he'd done plenty of the dirty work himself, trying to intimidate—in her case—and beat—in Laurence's—information out of them. "No," she whispered, and tightened her grip on Tracy's arm. That was the other thing she'd done, grabbed the younger woman to drag her out of danger as well, though that was absurd, Faith assumed. A female Were could undoubtedly take care of herself. Tracy looked merely confused at the moment.

Laurence stood as tall as he could manage and growled, an instinctive puffing up she remembered from when she'd first met him and he'd spent a lot of time terrified and angry to cover it. It drove home how much he'd managed to shed that until now. Pierce didn't posture, but he added his own deep, rolling growl to the mix. Apparently he was no fan of Mikhail's either.

"What in the Lady's name?" Tracy protested. She peeled Faith's fingers off her arm, but then kept hold in apparent protectiveness in the other direction.

"No!" Faith said again. She should explain to Tracy, but first she wanted Mikhail *gone*.

And Mikhail…prostrated himself on the brown, scrubby grass in front of them. That stopped the growls, and Faith stared at him a little open-mouthed herself. "For the hurt I did all of you, I am sorry," he said in an even thicker accent than Tatiana's. "I followed orders that were wrong."

Faith couldn't see his face to see if he was still as smarmy as she remembered, but he did make quite a picture, dark golden head and tall graceful body bowed down. She wondered if he was aware of that picture. "I regret what I did under them. And now we are all trapped—if I stay, the new alpha must kill me. I have come to not force her to make that choice."

And to save himself, of course. But could Faith blame anyone for that?

"He is right," the other man spoke up. His accent was no worse, but he picked his way through his choice of words with painful slowness. "At home, he is probably killed. He has no moon knives, I watch him with both eyes." This one would be Alexei, Faith presumed, the one Tatiana had actually vouched for.

"Or I could kill you instead for your crimes," Laurence snarled, and rocked his weight forward. Little as she wanted to even be in the same county as Mikhail, Faith didn't see that Laurence attempting such would help anything, so she pulled away from Tracy and went to put her hand on Laurence's arm instead.

"They are our ancestors. We have a right to be here as you uncover our history," Mikhail said. Faith caught her lip in her teeth hard enough to hurt. There was no way he could know how he was turning her own words back on her, but Faith still dearly wished to grind her teeth.

"But I do not blame you for wariness. I swear on the Lady." He paused. Faith supposed he wanted the others to acknowledge the weight of the formality in his voice before he continued. "That I will not even touch the human, to harm her in any way."

"And what about Were?" It was Pierce who voiced the objection. Laurence's hands were clenched into fists, and he seemed too angry to get any more words out.

"I will only defend myself, nothing more. I think that is the necessary promise, yes?" Mikhail raised his head to look at Laurence pointedly, though he quickly dropped his eyes. Faith assumed it was to avoid any kind of dominance challenge. When no one jumped him for the space of another breath, he rose to his knees, chin dipped down but definitely not as low as before.

Tracy cleared her throat, awkward. "If the alphas have given their permission already...?"

Which was another painfully true point. His word on the Lady must have been good enough for them. Pierce shook his head, a sharp, snap of a motion, then gestured them all aside. All the way up to the house with the door shut, in fact, but Faith supposed that was needed for werewolf hearing. "Did they, though? To him specifically? Why didn't they warn us, specifically?"

Laurence's lip curled in an unvoiced snarl. "Because it's undoubtedly a political necessity they didn't want us spoiling."

Pierce's frown hardened. "Which, if it was, I see no reason they couldn't have also told us, in so many words. Call them back. Make *sure* this is what they agreed to."

Laurence turned into an abortive step—away from Pierce, into pacing, or simply to bleed off frustration? Faith couldn't tell. He glanced at the front door with the Russians beyond it and stepped right back again, reclosing their rough circle. "The reason to hold it back is so we don't *instantly refuse*. How is that call supposed to go? Sorry, alphas, the hunt just got more difficult than you initially said, we're wimping out two minutes in and plan to whine until you let us slink home?"

Tracy looked from one to the other of the men, and maintained a tight silence. Above her pay grade, Faith could read that in her face—and in a different grading system entirely than Faith's, she figured. Faith was standing closer to Pierce than Laurence given how the latter was vibrating with frustrated energy, and she *thought* she heard Pierce mutter, "Your shit with authority..." But then wouldn't Laurence have heard it too? Perhaps his deafness was selective. Or perhaps he doubted his own senses too because Pierce spoke almost immediately after at normal volume, smooth and diplomatic. "Perhaps we could give Tom a chance to weigh in. Or reach out through Felicia..."

Faith didn't know if another random member of the pack would have any particular insight into the alphas' motives, but at least she'd be on the spot. To be honest, Faith was with Laurence on his read of the situation—just because this was his sore spot didn't automatically make him wrong—but more information from an unofficial source couldn't hurt.

Laurence set his jaw and finally stilled, facing Pierce straight on. "Fine, you want to take a *vote* to overrule me, do it. We're all mid-ranked out here, after all."

Or maybe more information would hurt in this case. Hurt Laurence, if he had to be overruled. Better to work from their own deductions, in that case. Pierce must have come to the same conclusion as he sighed, tipped his head—not down, to the side—and his frown smoothed away to a pretty, empty sort of neutrality. "It's not me he's going to be able to hurt. We can do what you think best. But you might also ask Faith."

Laurence shook himself, finally seemed to unwind a few degrees from his fear-fueled anger. With a gentle hand on her shoulder, he nudged her a purely symbolic distance away from the other two. "He's right. Are you really okay with this? If you don't feel safe, screw politics."

Faith twisted her fingers tightly together. "Leaving aside the alpha's permission and stuff about who owns history—because it doesn't have to be *that* Russian we have observe—he's a bastard, but I'm not willing to say that means he has to be executed, if that's what happens if he goes home again. If that other guy really is going to be watching him all the time—I guess it kind of comes down to whether you think he'd keep his word about not hurting anyone. Are you guys serious about that, swearing on the Lady?"

Laurence automatically pressed his thumb to his forehead, which gave her her answer even before he articulated it. "Even though he's a cat's bastard, the Russians are even more observant than we are. I believe him when he swears on the Lady." He let out a long breath. "I guess I don't actually want to kill him either." Faith took one of his hands in both of hers and he layered another atop to cling to her.

"We can see how it goes," she offered him. And reassured herself, she supposed. "Throw him under the bus later if he deserves it."

And maybe he wouldn't. Certainly, when they went back outside, Mikhail accepted the news that he was allowed to stay from Laurence with the appearance of respect. Faith didn't entirely trust it, of course, but if he could keep pretending for

long enough to finish the survey, maybe they'd come out of this
without any trouble.

10

Everyone's probe locations were GPSed for the moment, so Faith wandered over to where Laurence was digging his and crouched to drag her fingertips through his small pile of backdirt. There had been a can scatter on the surface not far from here, but it had looked like it might have been beside an old road alignment, and sure enough, this dirt was showing an awful lot of what looked like road gravels.

"If you're claiming I missed something in that, I don't believe you," Laurence teased. His forearms were liberally dusted from his earlier screening, slashed by a hard line of much cleaner skin where his gloves had covered it in a different position. He wasn't sweating hard enough to do more than stick down a small patch on his shirt, but his forehead was damp enough that when he swiped the back of a wrist along his hairline it left a fashionable brown streak. Shovelbum fashionable.

"No, I'm no good at knapping. The best of those kind of anecdotes are always when someone slips a gorgeous obsidian Clovis point in someone's backdirt." Faith straightened, and dusted off her fingers on her hip before grabbing her own gloves from her back pocket and pulling them on. "Tell you what, I'll screen for you."

"Knock yourself out." Laurence levered a last load of dirt into the screen, then bit the shovel into the ground next to him to stand it upright so he had his hands free for the tape measure to check his bottom depth.

The screen had been laid down flat for filling, so Faith lifted the top, screen section up and back while her toes braced the bottom, leg section for leverage. When she had it upright, the leg section supported the back side of the screen section while she held the handles at the front, and the hinged join between the two sections was at around ninety degrees. A few rocking shakes back and forth on the pivot point of the legs and only the gravels remained. The dirt was relatively dry, which was why Laurence was so filthy already, but made for easy screening. There was nothing like trying to press wet, clayey sediment through a screen. In the rain, of course.

She did due diligence in case of any pre-contact lithic artifact showing up, using her trowel to scrape the gravels away from the main group from bottom to top, but road gravels were all she found.

Laurence added a last half-shovelful to her screen from the bottom of his level and then took a seat on an upturned plastic five-gallon bucket. It still amused Faith, they wouldn't be using the buckets for their ostensible purpose of hauling dirt unless she had them open some excavation units, but everyone carried equipment in them from probe to probe, and had discovered the other main use for them on their own. Laurence retrieved his clipboard to fill out his paperwork for the soil description of the level. At work, Faith sometimes used tablets, but the software was proprietary, and Faith hadn't seen the need to break the Roanokes' budget by trying to find something similar when a basic paper form worked just as well.

Laurence looked up and scowled. "Here comes trouble."

And indeed, here came Mikhail waltzing up. He held out a bottle to her, aqua glass and missing the finish and much of the neck. "Is this old?"

"Possibly." Faith hooked the front of the screen on her hip to hold it up, and frowned at the bottle. She wished he'd left it where it was and come to get her, but she supposed him doing what she'd explicitly told all of the Were to do was too much to ask. "Where'd you find it?" Before she accepted the bottle, she ran her fingers over the last of the gravels, lowered the top screen section to a steeper angle to shake them out, then dropped the handles to the ground to form a stable little A-frame of the screen and the leg sections.

"Back there." Mikhail gestured vaguely.

Faith looked up from checking the base for mold seams and skewered him with a sharp look. "Where back there? Show me."

"A couple steps away from the path to the house. I don't remember precisely." Mikhail shrugged. "Is it old?"

"You can't—" With anyone else, Faith would have sat on her anger and tried to convey the importance of careful data collection again—it was just one surface find—but she found she had no wish to give Mikhail the benefit of the doubt. "You can't just *pick shit up*. Okay? We have to record where it comes from or it's *meaningless*." She jerked a hand to Laurence, sitting stone-faced with his paperwork on his knees. "We're not writing all of this stuff down because we're bored and have nothing better to do. We're writing it down because we're doing *science*, and that's the only way we can form any conclusions about the history you claim you're here to learn about!"

"It belonged to my ancestors, I can do what I want with it." Mikhail swiped the bottle back out of her hands. The broken edge sliced the web between his thumb and forefinger, and he didn't even appear to notice as a line of blood oozed free before it healed up. As if she could possibly have forgotten she wasn't talking to a human. "I brought it to you because you claim to know about such things, but I can stop doing that if you wish."

Fuck, just what she needed, Mikhail running amok around the property like some kind of pothunter. If he decided to start digging random holes at midnight, how the hell was she supposed to stop him?

Laurence shoved to his feet and slammed the clipboard back down on the bucket with a thump before rounding on the taller Were. "You are *not* going to fuck up the Roanokes' archaeology."

"Oh, of course, sub-alpha…" Mikhail smirked. "Sorry, I forgot. You are not a sub-alpha anymore, yes?" He stepped into Laurence, looming over him with every one of his extra inches. "What authority do you have? You cannot even convince a Were to play chase with you."

Even with the holes in her knowledge of Were, Faith could guess that this fight needed to be interrupted or redirected five minutes ago. "It looks like a mineral water bottle," she said, and took the bottle back. "The aqua color is a result of impurities in the glass, I believe, so it's from earlier than when they started to be able to get really colorless glass. I'd have to look up the date range. There's a mold seam, but without the finish, I can't say if it was fully automatic machine-made." Faith gestured at the top of the bottle, where the finish would once have been.

Both men were looking at her now, rather than each other, and she decided to consider that a success. And moving their focus to her had had the side effect of easing them back away from each other. She knew Mikhail wouldn't believe it if she smiled at him, but she gave him a level look, and tried to believe herself that a pure interest in the truth of the bottle might distract her briefly from how it had gotten into her hands. "I'll let you know once I've looked it up."

Mikhail nodded, expression brightening with almost a smirky shade to it, so Faith just couldn't leave it there. "I wish I knew where it had been, though. It could have been tossed by someone traveling by on the local road, maybe. Or someone out working brought it along for their lunch? Or it would be really interesting if it was from someone's household trash, because then we'd know something about what that household was drinking. But now we can't know, I guess." Which was rather overstating the case, for one isolated bottle. But would he smell that? He didn't seem angry, but neither did he seem particularly cowed.

"When I find another, I note where," he promised, dipping his chin, but not pressing his thumb to his forehead as Laurence did when he was promising something really serious.

"Leave it there and bring me over," Faith said. This time, she did give him at least a lifting of her lips. "I don't mind being interrupted."

Mikhail waved a hand in acknowledgment, though Faith wasn't so foolish as to conflate that with agreement. He wandered off, leaving the bottle with her.

"Thanks," Laurence told the ground, shoulders slumped. "For deescalating that. I knew I should, I just...couldn't."

Faith set the bottle on the upturned bucket, so she could take his hands. "Hey, if there's something I'm better at, being a human, I'll take it. I don't give a shit where I am in the hierarchy." She grimaced, realizing she needed to amend that. "I don't give a shit as long as he at least listens to me enough not to dig illicit holes through a fucking site, if we find one."

Laurence pulled her close suddenly, and hung on, like the need to cling to her hit him like a storm and then passed a few moments later. He loosened the embrace, laughing awkwardly. "On the Lady, I'll get the others to help me tie him up and mail him back to Russia before he does that." A beat, then—"It's not that I couldn't play chase with a Were. It's that I wanted to be with *you*."

Faith's first impulse was to laugh. Of all the things swirling through her mind as sources of anxiety at the moment, that comment didn't even rank. Of course Mikhail was just trying to wound him. But laughing seemed likely to wound as well. "I'm not worried about that. Don't let him get under your skin." She found a lopsided smile as she turned it teasing. "All those other hypothetical Were don't get to have you now, anyway. Their loss."

"Ha," Laurence agreed, and his tension eased back to nearly normal as he let her go. "Back to work?"

"Back to work," Faith agreed. With her helping, they finished Laurence's current probe quickly and she lingered as he bit his shovel into the next, wishing vaguely she could provide him with some kind of archaeological win to throw shade on Mikhail's single bottle. But all of their current probes were so preliminary, without any positives to guide their way. Even the can scatter had been all on the surface.

At least the terrain indicated the new probe was likely out of the road alignment. Laurence laughed suddenly, and dumped several shovelfuls of dirt from the first ten centimeters into the screen. Even before he lifted it to shake, a white flash of ceramic was visible, and several rusty nails and flat glass fragments showed among the gravels once the dirt was mostly gone.

"I have no idea what this is," Laurence said, picking up a discolored white ceramic tube, about the length of a pen with a thicker bulb at one end. "But it's clearly something."

Faith accepted it from him and rotated it thoroughly to look for maker's marks. "It's a household insulator. Porcelain." She knocked it against the side of the screen to try to clear the dirt from the center to show it was hollow, but said dirt was too stubborn for that. "It goes in the walls, with the wire through the center." She picked at a spot of discoloration with her fingernail. "Looks burned to me."

Laurence's face lit up, and it killed her to have to dash the hope she hadn't realized she was inadvertently raising. "It won't have anything to do with the homestead, even though that burned down. Insulator means electricity, and these are all wire nails." She traded the insulator for one of them, rolling its length, clearly round even under the encrusting rust, between her fingertips. "At the time of the homestead, they'd have been using square nails. Wire nails are later, and completely replaced square nails because they can be mass produced." She lifted a largish fragment of window glass. "And this is pretty thin and very regular, which also says later."

She ducked to grab Laurence a plastic zip bag for this level's artifacts. "So I'd guess this was some outbuilding that they pulled down and then burned the debris, but we'll definitely do more probes around here to delineate the area of debris. You can look forward to counting hundreds of window glass shards in the lab later."

Far from being dimmed, Laurence's enthusiasm slipped free into a laugh. "Talk it down all you want, but I still think it's cool we found something."

A matching smile tugged on Faith's lips. "I suspect we will find cooler than a demolished shed eventually, but you're right in another way—we don't need to get so focused on the Were that we ignore what we can learn about those who came after them, even if we won't be excavating any of that."

As Laurence picked the artifacts from his screen, dropping them into the bag, Faith dusted off her hands and snagged Mikhail's bottle from where she'd left it by Laurence's field paperwork. After she washed that, it would be time to check in on what the others were finding in their probes again. And make sure Mikhail wasn't bothering them either.

11

To Faith's relief and more than a little surprise, for around a week Mikhail didn't cause trouble beyond sniping at Laurence whenever the two men were in the same vicinity. Pierce, on the other hand, demonstrated an almost preternatural ability to never be in the same place as Mikhail, which frankly impressed Faith. First, because of how long it took her to notice—and how Mikhail still hadn't seemed to—and second, how Pierce still got all his work done. For his part, Alexei pulled his weight as far as lugging buckets of dirt—which given he was not only a Were, but a built one, was a hell of a lot of weight.

And there was dirt to lug, as by the end of the trouble-free week, they'd finished with shovel probes, and Faith admitted to herself that Roanoke Dare had been right: there was at least one site related to the homestead on the property, if not more. She found the idea of breaking the law had grown familiar with time, and without any more hesitation she'd had her "crew" open a few units in promising artifact concentrations.

In the evenings, the two groups tended to clump separately, which Faith figured was all to the good. Tonight, Tom and Laurence were consulting over some kind of bonfire plan of theirs on one of the more grass-denuded patches of the front lawn, and she let herself back into the house to bang around in the kitchen in vague hopes of a better method of spearing marshmallows than random sticks from the ground outside, since on their last grocery run they'd thought of the snack but not the apparatus.

Voices rumbled low from the dining room, and Faith glanced in, doors of the current cupboard still in her hands. Alexei and Mikhail were at the rickety table, which she probably should have guessed given the words hadn't resolved themselves into anything she could understand. They'd laid out some kind of cloth, bright yellow circles on a dark blue background—moons, she supposed. Alexei set a bottle of wine ceremonially in the center of the cloth, then dispersed two glasses from a larger stack. They had bases that seemed almost too round to be stable, and he placed them like hands of a clock around the bottle, pointing to himself and Mikhail. Alexei's back was to Faith, and while Faith didn't kid herself they weren't aware she was there, Mikhail ignored her, watching Alexei work with an opaque expression.

"Did you find anything?" Tracy asked, coming up behind Faith and making her start. Then her attention was caught by what the Russians were doing as well.

Mikhail's lips lifted in a smile that was disquieting in a way Faith couldn't put her finger on, and he gestured Tracy forward. "Come. Alexei, a glass for the young woman. We can show how to proper honor the Lady."

Alexei filled the two glasses about half full, replaced the bottle, then turned with an arm slung over the back of his chair. He said something dubious, to which Mikhail laughed.

Tracy approached cautiously. Faith could practically see a canine nose questing urgently forward. Faith trailed in her wake, because all right, yes, she did want to observe the Were ceremony if it wasn't private.

Mikhail offered his glass when they arrived at the table, unclear to which of them. Alexei's spine snapped straight. "No, human," he said, then some urgent word, presumably in Old Were. He frowned thunderously and failed to find it in English.

Faith held up her hands placatingly even as frustration bubbled beneath the surface. She was, what, twenty feet closer than she'd been before? But fine, the human was leaving, the ceremony wasn't going to be tainted or whatever.

"Poisonous," Mikhail translated. "To humans. But this one is too clever to be in danger, I think."

"I know better than to take drinks from strangers, yes," Faith countered, and settled her weight back, trying to parse the backhanded aspect of that compliment she could hear perfectly well in his tone.

Tracy shied back from the glass as well. "Is that wolfsbane? It almost killed the Roanokes."

Mikhail, not one to miss such an elegantly crafted set-up for him to show off, shrugged, and tipped his glass back himself. "Only in the wrong dose."

Alexei growled something Faith decided to pretend was "stop being such a fucking tool" and made a circle over his own glass, thumb to thumb, forefinger to forefinger, and spoke something with the cadence with a prayer. Only then did he sip too.

"Wisdom, or courage?" Mikhail asked, in English, but even then not particularly comprehensible.

Alexei waved him off, finished his wine, and stood. He shoved the glass at Mikhail, then pointedly turned his back on the other man. "You see—seen Pierce?"

"Outside," Tracy said, tipping her head that way. "We're going to roast marshmallows if you're interested." She spoke very intently to Alexei, but spoiled her plausible deniability that she wasn't trying to exclude Mikhail when she flicked a worried glance to him. He snorted, and poured himself more wine, clearly with every intention of staying where he was to enjoy the high. Faith assumed that's what this was—a religious drug that killed you only in large doses.

"Yes," Alexei agreed. "I follow, one minute." He turned off into the dim hallway into the rest of the house, floorboards protesting at his step, presumably heading for the bedroom the Russians shared. Faith wondered if that was merely him trying to be polite about turning down Tracy's offer. The two of them headed back out into the heavy orange weight of the late evening light.

"No luck on skewers, someone's going to have to mug a pine tree," Faith told the three other Were gathered around a tidy stone-ringed campfire as she approached.

Pierce held up his hands, denying responsibility for any such activity, but then he noticed Alexei coming up behind and his whole face brightened as his hands drifted down like he didn't quite know what to do with them. After an awkward moment, he stuffed them into his pockets. "Time for the moon blade lesson?" he asked.

"Yes," Alexei said simply. He dug in a shoulder bag and held out some kind of leather harness, which only resolved itself for

Faith when Pierce shrugged it on over his T-shirt, becoming a shoulder holster for a pair of blades.

"What about you?" Pierce said, head down over one of the blades, testing the motions he might use to draw it, but not doing so just yet. A few locks of hair made it free of his gel, a little impressive in the way he achieved "mussed" without going so far as "movie villain losing his cool."

Alexei set his bag down and gestured Pierce to draw his borrowed blades, face filling with delighted anticipation. After all Mikhail's smirking, Faith found herself smiling along with Alexei, even more affected by the kind of delight that grew by inviting others to share it, rather than at others' expense. Pierce complied and lifted hands curled around the handles of curved blades that were really more like brass knuckles.

And Alexei, laughing at the culmination of his carefully set up joke, drew out a pair of pastry cutters, mismatched in both size and composition, one with a wood handle with peeling varnish, another with soft, rubbery, black plastic, clearly thrift store finds from the last trip into town. After a moment of surprise, perhaps not recognizing what the objects were, Pierce joined in the laughter, forging a connection that clearly transcended the language barrier.

Faith snagged Laurence's elbow, in case she needed to drag him off. "Are spectators allowed, or do you want some privacy?" she asked, laughing too. She was as curious about moon blade fighting as everything Were, but she was happy to avoid stepping on their flirting if she could.

"It's fine," Pierce mumbled. Then he turned his attention back to Alexei, easing into readiness as Alexei chose his patch of relatively flat ground a little ways away, and gestured the sweep of the area they'd use.

Faith left Laurence to claim herself a bucket seat, rather than one of the old lawn chairs they'd found in the shipping container that seemed likely to infect you with tetanus or black mold just by looking at them. Tom had set them up optimistically around the fire, but Faith noticed he was the only one to settle rather dubiously onto one once he'd reoriented it to face the practice fight.

Laurence selected his own bucket and set it between Faith and Tom, forming a proper peanut gallery once Tracy appended herself to the other end of the line. "I suppose I did smell that, then."

"Told you," Tom crowed. The two men lifted their weapons a little like boxers squaring off, and then Pierce threw a few slashes that Alexei blocked with ease with the pastry cutters, one hand and then the other.

A blur of motion, and finally Alexei took a slash across his forearm that made Faith hiss to see it, but of course it bled for under a second and he seemed to hardly notice. Instead, he nodded in approval, and demonstrated some other move in slow motion in return. Perhaps Pierce had dropped his guard after the successful hit—Alexei certainly had no trouble tapping the edge of one pastry cutter against his collarbone.

He crossed behind Pierce, and demonstrated an angled slash, then waited pointedly for Pierce to copy it. When he corrected Pierce's position with nudges at his elbow and shoulder, his touch looked fully professional, but Faith wasn't sure who he thought he was fooling. Not her, and she couldn't even smell whatever the others apparently could.

Laurence *hmph*ed, and turned back to face the fire to give the privacy that was clearly needed after all. Tom moved as well, curling the line around the fire, but Tracy pushed to her feet.

"I think I'm going to go for a run before bed," she said, a little overloud, then bounded off. The power of suggestion making her restless, Faith figured.

Laurence adjusted his position closer so Faith could lean on his shoulder. "I honestly thought Pierce dated women."

"He used to," Tom verified.

Faith straightened and frowned at Laurence. "Laurence. *You're* bi, aren't you? Or am I missing something…? Were you joking, about Chris Evans?" She scrubbed the heel of her hand against her cheek, hoping her flush couldn't be seen in the twilight, or could be ascribed to the fire. That had sounded dumb out loud.

"Chris Evans…?" Before he quite finished saying it, Laurence's memory seemed to catch up. "Oh, that was about playing chase. Every Were has a roamer's chase or two before they figure out their type. I was talking about dating in terms of, you know, relationships. Falling in love."

"Oh, so bisexual versus biromantic," Faith said. That was another interesting piece of Were culture. She wondered how the Russians thought about sex, not that she would ever ask in a trillion years. "How do humans fit into all of that? Are they part of the roamer's chase experience?"

Laurence pulled her against his shoulder again, slid an arm to hold tight along her hip. "Not in my opinion. Better to be a bit more mature before you dive into those waters."

"Especially if you're a man." Tom grimaced, the rest of his body language going uncommonly sober. "I remember the first time I was closing up after the late show with only one of my younger female coworkers. She was vibrating with tension, and I couldn't figure out why at first." He called up a smile, lopsided. "I think any decent Were man does his best—it's kind of like the art of derp, you know? Give off the right signals to show you plan to leave them alone."

Laurence nodded. "I think it's easier for me to pull off than, say, John. Being smaller." His lip lifted in a silent snarl. "I can't understand why any Were man *wouldn't*, being able to smell the fear, but I guess if you get off on that kind of thing."

"The former Sacramento's son had a habit of raping human women, which was why Dare had to execute him," Tom agreed.

Faith was glad to hear about justice being done, but it made her feel a bit shivery to hear it so stark: executed. What other crimes were capital, for the Were? And how did she match the relatively mild man she'd talked to at his dining room table with an executioner?

The Were seemed to have plenty to keep the conversation going themselves without her input, however, discussing other Were she knew nothing about. "Honestly, the former Sacramento himself was a real cat's bastard," Tom was continuing. "Just a bit smarter to get away with it longer, I guess."

"You were there, weren't you? When he went after Silver?"

Tom grinned, more predatory than normal. "I was. But it was Susan who killed him."

Laurence released a pleased huff, while Faith's muscles all seized up at once. Was that what it took, to be a human among Were? God, she hadn't signed up for that.

But she needed to be careful or Laurence would notice she was upset. She supposed the smoke from the fire was the reason he hadn't smelled it immediately. Carefully, she focused on the comforting weight of his arm across her back. She felt safe with him, that was enough for the moment. And then Laurence snapped her attention tightly to him. "I suppose you could say that about Rory: he only scared humans because he didn't bother to give a shit about their reactions to him. Like they were beneath his notice."

Laurence never talked about Rory, the former alpha he'd been beta to, and who'd used to beat him, leaving him, pre-therapy, flinching from authority and lashing out. Faith didn't know if Tom realized that as viscerally as she did, but he was certainly as low-key about his response as she could have wished. "Wasn't he married?"

"Still is." Laurence frowned into the twist of spark and smoke over the flames. "He was different with Sarah. And Ginnie—his daughter." He wasn't looking at Faith, and she'd wondered for a moment if he'd forgotten about her, but now she knew he definitely hadn't. Tom would know who Ginnie was. "It was like if you were a Were he'd decided was weaker than him, he was—not protective, precisely, but bothering to think about the consequences of his actions. But if you weren't weaker, he left it to you to protect your own damn self, even if that meant against *him*."

Or not protect yourself, as the case might be. "How old's Ginnie?" Faith asked, for something neutral to say.

"Fifteen?" Laurence checked with Tom, who nodded. "Lady, she's getting old. I remember when she was just a bright little kid, but I haven't seen her since before her Lady Ceremony. I suppose it will be a few years yet before she's roaming or... out on her own..."

Where Laurence could possibly visit her without encountering her father as well. Tom hadn't said that out loud, but Laurence dropped his head miserably like he had anyway. "Why can't she visit? I mean, here, even. If you think archaeology might interest her," Faith said impulsively.

Tom straightened with a bounce, which wrung a worrying

creak out of the lawn chair. He ignored it. "That's a great idea! She spends the summers down in Boston, anyway, so she and her father don't tear each other's fur out, a couple of alpha personalities stuck together, so why can't she come a little farther?"

"If her father lets her," Laurence said darkly.

Tom snorted. "I'll invite her, so he won't have a reason to think he'd be nipping at Roanoke Dare, by refusing." His enthusiasm dimmed. "Unless you think it's you he'd want to thwart...?"

"I am *certain* Rory has more or less forgotten I exist," Laurence said. Flat, but maybe a little more balanced? "It's worth a try."

"I'm too lazy to find sticks now," Faith announced, judging a change of subject was called for. She checked over her shoulder, but Alexei and Pierce had disappeared off somewhere. To talk, not make out, she'd guess, judging by their level of new flirtation awkwardness earlier. Language lessons to go with the knife-fighting lessons, maybe. "I vote we let this burn down, and then buy some real skewers tomorrow, to do this properly."

Tom edged a hand toward the package of marshmallows, sitting in state on one of the other lawn chairs, since at least that weight wouldn't stress it too much. "We could just eat some raw."

Faith lunged to capture it first. She knew he let her win, but found she didn't mind. "No way, we're not opening it! Some will turn into *all*, disappearing into bottomless Were maws." She tussled with him in a much gentler version of how he and Laurence interacted. It proved a good way to wrestle the aspects of Were she was determined not to think about down as well. For now, at least.

12

A few days later, they hit what Faith had been hoping for in one of the excavation units. They'd been exploring an area of subsurface sheet midden—diffuse debris mostly spread flat as opposed to filling in a depression—that seemed to be about the right age, with square nails and a hand-blown bottle base, when Tracy called Faith over to the one-by-one—meter square, that was—she was digging.

"I found a whole bottle, so I left it—" Tracy frowned, then proudly pulled out the correct terminology. "In situ. And now there's a bunch of them. I point-plotted the locations and drew them on the form. Should I do anything different now?"

"Congratulations, looks like you have a feature with actual visible boundaries," Faith teased. "Technically the sheet midden you're all in is a feature of its own." She considered the base of the unit from several angles, standing outside the square, then stepped in and brushed loose dirt from around bottles and also a piece of ceramic flatware, plate or saucer. She pulled out her trowel and scraped carefully at the dirt around the edges, seeing if she could get the soil stain to resolve into something a little more distinct, then drew a line around it with the tip of her trowel so Tracy could see what she was talking about. "It might be a privy, which would be more straight walled, and you might find bricks or an old barrel lining the walls. Or it might be a trash pit, with the walls being more bowl-shaped.

"What I'll have you do is excavate one more level to make sure the stain continues. The dark, organic stuff, see? That's from the rest of the contents of the feature decaying. If it does continue we'll open the next unit over to come down on the whole thing. That way, you can excavate and bag artifacts from each level within the feature together."

She looked up from her crouch to summon the others to see what she was talking about as well, but she discovered she was already the subject of a square-shaped Were huddle, everyone except Mikhail. She stood. "There might be a lot of artifacts from this, so I think we should start washing and cataloging now, rather than waiting until the end. I'll head it up and train you guys one at a time, see who takes to it, yeah?" She wasn't wild about cataloging instead of digging herself, but better she not force anyone who actively hated it into doing the task. That was a guarantee of misidentification and lost provenience.

Nods all round, and Faith climbed out of the unit, and pointed back for Tracy. "Measure and draw the current boundaries of the stain and take a bunch of pictures, okay? I'll go get set up for cataloging."

Privy it proved, over that day and the next, and with all the industrious work connected with it, over the next week, came something like peace. Mostly. Mikhail apparently couldn't speak to Laurence without some kind of sly dig, but she managed to keep them apart, mostly, and Laurence showed heroic patience. Faith ended up mostly keeping him with her in washing and cataloging the artifacts, because his patience extended to that as well. Otherwise she'd be the only one doing it forever, at it far into the winter. Which was job security, but she doubted paying her for all those hours would be what the Roanokes had bargained for. Everyone else was working for free, after all.

They'd gotten the worst of the dirt off with the hose earlier, but Faith had a dish tub of water and a toothbrush at her elbow for any stubborn grime that might be obscuring the embossing on a bottle's maker's mark, for example. Sunlight sliced at an angle across a corner of the heavy-duty plastic table they'd set up outside to hold the various field lab equipment. Under a small marquee tent, no less, a far cry from a familiar blue tarp, fraying at the edges, tied to whatever piece of the landscape was high enough to make it throw some shade.

They were currently laying out the latest level bag by material type on different plastic cafeteria trays, the glass in front of Faith while Laurence sorted ceramic, metal, and "other" in front of himself. She lifted one dark shard to the light. Olive or green? She hated when things graded into each other, especially because she liked having easy categories for the others. Eventually, she solidified her piles—bottle glass sorted first by color, then into base, finish, and body shards, with a few other things like lamp chimney fragments in a pile of their own. She set the tray aside to count and bag in a minute, and stole the ceramics tray from Laurence. He could add any last particularly dirty fragments that had hidden among the other materials as she worked.

"Earthenware, porcelain," she told Laurence as she swept fragments to one side of the tray or the other, then started flipping them as necessary so any marks or decoration were uppermost. "I think this blue hand-painted pattern on the porcelain is Russian. Obviously I'm not an expert but it looks like some stuff I found pictures of online. Nothing with a mark yet, though, mostly rim shards. Clearly it's a set, though. Look, these are from different vessels." She showed two fragments, the arcs of their rims illustrating two entirely different sizes, a saucer and a plate, perhaps.

Laurence straightened with a snap, which told Faith who was approaching from the direction of the house, without even looking. In fact, she didn't want to look in case he had another artifact, shorn of its provenience, in his hands. When Mikhail came around to face her across the table, however, his hands were empty except for a water bottle. He had nowhere near the level of dirt of anyone else who'd been digging, but he'd at least worked up an honest sweat in his relentless walking of the property, and his shirt was stuck down along his sides and probably over his back.

"Did these belong to the pack?" he demanded, coming to lean over the tray of ceramics. Laurence reared back, then leaned forward, but managed not to growl. Faith imagined his hackles would have been up, had he had any at the moment, though.

"Very likely." Faith hovered her hand over the Russian pattern, then flipped over a few of the earthenware pieces. "This pattern though, the brown transfer print, there was a piece with a mark in another level, from the United States. East Coast. So it seems like they bought a new set of dishes, locally."

Laurence swallowed some kind of exclamation. When their attention turned to him, he dragged the bag of half-washed artifacts closer to his body, but Mikhail must have read in his expression—or smelled—that something of real importance was in the bag because he swiped for it. Rather than surrender the artifacts, Laurence lifted one out. Wood, simply carved and around the size of a pendant.

A cross.

Of all things to find. Before finding a moon stone, in fact. Faith stared at it for several seconds, then shook herself free of shock before Mikhail did and took it from Laurence. It had a hole at the top, too small for a cord, but perfect for a metal jump ring. "There must have been a human here," she said, not even realizing what she was going to say until she did. "A servant or laborer, maybe?" A stretch, without other evidence—but that cross. Someone had to have been living here, using the privy often enough to drop it in by accident. Unless it had been a visitor, though the probability of dropping something important during a single or handful of visits seemed low. And how many visitors would the pack have had, far from most other areas of European American civilization at the time?

A Were converting seemed even less likely. Where did that leave them, a Were picking up so utilitarian a religious artifact as a curiosity?

Mikhail reared back as if she'd slapped him, snarling his first words in Old Were. "No Were pack would have *human* living with them." His English, when he found it, was growled. "I know this."

Faith swallowed a growl of her own. If she spoke in a reasonable tone about archaeology, he seemed to accept it, so she needed to stay reasonable. "That's valid, as oral history, which is one line of information archaeology draws on, but it's not the only part of archaeology, the way it's not the only part of any scientific discipline. We have to see what the evidence supports, not just accept what we think we already know."

Mikhail had apparently regained his equilibrium, perhaps by editing out the existence of whatever he found inconvenient, as his gesture of dismissal was lazy. "What good is archaeology if it wastes time reinvestigating what we already know?"

"It doesn't matter what you think of archaeology, you're not the one paying to have it done." Laurence stood, folding chair juddering as one of its legs caught on a dead grass hummock. He stood tall and challenging, chin up, but Faith noticed he didn't go toe to toe with Mikhail, which would highlight the difference in their heights.

"Always quick to defend your chase with hot words, I see. You think I will not notice she is the one with authority over you?" Mikhail's smile flashed his teeth at Laurence. He didn't close the distance either, standing as if too lazy to bother.

Laurence closed his hands into slow fists, and his voice remained even. "Faith is in authority over this excavation. Why should that bother me? You must have figured out by now that one of the Roanoke betas is a human."

"I do not speak of humans in authority, I speak of *you.*" Now Mikhail prowled closer to Laurence, crossing behind Faith's chair. "Showing your neck to everyone you can."

Faith wanted to snap at him, but should she? Would that only prove his point? She wasn't even sure what his point was, tangled up in the complicated layers of status—public, private, intrapack, interpack—she only vaguely understood. She set the cross safely among the ceramics before twisting in her chair to follow them, then stood when Mikhail started edging Laurence along the table.

When Laurence reached the edge, he seemed to finally notice his instinctive movement and stood fast. Mikhail rocked forward a last step, sudden and sharp, and Laurence flinched.

Faith would have done the same thing without a hint of embarrassment, so she didn't realize the significance until Mikhail *laughed*, and Laurence flushed with humiliation.

He surged up into Mikhail, grabbing at a handful of his shirt over his chest, in a reaction Faith recognized all too well. Covering his fear with ill-considered violence. "If you want a challenge, fine. Let's make this a real challenge fight and see where that gets you, purse dog," Laurence snarled up into Mikhail's face.

"By all means." Mikhail's smile only grew, only congealed more sneer-like. He waited, unmoving, until Laurence released his hold, then backed up. "I will not even shift, to make it more fair."

Laurence muttered something incredulous, but seemed eager to seize the apparent advantage when it was offered. Was Faith being too human when she had a sinking feeling that if Mikhail had offered it, it couldn't possibly be an advantage that favored Laurence?

Laurence stripped rapidly, without a hint of embarrassment, only looking around as if in search of cover when he stood nude, boots dropped under the artifact table and his clothes loosely piled on a chair. But for the actual moment of shifting, there was nothing to step behind, under a tent roof on open ground. Faith tipped her head down and away, picking up on the discomfort, but that left her with a perfectly good view of Mikhail as he crossed his arms and waited, as if impatient. Staring. A beat, then she heard a grunt of effort indicating Laurence had shifted anyway, even under that gaze.

Maybe that was Mikhail's only planned advantage, that initial embarrassment, but Faith wouldn't bet on it. The man and wolf strode and loped from under the tent, measuring space and hummocks and awkward bushes in minimal, practiced glances until they settled on a relatively clear area in common accord. Laurence's lips were far off his teeth, his ears and tail were both stiff and high, and a growl rolled continuously from his chest, surging into a snarl at times.

Laurence attacked first, perhaps thinking to catch Mikhail off-guard. He leaped, impossibly to human eyes, launching his teeth for Mikhail's throat. Mikhail's throat wasn't there, as he twisted aside, hands coming down and ready around the level of his chest. While Laurence skidded and reversed direction back to him, Mikhail flexed his hands, perhaps feeling the lack of weapons. That was something, at least.

But not enough.

Laurence feinted several times, lunging in to snap at Mikhail's knees, until suddenly he didn't snap, he lunged around to the side and then slammed in his shoulder, aiming to land his weight on the back of the man's knees. Sound tactics, Faith would have said—little as she knew about such things—taking advantage of his lower center of gravity.

Laurence's slam landed, but Mikhail moved with the momentum and rebalanced himself within two steps, easy as dancing. The next moment, Laurence flew back, body arced from a kick Faith had to guess at in retrospect.

Now Mikhail was on the offensive, striding to carry each heavy new kick to Laurence. He aimed for the belly, throwing Laurence with most blows. And avoiding teeth, Faith realized. Laurence finally caught his ankle, and locked down, forcing Mikhail to keep his balance on one foot, and find it again and again as Laurence dragged and worried at the wound.

Hope formed a bubble in her chest, forcing open the tightness long enough for her to take a couple clear breaths. One last yank, and Laurence got Mikhail down onto his ass. But then Mikhail could get both hands in play, and he hauled at Laurence's jaw from top and bottom, slowly forcing it open. Rather than lose that battle slowly, Laurence gave up all at once and lunged for the throat again, now so temptingly close.

And hope popped and Faith couldn't breathe again. Mikhail had enough grip in Laurence's ruff to strongarm him back, and rolled the two of them until he somehow rose atop, Laurence on his side in the dirt and Mikhail sitting on his hips and leaning one hand down on his throat to keep him down. With one hand remaining free, he slammed punches into the side of Laurence's chest.

It was so *slow*, though it couldn't possibly have been more than a minute, as the damage built and soaked beyond what Laurence could take. Over the men's grunts, squeals of pain, and jagged panting, Faith couldn't tell if she'd heard ribs snap or not—what did snapping ribs sound like?—but her stomach heaved with nausea, combining with her difficulty breathing to double her over.

"Stop!" Her voice came out thin, like every *fucking* useless movie girlfriend. If she only had a brick or something, to swing—but what would happen when he turned to hit her back?

But he did stop. Mikhail stilled, gathered a few breaths, and then climbed free. He dusted dirt off his hands, lifted one pantleg to frown idly at the minor spotting of blood around his ankle. Laurence was breathing, his position made that possible to see at least, but the rise and fall of his flank was shallow. Faith took a step in, wavered, not able to bring herself to get within Mikhail's reach.

Mikhail tracked on her movement, smiled at her. "I am sorry you have to see such unpleasant Were business," he murmured. Then, still smiling at her, though he dropped his eyes to his work, he stomped his heel down on Laurence's foreleg. A precision strike, all his weight behind it, and this time Faith heard the snap for sure. And again on a hind leg.

Then he ambled off.

Faith was on her knees beside Laurence the next moment. She extended a hand to smooth his fur, but hovered without touching instead. It seemed so deeply wrong for there to be no blood, except spattered around his lips and teeth—from Mikhail's ankle, or from internal bleeding?

But his arm and leg would need to be set. Before they healed wrong, like his arm had the last time Mikhail broke it. Faith couldn't deal with that again. She couldn't. She surged to her feet. "I'll get Tom," she promised him as she did her best with human speed in running. Laurence might have made some kind of protesting whine, but she didn't stay to listen.

Tom would be either be at the house, or at the excavation units. But it must be nearly lunchtime, right? The house was closer, opposite the way Mikhail had gone, and Faith found she'd already made the decision of where to go first, right or wrong.

Right, as it turned out. Tom was at the front door, bending to the laces on his work boots, as those weren't allowed indoors. He straightened as she pounded up, building who knew what story from her stew of fear and anger and urgency. "I know you guys need to set bones as soon as possible—I *can't*, I'm sorry, I just *can't*, again, please, you have to—"

"Set *bones*?" Tom was beside her in the next moment. She'd expended all her air on that much, had to suck in more, and she waved him to follow her trail and not wait for explanations. He refused to leave her, though, and she allowed him to take her elbow. Protecting her, she realized. From the unknown threat.

She would have to explain at least a little, then, so he understood protection was secondary to speed. "Challenge—" There was an order here. Important to get that right. "Laurence challenged Mikhail—" Even if Mikhail had schemed and manipulated to put him in a position where that seemed his only choice. "Go, hurry."

Tom hurried. Faith trailed him at a bit of a distance, not admitting to herself that it wasn't about being out of breath until she heard the yelp. Even just hearing it, not seeing it, she gulped in a breath too fast, unexpectedly, and had to stop fight back a coughing fit. She stayed where she was, shaking, until the second yelp came.

Tom met her coming back, Laurence hefted easily over his arms, legs hanging. Laurence whined some kind of protest Faith couldn't interpret when he noticed her, but apparently it meant something to Tom. "I don't care, you're not walking anywhere until you've had something to eat and time to rest," Tom said firmly, no hint of humor anywhere, what would be a neutral tone for anyone else flat for him.

Laurence felt undignified, Faith realized. Her anger and desperate worry, denied a real outlet, surged up. "If you think I care about *anything* except you healing up after I had to watch you—" Her throat closed up on tears, though she couldn't find the words for what she'd seen anyway. Get half killed? With all that it apparently took to kill a Were, was that even half of it? Laurence dropped his head, relaxing, but Tom only seemed to tense more, drawing in some of her upset.

Then they were at the house, and Faith was busy opening doors for them. Tom laid Laurence down with great care on the bed they shared in the master bedroom—such as it was, it wasn't any bigger than the others, but it did have its own bathroom—and took Faith's elbow to orient her, then dropped it to stride off with greater speed. "We need to get him something to eat."

In the kitchen Tom grabbed a random plate out of the dish rack and dived into the fridge, reappearing with pretty much every piece of raw meat they'd bought on the last grocery store run. He stripped it efficiently out of plastic and Styrofoam, dripping juice on the counter in a deeply unsanitary fashion, but Faith paced between the table and the door and didn't interfere. "I suppose a challenge is a Were thing, but that wasn't *right*, what Mikhail did!" she burst out finally.

Tom gathered the heavy plate, hand on either edge, and extended it to her, head hanging. "You're right. That's not how challenges are supposed to go. If you want, I can be the one to call the alphas while you take this to him."

"No!" Faith didn't realize what she felt until the syllable came out so emphatic that certainty flooded through the rest of her body. She knew what she had to do. Not the details yet, but at least the rough shape of it. "I'll take care of it."

Tom's head came up, tipped with wariness. "And by take care of it, you mean call them yourself?"

"I can't do that to Laurence." Faith stood as tall as she could, not that that helped much in comparison to Tom. "Not only does he get his ass beat, but it has to get announced to the whole pack? No. I'll take care of it. It will be fine." She tried to stare Tom down, expecting to having to duck her gaze away from his after a few moments that proved her point, but he dropped his head again first.

She took the plate from him, and headed for the bedroom before he could come to his senses.

Inside, the tumbled, ugly flower-patterned bedspread was entirely lacking its burden of a huge wolf, and Faith stood in numb consternation for several seconds. What—?

Under. Under the bed. Oh, Laurence. Something felt like it broke a little in her chest, releasing a flood of liquid emotion into her body. She set the plate down on the floor, and folded down herself to see his shadowed bulk over against the wall. "Laurence?" What was the Were word—"Puppy?"

He edged out, a few inches at a time, enough so he could hold his head upright and then dip it to gulp down the raw meat. Faith waited until he was done, and then clamped a grip around his neck. She tried not to be too tight, but she wanted to assure herself he was solid and real, all right. One of his ears folded and then sprang upright, brushing the side of her neck, as she pressed her cheek to the top of his head.

They stayed like that for a long time, until Faith thought Laurence might have had a chance to heal some. "Can you get up on the bed okay? It would be more comfortable," she said, straightening, and he whuffed something she took to be positive.

She let him go long enough for him to climb up, less of his usual leap, and more of a scramble, but at least it was like a normal big dog, dealing with four limbs, rather than one seriously injured or arthritic. When he curled up on his side, she spooned his back, petting a hand along the fur of his flank, slow. "If you want, when you can shift, you could head back to Seattle," she said, keeping her tone slow and easy. She wanted this to sound like what it was, something offered to help, which should be refused if it wasn't helpful. "Take a few days, get an appointment with your therapist? I know you haven't had one since you've been out here."

He drew away from her, making Faith's heart stop for a second, but the next moment the muscles of his back rolled with effort and settled into bare flesh as he shifted, breathed for a moment, then scooted back into her arms. "Yeah," he said, and no more, like it helped not to be explicit about what he was agreeing to.

Faith wasn't at all tired, her mind racing in three directions at once, as she considered plans and details, but Laurence seemed to doze, which was good. So it startled her when he spoke again. "I love you."

"I love *you*." It was past time for her to say the word as well. Faith pressed her face into the back of his neck, to hold back tears.

Mikhail was going to *pay*.

13

Faith found Mikhail after breakfast the next day, comfortably watching over Tracy's shoulder as she organized excavation forms ready for the day, beside the units with the privy feature. She'd felt wound tight as a spring last night, when she went shopping for supplies after Laurence left for Seattle, and it had worried her that Mikhail might spot that something was off. But now she felt a sort of artificial, crystalline clarity, and she was sure he'd simply think she was still pissed about what he'd done to Laurence.

She braced her feet on the bare dirt of the nearest path. "Mikhail? Can I speak to you please?" she said with heavy formality. He ambled over to her, smiling with apparent smug self-satisfaction with the fact he was deigning to humor her little human hysteria. "In private," she specified.

He shrugged, and followed her as she led the way to the shipping container. Rather than clearing out the detritus of random, outdated furniture and rusty equipment, they'd added a layer of their own on top, shovels and unneeded screens from the shovel probe stage leaning against a couple folded card tables against the wall. Besides having no natural light, the place got approximately as hot as the bowels of hell in the middle of the day, so it wasn't really fit for any other use.

Faith stepped up into the container, and waited for Mikhail to join her, facing her across the rough aisle down the center of the space. She slipped her hands into her pockets as if awkwardly unable to find anything to do with them. "So what does this mean, now you've won the challenge or whatever? Are you going to leave Laurence alone?"

Mikhail shook his head. "I have no problem with Laurence if he doesn't make one—"

Bull-fucking-shit, but Faith didn't give him a chance to say anything else. She touched the remote in her pocket, and the toy from the shop in Spokane twitched into life. It was one of those motorized balls with an attached puff of a tail, that rolled around and twitched apparently at random, to the consternation of pets at home or people walking in the front door of the shop.

The movement was a bit subtle at first, but then the ball knocked into the metal leg of something, and Faith had a chance to cut Mikhail off with a shriek. "It's a rat!"

He couldn't smell it, of course, but he did look where she pointed with exaggerated, smarmy patience. He didn't snap to attention with quite the crispness a dog might have, but he was definitely interested. Faith backed up, and shrieked again for good measure when the fur of the tail flashed into view.

"Kill it!" she demanded, and jumped out of the container to mostly close the door and peer around it. By now, Faith rather suspected even someone like Pierce who didn't know her very well would have—well, smelled a rat—but Mikhail merely laughed.

"It will not hurt you," he rumbled, picking his way farther into the container.

"Kill it!" Faith said, and closed the door even more.

Now. She could never be faster than him, but if she could be faster than his realization something was wrong—

She pressed the door into place—no slam for even those split seconds of warning—and brought the small padlock out of her pocket and swung it open, through one set of holes in the container's latch, and smashed it closed against the metal of the door. She'd practiced that movement over and over last night, and the lock and her wrist both moved smoothly.

One done. Faith reached down into the scrub to the side of the container's door, and pulled out the heavy-duty storage unit lock she'd also bought, and wrapped with silver chains. That went through the second set of holes on the latch. She had to turn the shackle closed using the key, and that took a split second too long. A kick smashed into the door from low on the other side, and Faith instinctively jumped back, losing her grip on the lock with it half closed.

The little padlock held, though, and Faith got the big one shut before the second kick came. Then the third, then a rolling set of BOOMs that sounded like post-apocalyptic robot thunder. Apparently he was body-slamming the door. She drew the key out of the lock and set it into her left palm, then looped another silver chain over it, hooking it one-handed so it would be good and tight. She closed her hand over the lump.

A pause in the noise, and Faith started to think maybe they were done, but then the slams started up again, lower. He'd shifted, then. That would make it harder to talk to him. But she could be patient. She set a hand on the door, felt it shudder. There was perhaps a hint of a bow in the ridges of the metal surface, but not much of one. Certainly not a shoulder-shaped dent as Mikhail probably thought there should be by now.

Finally silence again for a space. "Why in the Lady have you trapped me, you—" That Russian-sounding spill of syllables was undoubtedly obscene. Mikhail's voice came as if he was speaking into the crack of the door, small scrabbles joining the sound as he perhaps felt after a place to pry.

"I'll let you out when you apologize." Faith put her fingers, perhaps mirroring his, to the latch, feeling the thickness of the metal. It would hold. It had to hold or she'd be torn to pieces, at this point.

"I did," Mikhail snapped. His voice dimmed for a second, and then more serious, metallic scratching sounds started up as something was shoved into place and then hauled on. She presumed he was trying various things as levers. Taking a page from the book of those pesky tool-using humans.

"You apologized for kidnapping us. I'll let you out when you apologize for everything you've done since you arrived here." Faith had meant to stay icy about it all, but her voice gained volume despite her best efforts. "Dismissing me, undermining my authority, I'll buy that you didn't even realize you were doing that, but you knew full well what you were doing to Laurence. Nipping at him, all those little insults, nip, nip, until you'd manipulated him exactly where you wanted him, which was giving you the excuse to hurt him and claim you'd kept your word. Did it make it *better*, that he'd been previously abused, so he was that much easier for you to hurt? Well, I'm not *stupid*, whatever you think, and I call that harm, and I don't call that defending yourself, so *I* say you broke your word and you can stay in there until you apologize for it!"

Deep breath. Faith throttled her voice a little more under control. "And you give your *word*, since apparently you value that enough to go to the trouble of wiggling around it rather than simply breaking it, you will cause no harm, by my definition of harm, to Laurence. Or me. Or any of the others here, for that matter."

"I'm not going to negotiate with you,—" Old Were word. "—human." A sound like maybe one improvised lever had clattered to the ground, to make way for another.

"Get comfortable, then. You're welcome to starve to death in there, if you like."

No more scratching for the moment. Maybe Mikhail was finally realizing his true situation. "The others will not let you keep me trapped."

Right. The others. Faith had been so focused on the door, she turned to find every Were on the property assembled in the yard beyond her, all staring with varying degrees of sick confusion. Of course they must have heard the earlier booms from one end of the farm to the other. She held up her hand, showing them both the key and the silver protecting it. "I don't know. Maybe the others aren't stupid either, and saw what you were doing as well." She held her arms wide to the others. "Have I got him wrong? Anyone?"

Of course, she supposed, as Were, they could simply rush her and rip off her hand or whatever the fuck they wanted to do. Which she should have thought of before embarking on this insane plan, but Alexei, the one she was most worried about, only shook his head sadly, and settled his weight on his back foot. Tracy chewed on a knuckle, hugging herself, and Pierce looked carefully neutral. Tom took a couple steps toward her, face creased with concern.

She didn't want his help, though. "It's easy. He just has to say the words, and I unlock the container, that's all." She spoke sharply, toward everyone at once. Tom rocked back, and didn't get any closer.

A sharper, focused blow, metal on metal behind her, made Faith startle badly enough she had to stumble to catch her balance. That made a dent after a few more blows, like Mikhail was whaling on the seam of the door with a leg yanked off one of the card tables.

"Don't worry, I've got all day to wait," Faith shouted into the seam, and settled herself seated with her back against the door, so she could feel the shiver of his every futile effort.

Time passed—possibly even a couple hours—in fits and starts. When Mikhail used English to scream insults at her, she answered in kind, which passed the time faster. When he grew silent, or body-slammed the sides of the container with a single-minded rhythm, it passed slowly. At least one of the other Were was hovering close, watching her, at all times, but they didn't interfere, so she ignored them after a while.

The container had originally been a dark red-brown color, which didn't gather the sun's heat as much as a black one might have, but it certainly grew hot even to her touch on the exterior as the day wore on. Shadows edged around, but Faith wanted to be at the lock when Mikhail finally gave in, so she ignored the blush of a sunburn when she didn't renew the morning's sunscreen she'd applied on autopilot, and curled up against the door in the full light, sweat dripping down her neck and back.

At some point, she'd started to get a real bitch—yes, she'd think it, a real bitch—of a headache, and now she was spending the latest quiet period with her eyes closed against the pain and light both. The pain throbbed in time with her heartbeat. "Just give up," she begged Mikhail, and he answered in Old Were, unmistakably negative all the same.

"Faith." Tom's voice. She opened her eyes to find him crouching in her range of view. "If he doesn't give in, are you going to let him die of dehydration? You're not a killer. You don't have to kill him."

Faith tried to think about that, but the pain wouldn't let her. She needed to—make a decision. "What do I do?" she begged Tom. She'd gotten this far, but she hadn't thought about this beforehand, and her thoughts weren't working. "What do I do?"

That increased Tom's frown. "What about you? Faith, are you okay?"

All right, Faith could work this through, even through the pain. "I can't let him hurt anyone. He has to promise." Which meant...what? Fuck, her head hurt so *much*. "What do I do?"

"Has she drunk anything all day?" Tom appealed to the others, then turned back to her. "I'm not letting you die of dehydration either." He reached out, and she batted at him ineffectually, then let him touch her forehead, feel the skin of her cheeks. "Lady, you smell sick."

"He has to *promise*." That, Faith could hang onto.

Alexei strode into her view as well, unleashed a torrent of Old Were at the door. At Mikhail's weak answer, he turned to Tom. "He promises."

Faith wasn't sure about that, but Tom was suddenly scooping her up, and the change in elevation made her head swoop so much she retched. She expected him to put her right back down again, but he only held her closer, despite the risk of vomit. She picked at the chain, finally got the clasp free, and dropped her hand to tip it and the key to the ground where Alexei dived on the key. He picked it up delicately with his fingertips to avoid the silver, jerked the lock open and free, then swung the door wide.

Mikhail, in human form, slumped onto the ground from where he'd been sitting leaning on the door. He was panting, gaze glassy, and it made Faith realize how shitty she felt herself, to see him so flushed. "Look up heat exhaustion," she said. "I'm not that bad, but he..."

"Tracy," Tom delegated, instantly, and Faith saw both her and Pierce take out their phones. "You are fully that bad, puppy. Should have checked you out from up close hours ago." He spoke low and husky, voice strained with his worry. But Faith's head hurt and it seemed she didn't have to figure anything out for the moment, so she closed her eyes on the sight of Alexei gathering Mikhail into his arms in the same manner.

"Air-conditioning, water in small sips, wetting down the body with cool water," Tracy reported, as Faith felt Tom start striding somewhere. Probably for the house.

That was all right for now, she supposed.

14

Sense came back to Faith properly sometime in the evening, and it was only then she realized how muddled her thoughts had been. She knew exactly what she needed to do now. Leave before the alphas found out what happened, leave before Laurence got back and her nerve failed.

Leave before the next time, when she had no choice but to kill someone.

But she was so *tired*, and she somehow let Tom chivvy her into bed and then she was asleep before she realized. She woke with that certainty filling her whole mind, though. Showered, dressed, packed, and she'd tell Tom to call the alphas on her way out the door.

She found the open front door before she found Tom or anyone else, though. The alphas were getting out of a crossover double-parked behind the line of other vehicles in the yard. Sunlight blazed up from Roanoke Silver's white hair and picked out the white lines in Roanoke Dare's, making them look far too glamourous for the scrub and dirt around them. *Shit.*

Of course someone had already called them. She should have thought of that. Faith dropped her pack against the wall inside the door, where it didn't look out of place among the other assorted dirty field gear, and retreated to the kitchen. All right. She'd have to argue her case, and escape when they were distracted or retreated to make a decision. They could always track her, but the question was whether she could make it enough of a hassle so they wouldn't bother.

Faith chose a chair, dragged it out from the table a little to face the doorway nearer the front of the house, and tried not to fidget as she waited. It was Susan who entered, however, apparently alone, much more at home in the space given her messy ponytail and ratty jeans. Faith supposed it only made sense. Send the human to talk to the human.

But how was she supposed to explain herself to someone who'd let the Were world make her a murderer, and was apparently okay with that?

Susan picked another chair, scooted it into the table, and brushed her fingers along one of the random lines made by adjacent speckles in the pattern of the age-yellowed Formica. "Can you tell me what happened yesterday?"

Could Faith tell it in a way that didn't get her in trouble, that was the question. "Over the past few weeks, Mikhail's been pretty much constantly verbally harassing Laurence, whatever he promised about not harming anyone. Mikhail backed him into that challenge fight."

Susan's lips thinned. "Mikhail did *not* have the alphas' permission to be here in the first place, no matter what he promised."

Faith stared at her for several seconds, lips still parted for the next part of her explanation. Did not have permission—

"So his alpha thought Alexei was coming with some rando, and told your Russian that, who told the North American executive suite—"

Susan lifted a hand, perhaps to ask for an explanation, but then she seemed to make the connection, and shook her head. "Apt enough."

"And Alexei thought Mikhail had told their alpha, so that every step on that chain already knew about Mikhail." Faith clenched her fists on her knees. "Par for the manipulation course."

Susan shook her head in apparent disgusted agreement. "You really thought we'd let him onto the continent? He *murdered* a sub-alpha, never mind kidnapping you two." She paused, then sought Faith's eyes with a human intensity. "Why didn't you *tell* any of us?"

Because she hadn't been able to trust the inscrutable, all-powerful alphas not to have some longer political game, even with Pierce's objections? That didn't seem so strange to Faith, but she figured she sure as hell shouldn't say it to the alphas' faces, or to the face of their beta. But what could she say, then? "I made a mistake," she told the floor, as sincerely as she could. "I'm sorry."

"No, don't apologize—" Susan cut herself off with an exasperated twist to her last word. She hesitated for a few moments, gathering her thoughts. "Have you had breakfast yet?" At Faith's shake of her head, Susan stood. "We stopped off and bought a ton of food this morning, since we're importing twice as many Were appetites. You should have some of that."

"Thanks," Faith muttered. Once Susan was gone, she told herself to go start the coffee, but instead ended up sitting there, staring at the table like the stupid speckles would form a pattern and jump out at her like one of those 3-D puzzle images. When had everything started going wrong, with her and Laurence's dreams of being together, with her a part of the Were world? She desperately wanted Laurence here right now. She desperately didn't want Laurence to be here.

She desperately needed to stop wallowing.

She'd gotten as far as pulling out the bag of ground coffee when Felicia arrived. She set down a huge grocery store pack of assorted Danishes on the table, and offered Faith a worried smile.

"Tagged along to visit Tom?" Faith wasn't sure why Felicia was lingering awkwardly here instead of finding him now she'd dropped off the food, but she found herself suddenly grateful for company less threatening than anyone involved with the alphas. The alphas themselves undoubtedly being busy at the moment with an interrogation of various other parties involved in the incident.

"And to see if you were okay!" Felicia curled her fingers into the plastic wrap over the pastries and peeled it unevenly back. "Tom said you were sick. You should eat something."

Faith abandoned the coffee and sat back down at the table with a thud. The pastries looked terrible for her, as well as terribly tasty. She pretended to herself by ripping one in half and only taking the half. For now. "Not—sick, sick. Heat exhaustion, at the worst. Maybe not even that bad. You have to rehydrate and get cool, that's all."

Felicia was looking at her with big eyes anyway, as she took a whole pastry of her own and started chowing down. "Shoulda seen the other guy, huh?" she said, tone lightly teasing.

Faith didn't have it in her to tease back. "Yeah." She shredded the edge of her Danish, but that just made flakes that drifted out of her grip, rather than separating small bites. "I was just trying to get him to leave us alone."

Felicia stabbed a fingertip in the air. "After he slimed his way in here to fuck with you guys under false pretenses, that's the least of what that cat's bastard deserves."

Faith's shoulders dropped with the sheer relief of having at least one—admittedly young, probably hotheaded—Were agree with her. She ripped part of her Danish off with her teeth this time. "Thank you! You know, I hadn't realized he'd noticed he broke Laurence's arm last time. When we were kidnapped, you know? But after that charade of a challenge fight this time, he *looked* at me when he broke them. He remembered, he fucking *knew*. And an arm and a leg, that must have been so Laurence couldn't walk, even in wolf form, right?"

She lost a lot of her righteous momentum. "I'd have thought it would be easier, to set bones after doing it before, but now I understand how…terrible it is, having to hurt someone to—" She swallowed. "I couldn't do it again. I was only lucky I found Tom as fast as I did. I don't know if it was fast enough, to not have to rebreak, but I don't want to know."

"Faith." Felicia's voice was faint, as she stared at Faith. Suddenly she moved, casting herself off her chair to her knees at Faith's feet, where she hugged Faith's legs, cheek against Faith's knees, like a dog trying so hard to provide support, it attempted to occupy the same physical space as you. "You had to *rebreak his arm* when you were kidnapped?"

"No, Laurence did that. I had to watch, and then help him set it." The feeling of pulling, hard as she could and then harder until Laurence's arm ground and moved just that little, unnatural degree…Her stomach flipped over into nausea, and she put her pastry down.

"Lady's light, what did Mikhail do to *you*?" Felicia twisted to look up at her, but kept her hugging grip tight.

"When we were kidnapped? Not as much. Started to choke me once. Laurence jumped him, though, so Mikhail stopped and slammed his head into the wall." Faith's next breath hitched in, near tears.

"Neither of you told anyone about this," Felicia said, voice soft, but tone near a wail. In sympathy, Faith realized. Concern because no one had known so they could make it right.

"Who would I tell?" Faith scrubbed her eyes, and the tears receded again. "Laurence knows. Everyone else here is like— coworkers. I guess I never thought about whether he'd have mentioned it to anyone. Not even Tom?" It was slowly, slowly dawning on her: perhaps the alphas hadn't had all the information to weigh against their political games, even had they been playing them. That...changed things, Faith supposed.

Felicia shook her head. "He didn't tell anyone what exactly happened to him. You need to tell the alphas! They truly had no idea."

Faith tried to pull back, but there wasn't anywhere for her to go at this angle. Felicia felt the movement and released her clasp, though. "I can't tell the alphas now. It'll seem like some cheap play for sympathy. And it'll make it seem even weirder that I didn't tell them when he showed up. They've already asked me why I didn't, through Susan, and that's a question I can't answer tactfully."

"Why?" Felicia gracefully rose, gaining just enough height to slide back into her seat, and dragged the chair directly across from Faith, a few inches between their knees.

Faith looked down at the two pairs of knees and the small gap between them. "Why can't I answer tactfully, or why didn't

I tell them?" Her tone twisted ironic despite her best efforts.

Felicia gestured: either question, or both. Faith sighed. "They've got their own shit to worry about. I know I'm not high on the priority list—until I fuck up enough to come to their attention." She gestured helplessly around them. See: the current situation.

Felicia grimaced. Not how she saw the alphas, clearly, but she was polite enough not to voice her disagreement. "Did Laurence teach you that?"

Faith started to answer, stopped. Had he? She actually had to think about that. "His issues are different. I know about Rory…" She hesitated, but she could tell from Felicia's glower she knew about Rory too. From Faith's perspective, she supposed she might as well assume all Were knew all other Were. "I don't think the alphas are going to hurt me. Neither does he, I suppose, but—all right, I guess it's not so different. I know he worries about what they'll do when he fucks up because of his issues."

Faith pressed her lips together. Too much talking about Laurence. She shouldn't be sharing his personal information with others. "But my situation *is* different from his. I'm human. I know way too much for my own safety." She zipped a fingernail along a dried swipe of dirt on her jeans, making no particular headway in removing it. *Which was why Dare had to execute him.* He'd executed a Were for his crimes in that case. What about inconvenient humans, did he get rid of those too, or did he have people for that?

Felicia leaned across to take her hands again, giving her plenty of time to pull away once more if she wanted. Faith let her grip hang limp. "If I promise on the Lady that you *will not* be in any trouble at all, will you tell the alphas all this anyway?

They need to know, about the kidnapping, and everything."

Faith changed her mind and squeezed Felicia's hands, hard. "I know you're only trying to help, but you can't promise that."

"But I can promise to protect you." Felicia sat tall, rolling her shoulders back and open. "They'll have to go through me."

Faith drew in a shuddering breath. All right. She would have to do this anyway, so she might as well do it with an ally. She dropped her head in a nod of agreement, then stood. Felicia kept one of her hands, tugged her toward the living room. "Why?" Faith asked, as they walked.

"You're pack," Felicia said, like that was an answer.

The three of them were seated on couches in the faded ugly-orange glory of the living room, arrayed like a panel sitting in judgment. The morning light was on the wrong side of the house to reach the windows behind them, leaving things a bit dim with the weak bulb pitted against the sunlight streaming into the hall on the other side. The alphas' eyes were already on Faith, and Susan looked up when Faith entered. She must have been clinging to Felicia's hand hard enough to bruise—at least on a human—but the younger woman showed no sign. The alphas looked—well, she couldn't really tell. Roanoke Dare's face was hard in its neutrality, but at least Roanoke Silver seemed somewhat sympathetic. She kept glancing at the floor, though there was nothing in particular there.

Roanoke Dare raised his brows. "Felicia?"

Felicia said something in…Spanish? Something, something, Papa.

Faith twisted to frown at Felicia. "Papa?" she asked at the same time as Roanoke Dare spoke too.

Roanoke Dare repeated Felicia's phrase back to her in surprise, then, on getting a nod, shook his head in belated apology and provided the translation. "Another one of the European packs' concepts that don't translate directly, but she takes responsibility for Faith…no, takes responsibility for Faith's safety."

Which was nice, but Faith was still stuck on the earlier part. She tugged on Felicia's hand as a reminder. "Sorry." Felicia's apologetic grimace seemed sincere enough. "I didn't want to be intimidating back when we first met, so I asked Tom not to mention his girlfriend was the alpha's daughter. And step-daughter." She gestured to Roanoke Dare and Roanoke Silver in turn, which Faith wouldn't necessarily have guessed but seemed obvious when she compared Roanoke Dare's features to Felicia's.

Tom was a brave man. But maybe Felicia really could protect her. Faith decided to sit down before her knees gave out, and Felicia joined her on the remaining loveseat without apology, pressed along her side, hip to knee, and keeping hold of her hand. "Felicia said I should back up to what happened when we were kidnapped." She collected nods from all three of her audience, to stall, then hesitated a bit longer after that, just to make things more awkward.

And then it all trickled out. Faith tried to stay as concise and as factual as possible, but that possible wasn't very much. She kept finding later things relied on earlier things she'd forgotten, but she muddled through it eventually—the kidnapping, the confusion over calls about a Russian arriving, the way Mikhail refused to leave Laurence alone. What she'd done about it.

"You locked him in a shipping container," Roanoke Dare repeated, still quite neutral, when she'd wound down.

"It's—the old owner was using it for a shed." Faith twisted to gesture in the general direction of the front door. "You may have seen it when you first came in?"

"Not in any detail. Perhaps we could look now," Roanoke Dare said, and rose. He made a gallant gesture for her to lead the way, which she did with Felicia still beside her and Susan not that far behind. He held back to walk with Roanoke Silver, no doubt to discuss. Probably the real point of the field trip.

Nothing else Faith could do now, though. She would wait until they revealed the result of the discussion, and then plan from there. Plan when and how to slip away and run like hell, perhaps. Or maybe not.

She couldn't balance her read of the alphas as reasonable people against talk of executions, so perhaps it was better she didn't try.

15

This early in the morning, the interior of the shipping container shed was only a few pleasant degrees warmer than the outside air, or at least it seemed so when Faith edged into the open doorway to watch Roanoke Dare stoop to brush fingers along a wolf-shoulder dent in the wall. On the way here, they'd picked up a diffident tail of Tom, but that was actually a net benefit in Faith's opinion, as he'd pulled his girlfriend aside for some low-voiced conference. Faith appreciated Felicia's stated position as an ally, she really did, but any decrease in the number of eyes directly on her at the moment was a relief.

Even with fewer eyes, Faith desperately needed a distraction, so she focused her attention on the scratches and gouges along the inside of the doorframe. She traced those herself, until she realized they were probably rough enough to draw blood if she wasn't careful. Instead, she bent to retrieve the silver chain that still lay where it had been tossed, then wasn't entirely sure what to do with it. Pocketing it seemed a rather suspicious thing to do, but it wasn't like she could hand it over to anyone.

"I'm surprised you didn't use it on him directly," Roanoke Silver murmured. She caught a loose end of the chain and settled it with the main pool of links in the center of Faith's palm. It…didn't burn her?

"Don't give her ideas, love." Roanoke Dare stepped down from the shipping container and joined their little group.

Roanoke Silver shot him a mischievous look, then ignored him. Instead, she reached into her own pocket with her left hand and held up a fine, silvery-colored chain of her own, apparently in silent reply to Faith's confusion. Her fingers on that hand seemed too clumsy to actually clasp it between fingertips, but with the length tangled among her fingers, it didn't fall. "Long story. I'll tell you sometime. Meanwhile, it's no bad idea to keep that around to even the odds." She nodded to Faith's own chain.

Faith, still feeling like she'd suddenly fallen three steps behind the rest of the group in the conversation, slipped the chain into her pocket as Roanoke Silver did the same. Certainly no one else seemed surprised by what Roanoke Silver had just done.

Roanoke Dare settled his feet a little apart, formally "at ease" in a contradiction that still felt natural. "All right. As alphas, we can't have the pack just deciding on and carrying out their own solutions to any interpersonal issues that might arise."

"Can't just do what you feel like," Faith murmured, imitating John's delivery. Susan huffed a laugh, so perhaps she'd done a decent job of it. Laurence hadn't come off too badly from that, which gave her hope? Probably. She'd been wound so tight for so long, she wasn't sure what she felt anymore.

"Mm," Roanoke Dare agreed, still neutral whether he recognized the source of the quote or not. "That said, that is not true in every Were pack, and you are, to say the least, new to Roanoke. We,"—a tip of his head to Roanoke Silver, to unite the decision—"think in your pursuit of justice for others, you've already punished yourself far worse than anything we would have imposed."

"Time served?" Faith tried to make a joke out of it, but she felt suddenly woozy. Roanoke Silver was closest and propped a hand against her shoulder.

The Were all did their pointer impression toward the house, Susan a few beats behind, so Faith shoved off collapse a little longer by climbing back into the space of immediate action. Who was going to show up now? Mikhail, to try to appeal the decision?

A car door slammed from the driveway in front of the house, rather than the house itself. Laurence jogged into sight across the yard a beat later.

"Shit, I have to *go*." Faith didn't realize she'd spoken out loud until Roanoke Silver made a small noise of surprise. And how could Faith possibly explain what she meant without sounding like a heartless, icy bitch? "I can't—I can't deal with the Were world, but if I have to leave when I see how much it hurts him—" She'd rather rip out his heart at a distance, walk away like that left her hands clean? None of this was coming out right, but it wasn't right even in her head.

But Laurence had arrived too fast, and she saw him hear her, *saw* it. She'd seen him get stabbed in the gut literally once, and this looked—and felt, in her own gut—very much the same. She gasped with the force of it. He'd frozen, but now he crossed the last few steps, reaching for her. "Faith, please—"

"No," Roanoke Silver said firmly. She took a grip across Faith's shoulders, and nodded to her husband, who frowned, but did as she apparently directed and blocked Laurence's path. Laurence stopped before him like surf on the rocks, breaking rather than dodging. "I am in accord with Death on this matter. Sometimes love is not enough, and to pretend otherwise is to take a single hurt, however acute, and stretch it long, make it a misery of years. The Were have not treated you well, puppy."

Laurence was blocked, but Tom wasn't, and he darted closer as if to read the answer to a great riddle on her face. "But why, Faith? You *won*! Mikhail damn well knows he can't fuck with you now."

"It's not about winning!" Faith found herself shouting, into Tom's face, because she couldn't look at Laurence. "It's not about losing, it's about not having to fight *all the time*. I don't want to have to spend each day deciding whether to let harassment wear me down or to put myself in danger. I don't want to end up *killing* someone." She didn't mean to, but she did look at Susan then. The woman looked so normal, but maybe she was different than Faith, stronger somehow.

Susan made a low noise of frustration. "Who decided *that* story was the best introduction to 'how to be a human among Were 101'?" Tom ducked his head, shaggy hair flopping over his forehead to make him look even more young and contrite, but Susan speared him with a glare anyway.

"But it's true, isn't it? Better I should know what I'm getting into." Faith would have rocked forward, out of Roanoke Silver's grasp, to confront Susan in turn, but the alpha's grip was inescapable.

"She was defending me, among others," Roanoke Silver said, in the kind of soft tone that snapped all speech out of existence around it. "It is not such a bad comparison, as with you and your lover. More germane is to ask her as to her regrets."

Susan shook her head, emphatic. No regrets, but before she could underline the assertion, Roanoke Dare spoke with the same attention-commanding tone. "When you have charge of a pack of your own, Felicia, it's important to note a certain kind of mid-ranker. When anyone new joins a pack, there's always a certain amount of upset and jostling as people figure out how they relate to each other. Some enjoy the thrill and exercise of it all. Most people realize that most mid-rankers don't particularly care about their status and leave them out of it, but fewer understand there are those who actively dislike challenging, and will even allow themselves to be pushed quite low in the jostling, simply to avoid having to fight. Aren't they then simply low-ranked? you might ask."

Roanoke Dare paused, giving the rhetorical twist weight. "Only until they perceive someone must be protected."

He was talking about her. Took her long enough to grasp the obvious, but Faith wasn't actually sure why it should have been obvious. He was talking about Were, after all.

At least Laurence was no faster on the uptake. "Protect—? Faith, *I'm* fine."

"You weren't," Faith said, voice so soft it faded out around the edges.

Laurence sidestepped, opening a clear path between them, but with Roanoke Dare still lingering close, Laurence used it only to catch her gaze, briefly, then drop his head. "All right. You're right. And we should have called the alphas, no matter what my fear made me do. Do what I say, not what I do, yeah? It's the other half of the social contract of being part of a pack, obeying the alphas, and the alphas protect you, and you have to *let them*. And before you say it—of course you'd be pack, if you stayed."

Faith huffed something that was almost a punchy laugh at the surprise of hearing Laurence use "social contract"—had he gotten that from her? Or maybe his therapist. But then too many ill-considered responses were pushing to get free all at once, and she had to let one free. "And when we were kidnapped?"

That earned the first visible sign of anger from Roanoke Dare, brows drawing down as a growl rumbled around his words. "If you understood what Silver did to have you freed—"

Roanoke Silver held up a hand, and Roanoke Dare's words snapped off. "We failed them nonetheless, that such release was so long in coming. It will never happen again, my word on the Lady on that. From your account of your recent experiences, I take it that you have some understanding of the import of that? Though it was used by someone who wished to wiggle out from beneath it. Death take my voice before my time if I fail to keep that word in both spirit and letter."

"I—" Faith believed Roanoke Silver, and felt almost embarrassed by the honor of having such a promise made to her. She was abruptly back at the point of wooziness again, from too much emotion layered on top of emotion.

"Unless Chris Evans called, and then no one could blame you if you didn't want to stay and compete with him," Tom said, and Faith was suddenly laughing, beyond punchy, nearly to the point of hysteria. She walked the line of tears, wavered back onto the correct side. For now. Laurence subsided into giggles as well, and Felicia's lips quirked. Poor Roanoke Silver looked completely at sea.

"I couldn't leave until I explained the cataloging system to someone anyway," Faith said. "I don't think after heat exhaustion is a time to make life decisions, but I won't randomly disappear." She held out a hand to Laurence. "Promise on—I don't know, something serious. I'm no good at that kind of thing."

Apparently that was okay, though, because Laurence had wrapped her up in his arms. She ignored everyone around them for a few seconds, pressing her forehead into his shoulder, and when she looked up again, they'd dispersed somewhat, Roanoke Dare drifting over to his daughter once more.

"Your grandparents are mid-rankers, but my mother is much more the type I was talking about earlier," he said. "In this kind of situation, it's another of a sub-alpha's many jobs, to calm the waters, protect those who don't want to fight, and protect any they might worry need fighting for, Spokane." The context and Roanoke Dare's intonation told Faith he meant the city name as a sub-alpha title, but there wasn't a Spokane, was there?

Felicia gaped at her father, poured out something incredulous in Spanish, remembered herself, and returned to English, more heavily accented. "You're serious?" She looked to Roanoke Silver for confirmation.

"We had thought it would be time for some small sub-alphaship after you finish learning with the humans, but for the space of the summer, it seems to fill an urgent need." Roanoke Silver's smile started small but only grew brighter with delight over Felicia's reaction. "Should Faith stay, I think she would feel better with a less-intimidating authority here in person."

"And then we can see where we are when you start classes again in the fall," Roanoke Dare agreed, and fielded a tackle hug from his daughter worthy of the beefiest football player.

"And we can invite Ginnie, too, right?" Tom beamed, not just with his grin, but his whole body, and then he was in for the next tackle hug. He turned neatly with it, spinning her off her feet, both of them bubbling over with laughter.

"Suppose we should go deal with Mikhail," Roanoke Dare murmured to his wife, a good-natured note bleeding over into his tone just from watching the younger Were.

"Can we watch? I want to see how this finishes," Faith asked Laurence, into his shoulder.

"Of course, if you like," Roanoke Silver answered instead because Were hearing. Laurence released her to sling his arm across her waist and allow them to walk.

Susan disappeared on up ahead while the alphas wandered up to the house with stately slowness just in time for Mikhail to be escorted out to meet them in the front yard. He looked *bad*, pale and haggard, having to be half-carried by Alexei. On Mikhail's other side, not touching, was a golden-haired woman Faith didn't recognize.

"The alphas have made their judgment?" she asked, as Roanoke Dare and Silver planted themselves before Mikhail. Faith recognized her voice from the phone. She was the Russian living out here. Tatiana.

Mikhail muttered something in Old Were. Tatiana snorted. "Perhaps they'll put you back in that box to die, and finish what the human started." For all her flippancy, Faith noticed that she was still standing at his side, not that of the alphas'. Her tone tightened to frustration a moment later, verifying Faith's impression. "Why couldn't you simply leave the human alone, without tormenting her?"

"Oh, I don't think he spared a thought for me," Faith said, punchiness making her bold, even when Tatiana's gaze snapped to her. "Laurence was the one who was just too juicy a target.

Because he'd been hurt before?" Mikhail had no response, as she'd expected. "But the fact that he ignored me was his undoing."

"So it was," Roanoke Dare said on a breath of a laugh. Apparently he appreciated boldness. "Mikhail. You will leave Roanoke territory by the next available flight, and if you step onto it ever again, you will be executed immediately."

"If I go home, they kill me there too," Mikhail spat, bitter. He turned a look of appeal to Tatiana. "You cannot want—"

"I don't know what I want. Or perhaps I do: I want you to not feel the need to court your own death by being unable to give up tormenting those who are weaker than you."

Alexei rumbled something, and Tatiana's eyes went wide. "Prague. Yes. Didn't you have a chase there you lived with, for a while, on a mission?"

"She does not know who I really am," Mikhail whined.

"And I am extremely reluctant to inflict you on her, except I know you must have acted as someone worthy of her, for that time." Tatiana stooped a little, putting their faces level, where he was somewhat slumped against Alexei. "Be that role, without break, without stumble, and perhaps her pack will continue to accept you. *Be* that role, like your life depends on it, because it does. And perhaps it will become true, given long enough."

They descended into their native language then, and Faith let a long breath trickle out. Yes, that was a just finish. "I should probably eat something properly," she told Laurence. "And possibly drink more water."

Laurence guided her past the others, and helped her do just that, without any more conversation, just the comforting weight of his presence alongside her. "Forgive me for—" she started, when breakfast was only crumbs.

Laurence shook his head emphatically. "No. Nothing to forgive. Clean slate going forward now, okay?" At her nod, he glanced back over her shoulder in the direction of the front door. "You should take the day off, but do you want any of us doing some cataloging or something?"

The mention of cataloging sparked a thought that linked to a couple others, now there was a little space open where her tangle of anger and fear had been ever since Mikhail baited Laurence into challenging. "Actually, I want to check something. Where—?"

Laurence pressed a hand to her knee to symbolically hold her into her chair, then stood. "Whatever it is, I'll get it for you."

"Well, first, I need the folder with all the background research. But after that, can you get that cross—make sure you mark the level bag's provenience on its individual bag—and get the alphas back in here? If what I suspect is right, I think they'll be interested to hear about it." And she could clearly demonstrate her worth as an archaeologist. Not that she had to, but she *wanted* to.

The folder with all the information was only across the room on the counter, swept away to the nearest flat surface after the papers been spread out on the kitchen table just before a meal. Faith didn't begrudge Laurence the satisfaction he clearly got from being able to fetch it for her, though.

Laurence disappeared to collect people—more than just the alphas, she suspected, by how long he was gone—and Faith skimmed through the pages of background, setting a few out in a fan before her as she worked. When she had her case as strong as she could make it, she was still alone, so she returned to a transcribed journal, reading through the narrative of it purely for her own interest.

When the alphas arrived, she stood, and came around the table to take the bagged cross from Laurence's hands. She hadn't told him to keep it a secret, but Roanoke Dare's brows snapped up when he got a look at it properly in her hands. Roanoke Silver was at his side, but she yielded her place to Tatiana without even looking at the artifact. The rest of the peanut gallery was blocked from entering the kitchen and rather than bother to crane to see, Faith just assumed everyone was back there. Faith handed the cross over for Roanoke Dare to examine up close through the plastic.

"So that's from our excavation, which I placed based on some artifacts in shovel probes which were the right time period for the Were homestead. We found it in a privy feature, which is where people threw their trash. Or dropped things accidentally, which is what I would suspect is the case here. Which implies a human was living here, short of conversion—" A laugh fluttered at the base of her throat at the sheer, blank incomprehension of the idea painted across every Were's face, but Faith swallowed it. She walked them through the rest of her logic as to why the cross being picked up by a Were or dropped by a casual visitor seemed unlikely.

"And that's as far as I got at the time, because I was distracted immediately after." Faith avoided glancing at Laurence—and then Roanoke Silver went ahead and did so anyway. "But then it suddenly connected for me over breakfast. We'd also been finding evidence of two sets of dishes—a Russian one, and an American one. Like they'd got a new set, locally, after too much of the other one broke, or as they began to acculturate, or…" Faith had enough showmanship in her she had to pause meaningfully. "As if someone married in, and brought a set with them."

Rather than wait for reactions, she dropped her head over the pages she gathered from the table, crumpling them a little at the edges with nervous fingers. "I remembered that in the pictures of the gravestones, a lot of them had two names, couples together on the same stone. But there was an adult woman, alone, who probably died in the fire, since it's the same year as the majority of the others, 1884." She handed off the translated print-out of that picture to Roanoke Dare. "Anna Lady-beloved. Is that a real surname, or...?"

"At that time, it was one of the placeholders we used for human records," Tatiana confirmed. She held up a hand in denial when Roanoke Dare would have automatically passed the picture to her, then remembered herself and passed it back over her shoulder instead. "I remember it from when I did the translation."

"Well, Anna, you might notice, is also not an uncommon Anglo name." Faith gathered up her next page. "Wazzu—WSU—has a whole collection of journals and letters from wives of the missionaries who were in the area starting in the 1850s. That's too early for any of the women writing to have known the pack, but one of them kept up correspondence with friends in smaller missions in the area. '...I have had news of my friend Maria, much excited by the prospect of seeing her oldest daughter *Anna* married to a local rancher living quite comfortably with his brothers and sisters-in-law...' " She extended the page with the typed transcription to Roanoke Dare, but this time Tatiana snatched it for herself before he could move. "Dated 1878. No name on the rancher, or surname for Maria, but it certainly fits. Anna, daughter of a local missionary, married into the pack, then died in the fire, and her husband must have survived. He moved on, with any other survivors, so he's not with her in the cemetery."

She dared to lift her head for a smile of triumph, but everyone still seemed too shocked to return it. It grew lopsided and Faith shrugged apologetically. "You should have your researchers follow that lead, but it may well be that's as far as we get. That's archaeology—you can only go so far, often, before there's no way to prove things one way or another. And frequently you can't tie things even this closely to individual people." More silence, in response. Faith tried not to fidget. Did they not believe her, proving much like Mikhail in the end?

Finally, Tatiana traded Roanoke Dare page for cross, which she held with something like reverence, extra plastic of the bag draped over the back of her hand. "That is an answer to the biggest question, yes?" Her accent had grown more pronounced. "They would never have gone home. Not after one married a human."

"Even after she was dead? There would be nothing forcing him to speak of her." Roanoke Dare turned to Tatiana, his tone that of someone playing devil's advocate.

Tatiana met his eyes, a quick flick up and then head tipped to the side. And maybe a little down. Faith wondered if she'd ever get used to reading the meaning in those tiny little changes of angle. "No. Not when every aspect of his life in Russia would have been a denunciation of his love, and his grief." Her voice wavered a little with personal associations Faith couldn't parse.

Laurence made a whine deep in his throat, perhaps thinking of personal associations of his own, and settled a hand, loving, protective, at the back of Faith's neck. Once more, her thoughts had stopped short of the true conclusion to be found in the situation, she realized. She hadn't thought of the light Anna's situation might shed upon hers.

And now, finally, everyone was exclaiming, shaking themselves out of what Faith had realized was shock alone, not disbelief. She abandoned the artifact and research print-outs to be passed hand to hand, relying on her crew to make sure the cross wasn't taken out of the bag. Together with Laurence, she slipped out to the living room.

"So. Taking the day off. Going to actually try to do that now," she said, laughing apologetically. "I think I'm going to declare this a holiday for the whole crew. You guys wouldn't be getting much done with all the visitors around anyway. Anyone who wants can join me in binge-watching something." The house didn't have TV service anymore, but they'd made sure to have broadband started back up, so a laptop connected to a secondhand set new enough to accept the input did well enough.

Tracy appeared almost immediately to join them and by the second or third episode—Faith couldn't be sure, she was mostly dozing against Laurence's chest on the couch—a wolf arrived and claimed the rest of the couch to curl up on, including her feet and much of her lower legs. It was a bit hot, but very comforting. She didn't actually know what anyone except Laurence looked like in wolf form, but this one was pretty burly, so she assumed it was one of the men. He had a scar across his back, fur along there pure white and wiry.

He was utterly relaxed, so Faith didn't worry too much about waking up completely for a proper identification. This being pack thing was all right, after all.

16

When the "sub-alpha needed" whistle reached them through the scrubby pines Faith, as the south team's "flag," was being carried piggyback by Tracy. Tracy set her down immediately and the other north team members clustered around for a quick conference. Under the circumstances, Faith didn't exercise her right to escape on being set down. "Do you think we should call off the game?" Tracy asked, frowning.

"Depends if anyone's needed besides Felicia," Faith pointed out. It was honestly delightful not to have to worry about whatever it was, unless she was summoned specifically. "If we lose more than one, we should gather to redistribute teams."

"Laurence! Faith!" Felicia bellowed from the direction of the house.

Faith saluted her capturing team and set off at a jog. Something archaeology-related, then. Despite the fact that everyone—Laurence most of all—was busy pretending otherwise, he was acting as beta, so that would be why he'd been called too.

Maybe a new roamer had shown up and needed interrogating as to their ability to follow directions and keep field notes. The late evening sunlight was oblique but the heat hadn't eased off yet, meaning Faith was sweating off her sunscreen along her hairline especially, but she did slow her pace long enough to smooth and reset her ponytail to look at least vaguely official.

It was the alphas in all of their dignity that greeted her when she arrived at the vehicle pull-out, though. Or perhaps less dignity than usual, as they were both in jeans, standing with asses leaned on the side of a car rather than one of the pack's higher-occupancy vehicles.

"Just visiting," Roanoke Silver assured her, the moment she came into range.

"I said they should look at the open unit anyway, while they're here," Felicia said, corralling her own mussed hair up into a vague bun, from which a tendril immediately slipped free to her shoulders.

"And how are things going other than the excava—what is that *smell*?" Roanoke Dare reared back from her like a puppy discovering a vicious lemon on the floor for the first time.

Laurence, arriving not far behind her, cracked up. She glanced at him, but he grinned at her, and gestured that the explanation was all her.

Well, fine. It sounded a bit juvenile, but that was pretty much the order of the day around here, and Faith would be lying if she said she didn't enjoy it. "Air freshener." She shrugged off her small, draw-string runner's pack and pulled out the spray can. "I'm always a flag when we play capture the flag, and I can't sneak unless I stink up the woods a little to confuse everyone." She slipped the can away again, though that wouldn't help the general miasma hanging around her, she was sure.

"Always a flag?" Roanoke Dare repeated, blankly, while his wife tented her fingertips over her lips to hold in a laugh.

"If we play with normal rules, I can't keep up. So we made up new ones." Faith was going to leave it at that, but Roanoke Silver's obvious delight tempted her into continuing. "You have to ask the flag's permission before you pick them up. And then if you're not moving, you have to put them down and can't keep hold. So they can sneak back to their base if you're not careful. Or you can try to persuade them otherwise." She fanned her fingers wide, effected a showman's cadence. "There's a world of new strategy."

"Who's the other flag?" Roanoke Dare asked, and that was when Faith noticed the laughter in his eyes as well.

"We switch it around. *Not* Alexei," Laurence said, and winced as if from carrying a heavy load.

"And here your father was worried, hearing the number of roamers you were accumulating," Roanoke Silver said, and embraced Felicia.

"How many are you up to now?" Roanoke Dare said, relaxed in his lean on the car, probably having greeted his daughter properly already. "Are you comfortable keeping them all in line?"

"Well, Ginnie doesn't count. The two from Billings, and then…" Felicia listed them all for her father, ending with a bounce to her toes that was pure Tom. "It's very…" She looked to Faith. "What did you call it?"

"Ten pounds of chaos in a five-pound bag?" Faith had called it any number of things, actually, some less benign when her workforce declined to show up some mornings after particularly wild partying. That idiom had been a new one on the Were, though, to much hilarity.

Felicia shook her head. "Well, yes. It's that too. But the other thing. Inmates?"

Faith barked a laugh of her own. "Inmates running the asylum." Felicia shot her with a "that's the one" finger-gun.

"Speaking of which, I better go redivide teams." Felicia glanced at her father for permission, and at his flick of a hand, she darted off.

"I'll get the mundane details of how things have been going from the beta," Roanoke Dare murmured, looking to Laurence. Something passed between the two men, in silent body language. Laurence winced, initially, at hearing what he hadn't faced up to yet, but then his posture firmed up, and he nodded decisively.

They strolled a little ways away, deep in conversation as they walked, and Faith watched them with a helpless little smile of relief on her lips. Roanoke Silver watched them too, or perhaps watched Faith watch them.

"That's been a long time coming," Roanoke Silver murmured, as Roanoke Dare suddenly embraced Laurence, then stepped back and kissed his forehead. Faith had to smash her cultural conditioning down a little to see the male platonic affection with clear eyes, but she nodded.

Roanoke Silver slipped an arm around her shoulders and gifted her with a side-hug of her own. "You might start thinking what sub-pack you'd like to join at the end of the summer."

"Faith! We need you! We only have one flag!" Another bellow from back on the playing field. Ginnie, this time.

Faith disengaged from Roanoke Silver with a laugh. "Should I go tell them the alphas want the excavation report immediately?"

"You stay here, I'll tell them." Roanoke Silver tipped her head to her husband. "The details mean more to him than to me anyway." She held out her hand, which Faith couldn't figure out until she made a "gimmie" gesture. "The scent! A flag needs scent, doesn't she?"

Bemusedly, Faith handed over the pack with the air freshener, and Roanoke Silver strode off in the direction of the game. Then she went to join her boyfriend, and her alpha.

ACKNOWLEDGMENTS

The stories in this collection span a number of years, so I apologize in advance for the inevitable omissions of people who have helped me with one or more of them. As usual, even more friends and family have provided the abstract qualities of inspiration, sympathy, and support.

Thanks to Jeremy Zimmerman and Dawn Vogel for publishing *Lead and Follow* among excellent company. Erin M. Evans and Susan J. Morris provided critique on the craft aspects of *Contested History*, and Cyrena Undem, Karry Blake, Michele Parvey, Lorelea Hudson, Simone Carbonneau-Kincaid, and Dawn Vogel provided notes on the archaeology (getting every aspect even of your own specialty correct is harder than one might think!). Kate Marshall provided beautifully designed covers and layout not only for this collection, but for all the original short stories as well.

Finally, I owe special thanks to Mitchell Fund for bringing the world of the *Silver* novels to astonishing, beautiful life in music.

www.ingramcontent.com/pod-product-compliance
Lightning Source LLC
Chambersburg PA
CBHW020405260626
47156CB00007B/2236